1

A week had passed since the Bradford bombing. The two photographs lay side by side on Wilson's desk. Beside them, a detailed report confirmed that by every measurement conceivable they were of the same woman. Wilson rubbed at his eyes with the balls of his thumbs. He had his killer, but he had nowhere to go from there. The car was a Mercedes with false CD license plates. Five of the same make and model had been reported stolen in the months prior to the bombing. Three had been accounted for. There was not a large enough piece of the bomber's vehicle left to tie it in with the other two, not even an engine plate. They were still sifting rubble up in Yorkshire but Wilson was not optimistic.

He glanced at his watch. It was almost noon. There was a National Security meeting at 2.00 PM. In Number 10, they didn't come much bigger. What did he have? He knew who the bomber was, one of them at least. The second, a white youth, had been caught by the camera just as clearly as had Alice Craven, had received the same coverage, but so far, they had not identified him. He let out a long sigh, the bottom line was that he had not prevented it, didn't have a clue as to who had masterminded it, and like as not wouldn't be able to prevent the next one or the one after that. He scooped up the photographs, opened his desk drawer, and tossed them into it. It would not be an easy meeting.

Wings

END GAME

by

David Toft

A Wings ePress, Inc.

A Fantasy Novel

Wings ePress, Inc.

Edited by: Rosalie Franklin
Copy Edited by: Sara Olds
Senior Editor: Elizabeth Struble
Managing Editor: Leslie Hodges
Executive Editor: Marilyn Kapp
Cover Artist: Richard Stroud

Wings ePress Books
http://www.wings-press.com

Copyright © 2009 by David Toft
ISBN 978-1-59705-630-4

Published In the United States Of America

August 2009

Wings ePress Inc.
403 Wallace Court
Richmond, KY 40475

Dedication

For my wife, Mary, with thanks for her patience and support.

One

Alice Craven banged against the bars of her cell with flat palms. She was too weak to tighten them into fists. A stab of pain travelled the length of her arm, and exploded into red sparks behind her eyes.

Today, she thought, *I'm going to die.*

She had thought that on the previous day, and on the one before that. Her lips were cracked and dry, and her tongue had started to swell once again inside her parched mouth. She was not afraid of death. It would come, she believed, as a slow drifting into sleep; a caring mother pulling warming blankets over a half-awake child.

She turned her head from the bars, which formed the whole of the front of her cell, to the window high in the wall behind her. A knot of blue fabric tied around the central of five iron bars marked the place where her uniform hung. It was on the outside of the opening to catch the moisture from the regular afternoon thunderstorms, which up to then had sustained the little life that she had left. The rain would continue to do so only for as long as her starved body had the strength to pull itself upright, retrieve the soaked material and wring

1

its life-sustaining cargo into the aluminium bucket, which stood on the earthen floor below the window.

Alice had only been in Somalia for three months. She had arrived full of hope and enthusiasm, there to give something back to a world that had seen her born, healthy and intelligent, into a developed economy. She had to admit, however, that there were also more selfish reasons for that final decision.

~ * ~

Six months earlier, following an unusually fraught day at the clinic, a television documentary watched after too much red wine with dinner had reduced Alice to tears.

The memories of that evening were so fresh in her mind that it might all have happened only yesterday. Tony, her husband, had watched her write a cheque for five hundred pounds. She had been uncomfortably aware of his scrutiny, as she made it payable to The Somalia Children's Appeal..

Five hundred pounds. He had kept his anger in check, but she had known that his mind was seething: could almost read his thoughts. Didn't she know anything? The hi-tech sector was a shambles. His business, their business, was heading for the rocks. Orders had almost dried up and there was nothing hopeful on the horizon. He would have to lay off workers, decent, loyal, English workers. Alice had heard it all so many times before.

"The children of Somalia," he had said, as she concentrated on addressing the envelope in her neat copperplate hand, "will see about sixpence of that." She'd looked up at him then. He'd swirled the remains of his wine around his glass. "When the U.K. administrators have had their cut, and the Somali authorities theirs, and the local militia theirs, there'll be fuck all left for the poor little children."

The cynical glint in his eyes had infuriated her despite its familiarity. Normally, she would have dispelled the feeling with a playful slap and an acid comment. The alcohol swirling about her brain triggered rebellion instead.

"Then I'll go and do something about it my-shelf," she slurred.

Tony had laughed then, and leaned forward, arms outstretched, to pull her toward him.

Alice had twisted away from the attempted embrace, pushed herself to her feet and retired in silence to the bedroom.

"I'll be up soon, my little missionary." Tony's voice had followed her up the first three steps.

In the darkness of the bedroom while she waited for her husband to join her, the seed that she had planted spread roots into every thought. By the time the strip of light, which outlined the door from the landing, widened sufficiently to allow Tony access, her mind was made up.

During the following three months of interviews and administration procedures, medical tests and inoculations, Tony's arguments had become more logical and more persistent, and Alice's resolve only firmer.

~ * ~

Sobs convulsed her chest and shoulders, but Alice hadn't enough moisture left in her body to provide the comfort of even a single tear.

An earlier bombardment had blown away the rear wall of the cell opposite. The body of its occupant lay, contorted and fly-ridden, just two feet short of freedom. Alice tried not to look at it but across the yellow dust of the compound to a distant range of snow-capped mountains. Of her guards, she had no idea. They might have been killed during the attack or fearing a follow up assault, they may have fled.

A dull rumbling encroached upon her consciousness. Her gaze switched to the concrete wall on her right. The shadow cast by the bars of the window had another three feet to travel across its pitted surface before it was time for the skies to darken, and the rain to begin. Her mind concentrated on the sound. Was it thunder? Was her life giving supply of water going to arrive early that day? Or was it artillery? The noise intensified and took on a regular mechanical beat. A helicopter, it had to be a helicopter.

Alice's eyes, bright and alert, scanned the horizon through the jagged blast hole. She could see nothing, but the sound was getting louder. It was above her prison then. Small branches and leaves appeared, blown across the swirling dust of the compound by the downdraft of the machine's rotors.

Inside its own cage her heart beat wildly, matching note for note the throb of the invisible engine. It didn't matter if the storm came early. It didn't matter if the storm failed to arrive at all. She had made it. She tried to stand but even with the assistance of her hands pulling against the bars she no longer had sufficient strength.

Somewhere outside, the beating of the machine slowed and then stopped, that inside her ribcage continued. She heard shouting voices and running, booted feet. All around her sounds, which were indiscernible, and yet at the same time familiar, suggested that some kind of work was going on.

~ * ~

It seemed as though long hours passed before a door, out of sight to her left, crashed open, and the barrel of an automatic rifle appeared around the corner of her cell.

The man was not in uniform. A tribesman, Alice thought, Anti-government. But the sight of him would not have been more welcome had he been wearing the blue helmet of the United Nations.

There was no indication of rank on his tattered, desert clothing but he carried an air of authority, which negated the need for stripes or insignia. His attention was on the body in the cell opposite. He aimed his weapon at the lock and opened fire. The noise echoed from the concrete walls and around the inside of Alice's dehydrated skull.

The fighter shouted a command to someone behind him, and kicked at the demolished lock. The iron bars swung inward. Then he turned and looked at Alice. His eyes smiled as they scanned her scrawny nakedness, but there was no pity in them. He raised his weapon, and destroyed the lock of her cell door with one sudden burst of bullets and noise.

Two other men appeared. They were stripped to their waists, their bodies covered in dust and sweat. They hoisted the body opposite, one by the arms, one by the legs, and carried it from the cell.

The fighter who had blasted the lock of Alice's door tested his work by kicking it open. Then he turned and strode away along the corridor, shouting out more orders as he disappeared from Alice's sight.

Another two men appeared. They lifted Alice from the packed soil of the floor with no more consideration than their colleagues had granted the body. Her ribs crashed against the metal doorframe as they negotiated her through.

They were through the outer door then, and the sudden brightness of the sun caused Alice to turn her head away from its glare. She saw the body swing three times between its two carriers before they launched it into the mouth of an open grave.

The realisation that she was being carried in the same direction hit her in a nauseating wave of horror and confusion. She looked up at the head of the man who held her legs but his face was away from her, intent on the direction in which they were travelling.

When they stopped, Alice could see the edge of the pit but not what lay beyond and below it. She felt the breeze against her bare skin as the hands that held her swung left to right three times before releasing their grip. She spun almost gracefully through the air, and landed, face downward, on a pile of decomposing flesh. A cloud of bloated, black flies, disturbed by her sudden interruption of their meal settled to their task once again. She could feel them on her bare back and at the corner of her lips.

A shout sounded above her. The first shovel full of soil half covered her mouth. She could taste its damp earthiness. Its smell carried her back to her small cottage's herb garden and the blue wooden-handled trowel with which she removed, with surgical precision, invasive grass and weeds from between clumps of ginger mint and thyme. She realised with the calm impartiality of a trained observer that she had not screamed, had not begged, or appealed for mercy.

Tony had crept up behind her as she weeded. Startled, she had turned, raising her hand to her face and leaving a black smudge of damp earth across the width of her cheek. Tony had laughed, and she had laughed back.

The next heavy scattering of soil blocked out the light.

~ * ~

Alice looked down at her hands. Her fingers had fleshed out. She released their grip on her glass, and turned one of them over to study the palm. It looked strange somehow, as though it belonged to someone else.

"Another?"

She looked up. A barman was holding her glass. He waved it toward her, emphasising its emptiness.

"Sorry, yes…please."

He turned away, busying himself with a clinking of the bottles that were hidden from Alice's view by his bulky frame.

Alice pulled her purse across the marble bar top and unzipped it. Without having to look down, she pulled out a folded note and waited for the barman to return.

"Ice," he said, without turning, and walked off along the bar.

She unfolded the note and looked down at it. Her brow creased, ten Euro. Her tongue flicked across her upper lip as she tried to slot this new discovery into a memory that would make sense.

The barman returned, tweezered two cubes of ice into her glass and placed it onto the cardboard coaster in front of her.

"Thanks." She held out the note.

He raised one hand. "Taken care of."

Alice looked around. The bar stretched away to either side of her. Not one of the equidistantly spaced stools along its length was occupied. She turned. The six, tall, dark-wood tables that centred the room were empty. So were the lower, square ones that lined the walls. All of the furniture looked new—trying to look old. The carpet was predominantly red paisley and unstained clean, the walls half-panelled, half, cream paint. Prints of racehorses broke up the expanse of paintwork.

Bright sunlight shone through a half-glazed door, central to the wall behind her. The word 'lounge' stood out, mirror written, in clear glass in the centre of its frosted pane.

Alice returned her attention to the bar, refolded the note and slipped it back into her purse. She lifted her drink to her lips, not expecting any taste because she had no recollection of what she had been drinking. *Strange,* she thought, but the strangeness faded into acceptance. She took a sip of the clear liquid. It was vodka and tonic. A thin slice of lime broke free of two restraining ice cubes and floated to the surface. Alice pushed it back down with the tip of a red painted fingernail.

She wondered whether she should be concerned about the fact that she did not know where she was or how she got there. She was not. She shrugged.

She knew who she was. She was Alice Craven. "Alice Craven," she said, letting the words hang as though expecting other words to follow of their own volition, any words, wife and mother, spinster of this parish. None did. Her shoulders hunched, and she focused her attention on the face that stared back at her from the mirror behind the line of bottles at the back of the bar. Her hair was long, blonde and well cut to frame a smooth-skinned round face. Her eyes were large, and made to look larger by a careful application of colour that also gave them a feline slant. Her lips were full and red, more paint. She smiled. The woman in the mirror smiled back. "Tart," she said, and the smile broadened in genuine amusement. "Alice Craven…tart." The smile disappeared. "Miss Alice Craven, Mrs. Alice Craven." Nothing. She took another drink.

The door behind her opened. She did not turn but watched in the mirror.

~ * ~

Arthur Molloy settled himself into the bay window seat of his first floor, South Dublin, apartment. His movements were measured, almost sloth-like. A whole day of inaction lay ahead of him, to rush anything would only make its remaining hours longer. He interlocked his fingers behind his head and let his mind trawl through the events of his life up to that point.

He was twenty-two. In two years, four months and seventeen days he would be twenty-five, and the apartment, the one above it and the one below, would be his, so would his dead mother's considerable portfolio of investments. Until then he was broke. His mother had left him to survive without a penny when he was nineteen.

"When he is twenty-five and, God willing, mature enough," she had said, through the medium of the family solicitor the week after her death. It had also been the year after she had disappeared to Italy with some actor that Arthur had never even met. At least she had not married the man and complicated things even further. "Until that time," the solicitor had continued, "he may live in the apartment rent-free." Fat difference that made, it only meant that Arthur was unable to claim a rent allowance from Social Welfare.

His father had disappeared four years before his mother. Arthur did not blame him though for wanting to escape from the tight cow who nagged about his football, about his drinking, about just about anything. Arthur had not heard from him since the day on which he had not come home from the pub.

Men should not be dependent on women, Arthur thought, *for their jobs, for their money, for their homes, for anything.* He only wished his father well, and hoped that, wherever he was, he had found some self-respect.

Things had gotten worse for Arthur after his father disappeared. His friends were discouraged because they used pubs. "Just like your father." He was allowed no money because he would spend it on drink. "Just like your father." The only girl that he had brought home his mother had dismissed as a grabber and tarty.

"Just like my mother," he said to the golden Labrador that had interrupted its morning stroll to urinate against the gatepost below his window.

The traffic, which travelled left-to-right below him, had increased in volume. The coming of evening would reverse the flow. It came in spasmodic bursts. A sequence of traffic signals fed the cars in controlled lumps of metal, allowing each clot to clear one stretch of tar macadam artery before releasing the next.

There were times, even during the rush hour, when Arthur could leave his apartment and walk straight across the street; at others two lanes of machines cruised passed him unseeing as he waited to cross.

Arthur's mind continued unguided along the tangent upon which the sight of the traffic had started it. What would the odds be? Was the road clear for longer periods than it was occupied? If he left his front door and just walked, would his chances be 50:50, 75:25, 25:75? He didn't wrestle with the problem for long; the mathematics held no thrill for him, but the gamble suddenly and inexplicably did.

He stood, and pulled the curtains closed. "That would be cheating." He grabbed his jacket from the back of his chair and then his Walkman from the table. Clipping the machine to his belt and slipping the earphones over his head, he pressed the play button and then increased the volume. It was Bob Dylan. It did not matter who it was. It was audio blackout.

He pulled the front door closed behind him, and skipped down the wide stone steps to the gate. He kept his eyes forward, focussing on the concrete lamppost opposite and seeing nothing else. "Tangled up in Blue," filled his ears and his head. He walked.

~ * ~

His outstretched hand hit the brass plate in the centre of the door, just below the word push. It swung away from him. The pub was almost empty. Bob Dylan had gone, so had the headphones. Arthur registered this without concern. The room's only other occupant had her back to him. She was perched on a tall stool at the bar, long blonde hair, nice figure, short blue skirt, long slim legs. He could see her reflection in the mirror, pretty, loads of make-up. His mother would hate her. He liked her, and he knew that that was why he was there.

~ * ~

Alice watched the newcomer cross the room toward her. He was young and walked with a swagger. The corners of his mouth were turned up, but he was not smiling. Not tall, probably shorter than she was, it was hard to tell through the mirror, broad shoulders though and no fat.

"Do you mind?"

She turned. In the mirror, he had looked to be further away. He was at her shoulder, gesturing toward the stool next to hers.

"Feel free," she said, and spun her legs away to give him access. Her legs, she looked down at them. Her skirt was very short. *Strange?* She thought. *No*, she decided.

The young man hoisted himself onto the stool and held out a hand. "Arthur." He smiled.

Alice took it. "Alice."

"Hello, Alice. Drink?"

"Got one thanks." She raised her glass.

The barman appeared and placed a glass in front of Arthur. "Taken care of," he said, and turned away.

Arthur looked at Alice and raised his eyebrows.

She shook her head. "Not me."

He looked around, shrugged, and then took a drink.

"Vodka?" Alice asked.

"Gin," he replied.

~ * ~

"Doctor Craven." The voice came from behind her. Alice jumped. She had not heard anyone else enter the pub. In addition, her subconscious had still been toying with her identity. Not Mrs., not Miss, Doctor, that was who she was, Doctor Alice Craven. She turned.

"And, Arthur, glad you could join us." He was a tall man, very tall. Alice craned her neck to look up into his face. It was weathered and wrinkled, but also high-cheek-boned and strong. The hair that framed it was white and lush, brushed back and hanging over the collar of a black, velvet-collared overcoat. His nose was long and hooked, the mouth beneath it tight and white lipped. His eyes flicked from Arthur to her, and Alice almost cowered away from them. One was blue, the other brown, both were piercing. He smiled then and they became warmer, but not friendly.

"Come, my car's outside."

Alice hesitated. There was a buzzing in her head. Her body ached. It was hot. She was thirsty. Her mouth was full of something. It felt like soil, tasted like dirt. She stood. The feeling disappeared but its memory hung on, tugging at her mind but just beyond her reach.

"Arthur."

The young man picked up his glass and raised it to his lips.

"Now."

A flash of pain crossed Arthur's face. He put down his glass and stood.

"Good." The tall stranger turned and walked toward the door.

Alice and Arthur followed.

A large, silver Mercedes had been parked, halfway onto the footpath, outside the pub. The man turned as Alice exited onto the street, and handed her the keys. The car's rear seats were stacked with bulky cardboard cartons.

Arthur walked around the back of the car to its front passenger door and waited.

Alice released the central locking, and looked into the rear seats. There was no room for the stranger. She looked around.

He was gone.

~ * ~

Alice slid behind the wheel and stretched her feet toward the pedals. The positioning of the seat was perfect. In the seat beside her, Arthur stared straight ahead in silence. She checked the mirror, and then guided the car from the footpath and along the narrow street. She knew where she was going, and she knew how to get there. She indicated right and pulled into a steady flow of traffic.

Ahead of the Mercedes, a set of traffic signals shone green. Alice slowed the car to a crawl. A driver behind hooted his impatience. Alice reached into her purse, pulled out a mobile phone and dropped it into her lap. Ahead the traffic signal turned red. The road in front was clear. O'Connell Bridge was wide and empty.

To either side of the car crowds of shoppers and tourists teetered on the kerbside waiting for their signal to cross. On the post beside Alice's window, the little red man disappeared. She picked up the phone and punched out a sequence of numbers. A green man replaced the little red one. From both sides of the road a sea of pedestrians surged around the Mercedes. Alice pressed send, and the signal from her phone made contact with the receiver in the bottom-most carton on the rear seat of the car.

Two

The air above the polished boardroom table was thick with cigar smoke. *Another hour,* Stuart Wilson thought, *and the head of the room's tallest occupant would become engulfed. That would be Rubek, the American, one of the non-smokers.*

The day had gotten them nowhere. Wilson scanned the faces around the table. Someone to his left was talking but he had long since lost the ability and the will to concentrate. *The Spaniard would be next,* he calculated. *He was three inches shorter than the American and would last perhaps an hour and a half.*

He glanced down at the thick manila file in front of him. It was closed. Scribbled on its cover were the results of Wilson's morning musings, down its left hand margin a list of towns: Dublin, Bilbao, Newry, Jerusalem and Colombo. Wilson had listed the obvious suspects next to each town: UVF, ETA, CIRA, Hamas and Tamil Tigers. The latter list had been headed: Suspects. Wilson had added, "Supposed", half an hour earlier. Now he crossed out both words, bracketed the first column and added a large question mark that almost obscured the second.

There had been fourteen suicide bombings in the space of three days, spread across the hotspots of the world. The usual suspects were always first in the frame. No group had claimed responsibility for any of the atrocities. The usual crank organisations had. The ones that everyone knew did not have the resources, the expertise, and like as not the balls to carry them out.

Next to the question mark, Wilson jotted down the common factors: big car, two passengers, massive explosion, maximum casualties, no warning, and no remains. He underlined the last three times. That was the real mystery. They had found remains of the devices and remains of the vehicles. However, there was no trace of the bombers themselves, not the smallest particle of tissue or spattering of blood, nothing. He threw down his pen.

"Adjourn." The word stabbed into Wilson's consciousness. He looked up, and was sufficiently alert to also catch. "Until 9.00 am."

Around the table, chairs scraped across the conference room's wooden floor. Twelve men pushed themselves upright. Wilson's eyes followed their ascent. Tobacco smoke engulfed twelve heads. He considered crawling from the room to avoid the pollution, but then he stood with the others, and took his turn to file through the suite's double doors into the lobby.

The space looked small because it was full of big men. Every delegate had brought his own protection. Times were scary. Wilson looked around for his own Special Protection Unit, and spotted the two burly police officers to the left of the main entrance. He signalled, and they crossed the room to join him, one to either shoulder, slightly to his front. Their overcoats hung open, and their eyes were alert even amongst the crowd of agents protecting all of the other delegates.

Wilson felt a light tap on his shoulder. He looked around, and then up into the pockmarked face of the tall American.

"Beer, Stuart?" Rubek asked.

"Sorry, Bill but I'm knackered. Catch you tomorrow."

"Count on it."

Then Wilson was out through the door, into the front seat of his official Jaguar, and heading into the London traffic. Lights flashed and camera motors whirred from behind the protective cordon that had been thrown around the hotel. Wilson shook his head. There was not a blue uniform in sight, not a bobby's helmet, not even the black shields and helmets of the riot police. What there was, were the camouflage green, automatic rifles and red berets of the parachute regiment.

"Who'd have believed it?" Wilson mumbled but got no reply from either his driver or from his protection in the rear seats. He laid his head back against the Jaguar's headrest and closed his eyes. He was tired. Fifty-five years old, he had headed Scotland Yard's Anti-Terrorist Squad for the last seven years. Now the peace process in the North of Ireland was in tatters. The hopes of the late Nineties had been blown away with the lives and limbs of the Orange Order in Newry and the SDLP meeting in Derry. The Orangemen blamed the Republicans, the Republicans the Orangemen. Wilson now knew that it had been neither, nor any other shade of orange or green. But when hatred ran so deep, he knew, the ears were the first organs to suffer.

It was not only in the North. Wilson's mind did an international tour of the more recent atrocities. Try to tell the right wing Jews that it wasn't Hamas that converted the Jerusalem synagogue into rubble, and one hundred and twenty worshipers into a scattering of body parts. The reprisals in both countries had been swift and bloody, the counter reprisals bloodier, and another peace process, built and nurtured over years had collapsed without trace.

The African Americans of Los Angeles had blamed white supremacists, could not find any, and so had used the police officers and businesses of their own neighbourhoods as outlets for their anger, fear and frustration. It had been the same in Bilbao and in Colombo, before that Macedonia and Indonesia.

The security forces had jumped to the same easy conclusions as the civilians, Wilson himself as much as the others. It had taken time, but eventually some of the pieces had fallen into place, or rather, the usual pieces had not fallen into place, and questions, not usually asked, had started to be asked. That was the reason for that day's conference.

The Israelis saw an international Islamic plot aimed at world domination. The Indonesians with their own internal problems were loath to argue. The Americans saw only Al Qaeda with the same blinkered loathing with which they once viewed the Soviets. Societies in collapse, they argued, made easy pickings for religious fanatics. They could be right. So could the Israelis. He could not possibly be right, because he did not have a clue.

He opened his eyes. The shop windows of the Edgware Road flashed by. There were few people about. They were scared. The country was on a virtual war footing.

The conference had only agreed on two things that day, firstly, that all of the incidents were related. Related, Wilson hated that word, it sounded to have been a minor traffic shunt on Oxford Street. More than related, he corrected his own thoughts. Related, could merely be co-operation. This was more than that. They had all been masterminded by a single source. The second thing was that it scared the hell out of them.

"Sir."

Wilson shook himself alert. A mobile phone was being dangled over his shoulder from the rear of the car. He took it. "Wilson." He listened in silence. Another five minutes, and they would have been on the M1, another twenty, and he would have been home. It was his youngest son's ninth birthday. Wilson would already have missed the cakes and the jelly but could still make it in time for Pass the Parcel and Pin the Tail on the Donkey. He had missed Gavin's previous three birthdays altogether. He would not, he had promised his wife, miss this one. He pressed disconnect and tossed the phone back into the rear seat. "The Yard and fast."

~ * ~

Alice woke with what felt like a furious hangover. She opened her eyes, and then snapped them shut again as bright daylight launched spears of pain into her skull. She tried again, and groaned at the effort.

She was lying, still fully clothed, on top of a made-up bed. She pushed herself onto one elbow and looked around.

The walls of the room were of bare stone, and the floor uncovered and unpolished wood. There was no decoration and no furniture other than the bed on which she lay. Above her head, an unglazed window admitted a steady warm breeze. A solid timber door opposite the window stood ajar. Alice could see along a narrow, stone walled corridor. She eased herself onto her knees and pushed her head into the window opening. The walls of the room were thick, and she had to lean into it to get a glimpse of the outside world. She gasped. She was high up, fifty feet, perhaps more. Below the window the solid stone blocks of the tower stretched down to bare, brown earth.

The landscape was flat and featureless. Nothing grew. The horizon curved across her field of vision as unbroken as a calm, open sea. Above this, the sky was a glow of orange and red as though beyond the horizon line the whole of the planet was aflame.

"Welcome back, Alice my dear."

Alice jerked her head around, grazing it against the rough stone of the recess, rekindling the earlier pain, and drawing a trickle of blood.

"I startled you. I'm sorry."

Alice recognised the man from the pub. She remembered the pub. That explained the hangover.

He was dressed in a floor length, loose-sleeved robe. It was black with silver decoration, which looked to Alice like ancient Greek letters. She recognised alpha and omega even though the symbols were upside down. The dark fabric exaggerated the silver of his hair. The symbols complemented it. She pulled herself clear of the window and stood to face him.

He reached out and brushed her grazed temple with his thumb, looked at the transferred blood for a second, and then sucked it clean. Then he was smiling at her, his eyes as deep and piercing as she remembered them from the pub.

She tried to recall his name, couldn't, and realised that she had never known it.

His tongue flicked across his upper lip.

"Leirbag," he said, still smiling. "Common enough in the Southern Baltic States but a little strange perhaps to the English tongue." His smile broadened.

Alice decided that she liked the man. She liked his angular features and his confident, almost aristocratic manner. There was a hint of mystery too and excitement, perhaps even danger. She returned his smile.

"You must be hungry," Leirbag said. "Please forgive my lack of consideration. Food always helps, I find, after a journey such as yours. Come."

Alice followed him from the room. Her door was the end one on the corridor, and faced along it. Regularly spaced to either side they passed others, all of solid looking timber. They mirrored one another along the whole, stone-walled length of the passage. All were closed.

Leirbag stopped at the last door on the left and pushed it open.

The room was much larger than the one they had just left. The bare stone of the walls and the timber floor looked the same. The ceiling, Alice thought, looked higher. At its centre, a long, rectangular table occupied over half of the available floor space. There were six straight-backed chairs to either side of it, and, at its far end, a single, ornately carved, wooden throne with arms in the shape of open-mouthed serpents. From the tops of either side of its backrest pointed-toothed, imps seemed to be staring at Alice. She looked away from their mocking gaze.

Places were set in front of the throne and the two chairs nearest to either side of it. On the table between the settings were plates of bread, fruit, meat and cheese.

Leirbag walked around the table and lowered himself onto the throne, gesturing Alice to the seat at his right.

Alice sat but could not look at the man without her attention wandering to the carvings, which seemed to be perched, one on each of Leirbag's shoulders. The more she looked at them, the more alive they looked, more alive and less friendly.

"Not the most attractive piece of furniture," Leirbag said, as though reading Alice's mind. "Family heirloom, you see, but it does grow on you." He smiled a white-toothed smile and stroked the serpent arms of his throne.

Alice returned his smile and tried to look at her tormentors through more benign eyes. It didn't work. She concentrated instead on the food in front of her.

"I'm sorry, please help yourself, Alice," Leirbag said. "Arthur will be along shortly. I'm sure that he'll understand if we start without him."

Alice was hungry. She took a wedge of cheese in the fingers of both hands, and bit into it.

Three

Wilson's private office was a square partition structure at the rear of a larger open-plan space. Only one of the seven desks in the main office was occupied. Seven people, his team, and in his opinion, the best officers of the best anti-terrorist squad in the world surrounded that. They stood in silence watching a TV that was hidden from Wilson's view by their clustered bodies.

"Initial reports put the dead at fifteen with forty injured, some of them seriously." The voice of the hidden announcer could have been relaying the soccer results. "Another one hundred people are still unaccounted for."

"Where?" Wilson snapped.

"Bradford, Guv." None of the heads turned toward him.

"Target?"

"Mosque."

Wilson's mind whirled. Bradford, what did he know? It was an industrial town in West Yorkshire, high Asian population, both Muslim and Hindu. There were the usual hotheads on file but there always were. Race relations in the city were good, remarkably good after the riots two years previously. Who would cop the blame for this one, Mossad striking away from home? Homegrown fascists? Hindu fundamentalists?

"Crabb, Searl, get our forensic team up there fast before the local boys do too much damage. Saville get me a 'copter in thirty, and grab a bag, you're with me…and a coffee and a sandwich now. The rest of you turn that fuckin' thing off, and get back to work." Wilson lunged for his office and slammed the door behind him. Then he sank into his chair, and dropped his head into his hands.

He should, he knew, phone home. Sarah would understand. He shook his head. No, she wouldn't, not this time she wouldn't.

A rap at the door interrupted his thoughts. "Come."

A plastic tray holding a polystyrene cup and a plastic wrapped sandwich preceded the young policeman through the door. "Coffee, Guv, chopper'll be on the roof in fifteen."

"Thanks lad, now grab your gear and meet me up there."

Another head rounded the door, this time female and pretty. "Guv, suicide bomb, Pamplona, police barracks."

"Jesus Christ!" Wilson pushed himself to his feet. "Forget your bag, Saville let's go." He shouted over the WPC's shoulder.

They were almost through the door of the outer office. A blond constable, who looked barely old enough to be out without his parents, manned the desk just inside of it. He held a telephone to his ear, but his hand shielded the mouthpiece. "Guv."

"Where?"

"New York, shopping mall."

Wilson did not stop until the elevator doors brushed closed. Then he leaned back against the smooth steel of its rear wall. He had never felt so old or so useless.

~ * ~

Daylight was fading when they put down astride the giant H on top of the West Yorkshire Police headquarters in the centre of Bradford. The air was damp, too dry to be rain, too wet for mist. It clung to Wilson's clothes and soaked into them as effectively as a downpour.

Above the throb of the helicopter's rotors, he could hear the screams of sirens. Flashing blue lights reflected from the glass front of an office block to his right. The door to the stairwell was open, and emitted a warm yellow light. A single, uniformed figure stood next to it.

"Sir, this way, sir, there's a car waiting."

~ * ~

Wilson did not know whether all mosques had domes or minarets. He knew that not all churches had steeples. He wondered for a second why this thought had occurred to him, and then he looked back at the pile of rubble and twisted steel that had so recently been a thriving place of worship. It was day again; or rather, the ring of powerful arc lights that ringed the scene suggested that it was. He looked up into a dark starless sky, and time dropped back into perspective.

A police cordon held back the surrounding crowd. The masses behind it emitted an eerie, banshee wail that ebbed and flowed, like an audible tide lapping at Wilson's senses. A fleet of ambulances, their rear doors open, stood ready. Small groups of yellow helmeted fire fighters crawled over, or bent to dig into the mound of rubble. Two sniffer-dogs worked higher up the pile. Their noses poked at the rubble. Their ears were pricked and alert.

Somewhere off to Wilson's left a loud hailer appealed to the crowd for quiet. The wailing continued. He looked around. A senior officer, all silver pips and medal ribbons, lowered the megaphone to his side and spoke to a less decorated uniform beside him. This policeman turned, and eased his way into the crowd. Seconds later, he reappeared accompanied by another man. The newcomer was Asian and old, he wore baggy white trousers and a knee length white smock. His hair and beard matched the colour of his clothing. He took the loud hailer from the policeman, and lifted it to his lips. Wilson did not understand a single word of what followed but the result was total silence.

One of the dogs raised its head from a protruding bar of steel reinforcement, and cocked it to one side. Its tail wagged, it barked three times and looked around as though for support.

The nearest group of fire fighters scrambled toward the animal and began to scrape away chunks of brick and plaster. From one of the waiting ambulances two paramedics hauled a stretcher up the mound and bent to assist.

Wilson watched until one of the ambulance men stretched down into the hole they had excavated, and then backed out again inching an arm and then a head into the bright arc light.

Wilson turned away. In London, his team had watched his failure to prevent this on TV. He had come to see it on the ground. He could not face seeing it in the flesh. He tugged at Saville's elbow. "Come on lad," he said. "Time for a drink."

~ * ~

Wilson discharged their driver at pub number four. They still had not had a drink. In pubs one, two and three TV screens had been broadcasting coverage of the bombing.

In number four, there was no TV. *No customers either*, Wilson noted, looking around the small bar.

There was a barman though. Saville headed toward him.

Wilson selected a table that faced into the room but had no others behind it. He watched Saville bend to examine the available beers and then point at the central pump of three. Wilson could not make out the brand, and then the young policeman was walking toward him carrying two pints.

"Quiet place," Wilson said, as Saville pushed his pint across the table.

"Not surprised, Guv. The selection's crap."

Wilson eyed his glass, turned it through ninety degrees and took a sip.

"Christ, lad, what's this?"

"Higginbottom's Bitter, Guv. Looked kind of local, I thought."

"Probably is. That's why the fucking place is empty. Back you go lad, large single malt, no ice."

Saville retreated

Wilson sat back and tried to persuade the day's events out of his mind, tried to grasp the overview. He couldn't.

28

The sirens were still whirling in his head, the arc lights still bright in his eyes. "Thank you lad." He took a drink and pushed the pint away. "That's better…so why didn't we know? Why didn't we have a fucking clue?"

Saville was persevering with his pint. The curl of his lips broadcast his disappointment.

"Oh, give it up lad, get a proper one."

"Thanks, Guv."

By the time Saville returned Wilson had managed to clear his mind of most of the detritus of the previous few hours.

"What does it tell you, lad, the fact that we didn't have an inkling, not even a whiff of intelligence that someone somewhere was becoming more active?"

Saville toyed with his glass. "That our intelligence failed. That it's not good enough."

"A little simplistic that." Wilson raised his glass and got the attention of the barman. A gesture toward Saville included him also. "Our intelligence is good, but only where we've placed it. We thought we had every base covered, every active group, every publication right, left and centre."

The barman brought their drinks to the table. Wilson handed him a crumpled note, and waited in silence until the transaction had been completed and they were left alone.

"We missed one, lad, and a big one." The screech of a siren drowned his voice and then faded. "A big enough one to have the means…" There was another siren, louder and closer this time, then another and another. The noise assailed them from all directions.

The barman left his position and made for the door.

Wilson drained his glass. "Come on, lad, something's going down."

The door swung open before any of them could reach it. A young constable peered into the room, saw Wilson, and visibly relaxed. "Sir, sorry sir, I'm to get you back to the hotel." A blue light behind him flashed shadows into the room.

"What's hit?" Wilson was still moving.

The policeman had already turned. "It's blown sir, really blown."

Two army trucks flanked by motorcycle outriders raced past as they exited the bar.

The doors of the squad car were open. The driver craned his neck to watch the door of the pub. He looked scared. Wilson slid across the rear seat. Saville followed. The door was still open when the driver slammed the car into gear and took off after the speeding convoy.

Ahead of them red traffic signals were ignored. The army carried straight on. Their driver swung a left toward the hotel. "Shit."

Wilson was pitched forward. His nose impacted the headrest in front and dripped blood. He was jerked back and then sideways as the driver swung the car around.

Through a mist of tears, Wilson looked along the street. To either side buildings blazed. In the centre so did a bus and two cars. A mob of youths, their faces covered, swarmed toward the car. Something hit the window beside Saville, and they were showered with glass. Their driver completed his turn, and the action was behind them. Wilson turned. Something bright bounced off the boot and burst into flames on the road behind them. Then they were at the corner.

To the left, a group of soldiers crouched in the doorway of a shoe shop. The squad car sped passed them. The soldiers raised their weapons and opened fire into the pursuing crowd.

Four

Wilson sat back in quiet contemplation of the two photographs on his lap as Saville guided the Jaguar from the gravel drive of Tony Craven's Wiltshire cottage. Tall hedgerows lined both sides of the lane; it was also narrow and winding. There were no other dwellings in sight. Wilson sighed, wanting to talk but not wanting to distract Saville's attention until they were off the lane and onto the motorway.

The first photograph had been a remarkable stroke of luck. The traffic-monitoring camera in Bradford city centre had caught the bombers beautifully. The driver of the Mercedes, a woman, attractive, blonde, late twenties to early thirties, was concentrating on a point somewhere below the camera. Wilson smiled, they couldn't have reproduced it more effectively using actors.

Wilson had had the picture circulated to security agencies worldwide and to every news agency in the country. The Times had reproduced it, and that was where five villagers had thought that they recognised Tony Craven's wife.

Wilson switched his study to the photograph that Tony Craven had allowed them to remove from his family album. It was the best of dozens. The photographer had snapped Alice Craven from one of the cottage's upstairs windows. She was crouching in the garden; retrieving a piece of litter from the lawn but her attention was on something in the direction of the house. The angle, even the tilt of her head, was identical in both shots. Wilson was convinced that it was the same woman. Tests back at the Yard, he hoped, would confirm this beyond reasonable doubt.

It had been an interesting interview. Wilson's fingers clenched; his anger rising just thinking about it. Tony Craven had been co-operative but detached. It had felt to Wilson that they were discussing an intellectual puzzle. He had detected no feeling of loss for his missing wife from the man. There had been no expression of outrage at the bomb attack and no show of disbelief that there could possibly be a connection between the two. There had been no anger at the suggestion that Alice was responsible for the bombing. He shook his head. He had been so close to slapping the man, would have but for Saville's, well-timed throat clearance. He looked at Saville, and smiled; his liking for his assistant drowning out his loathing for Craven.

He pulled his notebook from the top of the Jag's dashboard, and flicked it open. Alice Craven was a doctor. There had been no time for children; both were workaholics. She had volunteered for work in some Somali war zone. She had been missing for months. Doctor Alice Craven was presumed dead, or perhaps captured by some warlord's private army. No ransom demand had ever been made, and as time passed, dead had become the more likely of the two options.

"Unless whoever captured her needs a doctor more than money." Tony Craven had suggested, in a voice that was empty of emotion.

There had been just one spark of feeling, Wilson remembered. "Why did she go to Somalia?" He had asked.

"To spite me. No other reason." Anger had blazed in Tony Craven's eyes, and then they had seemed to cloud over once again.

Wilson snapped the pad shut, and looked across the width of the car at Saville. "What d'you think lad?"

"Well, it's the same woman."

Wilson looked back at the two photographs. He could not see one discrepancy. "Then why?"

"Could've been turned." Saville kept his eyes on the road. "She was a woman of principle or she wouldn't have been there in the first place."

"That's not what the husband says."

"You believe him?"

Wilson transferred his concentration to the passing countryside. The man's wife had been missing for months. She could well have already be dead. Her husband had identified her as a callous suicidal murderess, in which case she was certainly dead. All with the same display of emotion that Wilson had seen in the eyes of the goldfish that swam in pointless circles around the bowl in the corner of the room into which Tony Craven had ushered them.

"Not for a second," He replied. "And if she'd been turned by somebody in Somalia then why a mosque? And, why Bradford? It would make more sense if it had been the American embassy or some such." He stroked his chin between thumb and forefinger. "No, this was meant to alienate the Muslim community, no other reason."

~ * ~

A week had passed since the Bradford bombing. The two photographs lay side by side on Wilson's desk. Beside them, a detailed report confirmed that by every measurement conceivable they were of the same woman. Wilson rubbed at his eyes with the balls of his thumbs. He had his killer, but he had nowhere to go from there. The car was a Mercedes with false CD licence plates. Five of the same make and model had been reported stolen in the months prior to the bombing. Three had been accounted for. There was not a large enough piece of the bomber's vehicle left to tie it in with the other two, not even an engine plate. They were still sifting rubble up in Yorkshire but Wilson was not optimistic.

He glanced at his watch. It was almost noon. There was a National Security meeting at 2.00 PM. In Number 10, they didn't come much bigger. What did he have? He knew who the bomber was, one of them at least. The second, a white youth, had been caught by the camera just as clearly as had Alice Craven, had received the same coverage, but so far, they had not identified him. He let out a long sigh, the bottom line was that he had not prevented it, didn't have a clue as to who had masterminded it, and like as not wouldn't be able to prevent the next one or the one after that. He scooped up the photographs, opened his desk drawer, and tossed them into it. It would not be an easy meeting.

~ * ~

Wilson walked out of the Cabinet Office with head bowed, relieved of his post, full pension, pressures of the job, usual story, scrapped. He had heard all the words but understanding had come seconds later, when he was trying to listen to the next ones.

"Stuart."

The call came from the door of an anteroom to his left, and barely brushed his consciousness. The PM himself would make an official announcement to the assembled 'gentlemen of the press' in half an hour. That would give Wilson time to 'no comment' his way through the tabloid pack, and be most of the way home before they were loosed on him.

"Stuart." The voice was louder this time and accompanied by a hand on his shoulder. Wilson turned.

Bill Rubek was smiling down at him.

The hand on Wilson's shoulder guided him into a small office. He heard the door close behind him.

"Grab a seat," Rubek said

"No point Bill. Perhaps they haven't talked to the Americans. I'm finished. I'm out of it."

The arm guided him to a chair, and pushed him down onto it. "No, no, Stuart, far from it. We haven't even got started." The American released his grip, and moved around the table to sit opposite.

There was a file on the desk in front of Wilson. It had his name on it. He opened it just as a point of focus. Inside was a copy of the photograph of Alice Craven, captured by the traffic camera in Bradford exactly seven minutes before she blew one hundred and thirty-four innocent people to pieces.

"Got your picture," Rubek said, and tossed another on top of it. The car was different, the surroundings were different, but the woman was the same.

Wilson looked up at the American.

"We want you in on this, Stuart. Your PM's okayed it. We have the run of the resources of every civilised country on the planet, even some of the less civilised ones."

Wilson looked over his shoulder to the door, trying to tell himself that the meeting he had just left had actually happened. *If it hadn't,* he concluded, *then he really wasn't up to it.*

The American laughed. "This isn't a government thing Stuart, not officially. They wouldn't dare touch it." He laughed again but without humour. "This is X-Files stuff. That…" He pointed at the uppermost photograph. "…was New York, the shopping mall, exactly thirty-five minutes after Bradford. Every test that we can do tells us that it's the same woman."

Wilson rearranged the pictures so that they lay side by side. Both had dates and times recorded in the top right hand corner. He looked from one to the other. His brow creased.

"Don't worry about the time difference calculations," Rubek said. "Take my word for it. It's thirty-five minutes real time."

Wilson looked up into Rubek's face. It was set and serious. He looked back at the pictures. "It's impossible." He shook his head. "Impossible."

"No, not impossible." The voice was soft. Wilson jerked his head around to its source. He had not even seen the man who was sitting away from the table, in the far corner of the room.

He was small, and his crossed arms and legs bundled him even tighter. He was old too, with wispy, white hair through which his scalp shone bright pink. His brown raincoat was unbuttoned, so was the grey tweed jacket beneath it. Beneath these was a brightly striped v-neck pullover. The man cleared his throat. "Not impossible if she was already dead."

"Well, she was dead after Bradford." Wilson conceded.

"She was dead before Bradford." The old man countered. "Believe me, she was dead before Bradford."

"Sorry, Stuart." Rubek held out an introductory hand. "Ray North."

"Mr. North." Wilson stood, and held out his hand. The man grunted but made no attempt to uncurl himself from his seat. Wilson regained his chair, and looked at Rubek from beneath raised brows.

The American smiled, and looked at his watch. "Come on, we've still fifteen minutes before you're fired officially." He stood, and smiled. "We should be halfway to Hendon by then. There's a plane waiting."

"Plane for where?" Wilson asked, as he too gained his feet.

The American's arm slipped around his shoulder once again. "Somalia."

~ * ~

The heat was almost unbearable. Wilson had never been anywhere hotter than a family holiday in Torquay in July and, if he could possibly avoid it, he told himself, he never would again. The dust only added to his discomfort, turning to cement as it settled on his sweaty skin. It probably would not have been so bad without the excavators that were tearing into the packed earth at the north end of the compound.

Years of intermittent artillery and air bombardment had pounded the buildings around them into sections of freestanding wall interspersed with piles of rubble. In the far distance, a range of mountains looked cool and green. That only made things worse.

A group of Somali soldiers lounged against two ancient, three-ton trucks off to Wilson's left. They were there for protection against bandits. Wilson had little confidence in their ability to provide this, or to do the spadework once the first bodies were uncovered.

He turned. Behind him, three, dust-spattered but new four-wheel drives were the visitors' transport. Rubek stood in front of the lead vehicle. He was chatting with the two U.S. Rangers, who, together with the two SAS men, Wilson thought, were a more reliable protection squad than that provided by the Somalis. The two British soldiers were out of sight behind the middle vehicle, brewing tea.

A refrigeration unit that was close to being half as big as the Toyota itself topped the truck at the rear. That one, they hoped, would soon be carrying the remains of Dr Alice Craven back across the desert to a military airfield.

The USAF would forward them to a secure research establishment from there. No one had told Wilson where this was. *That secure,*he thought.

The smell hit Wilson's senses before the shout of the excavator operator. It was in his nose, in his mouth, sweet and repellent. Then it was in his stomach, which tried to eject it. Acid bile filled his mouth. He swallowed it down. Up it came again.

"Over here, sir." One of the SAS men led him between the vehicles. "We don't make tea just 'cause we're Brits you know."

His colleague stood up from a small stove, and held out a cup of thick brown brew. "Drink, sir, it'll do you good."

Wilson took the cup between two hands without speaking, took a drink, and his stomach settled. He hoped it was only tea. *No he didn't;* he told himself, once it worked, he didn't give a shit. He smiled. "Thank you, Sergeant."

"All part of the service, sir. Now, if you're okay, we'll go and get those idle native bastards working."

"Yes, of course, carry on Sergeant." He took another, longer drink. Rubek joined him. Wilson looked around.

The two Rangers had joined their British colleagues and the Somali infantry were prodding at the pit with spades and picks.

"They okay?" Wilson asked.

"Yeah, they're fine," Rubek replied, "Thank God, I had a look over the edge, not pretty."

~ * ~

There was only one white female corpse. Seventy-four native Somali ones were piled around and on top of it

They hoped that the body they had bagged and stowed in the refrigerated truck was that of Alice Craven. One of the Rangers was at the wheel. The second Ranger drove the supply truck. The two SAS men occupied the front seat of the third with Wilson and Rubek behind.

They travelled in silence, their driver attacking the pot holed desert road as though it were a child molester. Wilson tightened his grip on the door handle, and watched him from behind. The soldier had seen the bodies, Wilson had not. He looked at Rubek "What'll they do with the rest of them?"

"Put 'em back," the American replied.

Wilson shuddered, and returned his attention to the back of the driver's head.

~ * ~

Wilson's small apartment at the research centre overlooked a wide expanse of bleak moorland. When the sun shone, the pinks and purples of abundant heather lent his surroundings a cheery atmosphere. It rarely did. That day was as monotone grey as the three that had preceded it. Rain threatened constantly but never seemed to fall. He turned from the window. They had been in Yorkshire for over a week, and the investigation was not progressing well. Sometimes it seemed that it was not progressing at all. They had confirmed that the body, airlifted from Somalia, was indeed that of Alice Craven. North seemed to gain undue pleasure from this knowledge as though simply having the body was a major leap forward. Wilson did not like the man, but as a rule, he disliked small men. He had tried to compensate for this but his friendly overtures were brushed aside with cryptic remarks meant to make him feel out of his depth, a dabbler in things about which he knew nothing.

He was due at the meeting in ten minutes. He caught sight of himself in the wall mirror, and brushed a renegade tuft of hair back into place. He had nothing to contribute. He would listen; he would ask questions that seemed to be sensible. North would answer these through an undisguised sneer.

~ * ~

"Most operational planning is engaged with getting your men out safely afterward." Bill Rubek paced the floor around the meeting table.

Wilson and North watched his progress in silence.

"Take away that complication, and it becomes easy."

"Suicide attacks?" Wilson asked.

North snorted.

Rubek continued. "Yes, but the consideration then is limited resources. There are fanatics of course but they have to be targeted carefully and to optimum effect."

"What we have here…" North took over. "…Is a power that has turned suicide bombers into a renewable resource."

Wilson felt cold. He did not care how stupid his next statement sounded. "But that means power over life and death itself."

"Exactly." For once North's expression lacked contempt. "But people, however fanatical, can't just volunteer. These are not the terrorists you've been trained to deal with. They could be anyone, but they must be given, given by someone that they care for, someone that they love."

Five

Tony Craven poured himself a large brandy, and sipped at it as he watched the unmarked police car disappear around the corner at the end of his driveway.

This time they had taken Alice's hairbrush and a cosmetics pouch, bagged and labelled. They would use the magic of the forensic sciences and their new god DNA analysis to further verify the identity of his wife's body. He chuckled, and took a deeper drink.

His previous visitor had left with a silk scarf and underwear to work his own much more ancient magic. Tony had not spared a single thought for the possible consequences. Alice had walked out on him for her own selfish reasons. She had not spared a thought for him, for the loneliness that led to depression that led to the virtual collapse of his business. "Just a couple of personal items of which she was fond." The man had said.

Tony had bought both scarf and underwear as birthday presents, or anniversary presents, he could not remember which.

"And your signature."

That had been strange, but his business had been bled dry, a few drops of his own blood had seemed a small price to pay.

Tony had met the second stranger in his local pub on the night after he had sealed the bargain. They talked electronics and parts supply. The ensuing order had been huge, as had the deposit that lifted the pressure of his bankers from his shoulders, saved his business, saved his home. The Mercedes was new. It had all cost only a scarf and a pair of knickers, *and Alice's life,* he thought, and shrugged. He had done nothing criminal. A scarf and a pair of knickers, forty jobs saved, and twenty more created. Alice had only been extending the suffering of Somali peasants. He was creating security and happiness for hardworking Englishmen.

His glass was empty. He refilled it.

~ * ~

Sean Molloy invited the two police officers into his apartment. "Enquiries about the death of his son." They had said on the phone.

Sean wished that he still had the photograph, but he had given it away. He could not remember why. He had been drunk to the verge of unconsciousness. The man had bought him more drink. They had talked about their families. Sean had shown him the photo, the cigarette lighter and the wristwatch that had belonged to Arthur. Sean had kept them as reminders of the only thing in Dublin that he still cared for.

In his seedy London bed-sit, after yet another binge session in one of the local pubs, he would take them from his pocket, and he would cry. Now Arthur was dead, and he didn't have even those mementos left. There had been something else too but he could not remember. He looked at his thumb as though expecting to find inspiration there.

"Mr. Molloy." The policeman's voice broke into his thoughts.

"Sorry, please sit."

~ * ~

Molloy's seedy bed-sit was history. On the morning after his meeting with the stranger in the pub, with his hangover pounding inside his head, Sean had guided his shaking pen across the tight print of The Racing Post, seven horses, one accumulator, seven winners, three hundred and sixty seven thousand pounds. His luck had held, through Premiership soccer, Formula One and the dogs. It could not bring Arthur back but life had to go on.

Wilson and Rubek lowered themselves onto one of the room's three red leather chesterfields. "Thanks for your time Mr. Molloy," Wilson said. "We'll be as brief as possible. Before the accident did anyone approach you about your son?"

Molloy looked at the policemen. "No…why should they?"

Wilson and Rubek watched the man. Rubek cleared his throat. "Mr. Molloy, do you have any of Arthur's personal effects?"

"No, nothing. I had a photo and a lighter and watch, but they're gone now."

"Gone where?"

"A man in a pub."

"Why?"

"I don't know." Molloy's voice rose. "Look, I was locked see, blotto. We drank. We talked. We drank some more. I gave them to him...I think."

Wilson leaned forward. "Was there anything else, a bargain, a contract?"

"No. I don't think so." Molloy looked to be struggling for a memory, and then shook his head. "I don't know." He lowered his gaze. "Why?"

"We're just tying up a few loose ends."

"What loose ends? It was an accident."

"We're not so sure about that."

"You think he was killed?"

Molloy's gaze darted about the room, and then settled on Rubek.

"You think he committed suicide?"

"Mr. Molloy, we don't know." Wilson spread his hands. "But some things just don't fit. Anything at all that you can remember might help. What did this man in the pub look like?"

"I don't know."

"But it was a man?"

"Yes."

"Young? Old? Well dressed? Scruffy?"

"I don't remember...white hair though. I remember that."

Rubek scribbled this down, and then took over, "Did he approach you, or you him?"

"I don't remember...He approached me I think, because I didn't socialise, not then." His gaze dropped to the floor. "Not when I was locked."

"Which pub was this?"

"The Pickled Onion, it's just round the corner from where I used to live."

"Your local?"

"Was."

"Would you mind accompanying us there, see if any of the staff can remember?"

"Would it help?"

"It might."

~ * ~

The Pickled Onion smelled of stale beer and cigarette smoke. It was dingy, uninviting, and none too clean.

The barman looked up from his paper as they entered. "Sean, how the devil are ya? Long time no see."

Wilson introduced himself and Bill Rubek and then, needing no further confirmation that the barman knew Sean Molloy, he turned. "Mr. Molloy, would you mind waiting in the car for us? We shan't be long, and we may have a few more questions."

Molloy looked as though he was going to object. His mouth opened, and then closed. He looked at Wilson for a second, and then turned and headed for the door.

There were no other customers in the bar, but evidence of former ones lay everywhere, in the overflowing ashtrays scattered about the beer-splashed tables and in the crushed remains of potato chips trodden into the threadbare carpet.

Wilson bought the barman a large Irish. "Did you know Sean Molloy well?"

"Didn't know his last name but yeah used to drink here most nights before he moved away." He shook his head. "Started winning, like big time, funny old world…Always on his own he was, never talked to anyone, ordered his drinks, lots of 'em, got pissed then staggered home."

"You never saw him talking to anyone?" Rubek asked, nodding at the barman's glass, and permitting a hasty refill.

"Well, there was the one time, I noticed 'cause it was strange see. And because the man was strange, not the usual sort we get in here. Tall and sort of aristocratic, long white hair but combed back, neat like, wore a Crombie. You even noticed the coat because it fit so well, like it was tailor made. He had a stick too, not a walking stick, more like a cane, straight with a silver handle. There were animals engraved on it, dragons like. I copped that when I went to clear their table. He saw me looking, and moved it away like I was going to nick it."

The barman made to turn away.

Wilson pulled a roll of notes from his trouser pocket, peeled off a ten, looked at it, and then added another. "Anything else you remember?"

"Yeah funny, yer man…Sean, cut his thumb, deliberate like. I was going to sort it out but someone wanted serving, when I looked again it were all peaceful so I let it rest."

"Thank you sir, you've been very helpful." Wilson tossed the two notes onto the bar, where they soaked up a small pool of spilled beer before the barman snatched them up.

"Where to?" Rubek asked as they regained the street.

"We'll drop our man home, and then another visit to our Mr. Craven, I think. See if he can recall any Faustian experiences."

Six

From the outside, the building that North called his lab had looked no different from the other drab, windowless, concrete blocks that dotted the perimeter of the base. The interior was like nothing that Wilson had ever seen.

Swirls of black and red decorated both the walls and the ceiling. Figures appeared in the seemingly random patterns, and then were gone almost as soon as Wilson's perception locked onto them. For split seconds, and all around and above him, he saw cherubs and griffons, snakes and dragons. As soon as they were recognised, they were lost to him, as though the concrete of the wall itself was in constant flux.

Wilson and Rubek stood to either side of the blast-proof entrance door.

North was standing with his back to them, head bent forward and arms outstretched, in the centre of a chalk design that covered most of the floor. Around its edges, small stacks of Arthur Molloy's belongings were interspersed with conical piles of white powder and chalices of clear liquid.

Wilson looked at Rubek across the width of the entrance. The American shrugged, and forced a smile.

Wilson leaned his head back against the wall, and scanned the ceiling, searching for the source of the light show. His study uncovered no projector and no telltale wiring. He lowered his gaze to the walls, and then to the edges of the floor, convinced that somewhere there had to be a clue as to the source of the fantastic images but finding none. *Clever*, he thought, *very clever,* and reversed the path of his search. The constantly shifting patterns were starting to make his head hurt but he persevered. He stifled a yawn; his initial fascination retreating into boredom. His eyelids were getting heavy. He closed them, guiding his thoughts to revisit the events that had brought them there.

They had Alice Craven's effects and they had her body. North insisted that they retrieve as much as they could from Molloy's Dublin home. Wilson had assumed that they were using Arthur's effects because they had more of them. "Not at all," North had said, "we're using them because we stole them. Alice's were given, and by the person who gave her. They're not useless but they are certainly less powerful." The finality of the statement did not invite further probing. Wilson and Rubek had attempted none.

He opened his eyes. There was a lion on the wall opposite. He concentrated on the image, and it was gone. He thought he could still make out a part of the mane. He tried to rebuild the rest of the creature around it, but then that was gone also.

Rubek coughed.

Wilson looked at him.

The American nodded into the room.

North was on his knees, his forehead on the floor. In front of, and above him, the air shimmered grey, then gold, and then compacted into a swirling mist. A face and then a body appeared. Wilson recognised Arthur Molloy, and took a step into the room.

Rubek grabbed his sleeve, and pulled him back to the wall. Arthur's image increased in clarity, and appeared to be becoming solid. Then it screamed.

North's body lifted from the floor, spun onto its back, and slammed back down again.

Wilson moved again. This time Rubek did not hold him back but followed. They stepped between the piles of clothing, books and compact discs, and bent toward the old man.

North's eyes were wide. There was white foam at the corners of his mouth. "Had him, had him," he gasped, "lost him." His shoulders convulsed.

Wilson reached out. North grabbed his hand with a strength that he looked to be incapable of mustering. The old man held out his other hand. Rubek gripped its bony fingers. "We must follow him. We must." North's lips continued to move, but all that escaped them was gibberish.

Wilson's head began to spin, his vision darkened, and he felt himself falling sideways.

~ * ~

The bare, stone walls of Leirbag's tower exaggerated the sound of the scream.

At the table, and halfway through her meal, Alice jumped. Her fork clattered against the side of her plate.

The scream echoed around the room.

Leirbag leapt to his feet, and was almost at the door before Alice stood to follow. He turned. "Sit." His tone brooked no argument.

Alice sat.

Leirbag stomped out of the room leaving, the door swinging on its hinges behind him.

~ * ~

Arthur stumbled into the corridor from a door to Leirbag's right.

"Back." The tall man said with a hiss.

Arthur stopped, still clinging to the heavy, metal door handle as though, without its support, he would tumble to the floor. His mouth was open; his features distorted with pain.

Leirbag, arms rigid and swinging at his side, strode toward him. "Back." He accompanied his shout with a push to Arthur's shoulder that propelled him back into the room. Another vicious shove, and he was on his knees in the centre of a chalk circle.

"Stay there, fool." Leirbag stooped, and picked up a wristwatch and cigarette lighter that Arthur's flailing arm had sent skidding from the circle toward the door. He held them high in the air, closed his eyes, threw back his head, and began a high-pitched, melodious chant.

~ * ~

Alice peered around the side of the open door. Leirbag had his back to her. Arthur was crouched on the floor in the centre of the room. Above and around them, the air shimmered red and black. Alice thought that she could see faces in the swirling mist. Animal features, half formed, distorted and then disappeared. Below them Arthur's form was becoming fainter. As it faded, three other figures began to materialise in the circle. Two were crouched in much the same position as Arthur. The third was lying on his back.

Leirbag's voice grew louder, and his chanting more frantic.

Arthur was little more than a shimmering outline. Alice could make out that the other three were male but their ghostly images did not appear to be gaining solidity, and then they too began to fade. The red and black mist closed in around them, and suddenly the circle was empty.

~ * ~

Leirbag dropped his hands to his sides, and lowered his head. Then he turned. There were beads of sweat on his brow. He saw Alice. His eyes widened. He smiled, and held out a hand. "Alice, my dear." He beckoned her into the room.

Alice, reassured by the smile, returned it, and stepped into the room. Leirbag's left arm lashed out, striking a backhanded blow to her head that knocked her from her feet, and sent her spinning across the floor into the solid stone of the wall.

A sharp pain shot up her spine. She winced, and raised a hand to her brow. The blow had reopened the wound there. A thin trickle of blood ran down her cheek, and into the corner of her mouth. It tasted sweet, and then it tasted like dirt. It swelled under her tongue, and became solid and gritty. She spat, and watched a muddy mix of soil and saliva splatter onto the boards of the floor. Then there was more. She spat again, and again, each time there was more in her mouth than she had expelled. Her mouth was full. Her tongue was trapped. There was no room for more but still it came, forcing her lips apart, creeping down her throat. She gagged, and looked up at Leirbag. Her eyes were wide with fear. Then her mouth was empty. She clamped her lips together, and ran her tongue over a clean, taste-free palate.

"You must obey me, Alice. You must always obey me." Leirbag was smiling down at her. He held out a hand.

She hesitated. A hint of a taste made her tongue recoil. She held out a hand. The taste disappeared.

Leirbag helped her to her feet. "Always, Alice, in everything." He was still smiling. "Come, our meal was interrupted." He kept a gentle grip on her fingers as he led her from the room. In the corridor he turned her to face him. "You are beautiful, Alice, beautiful enough to be a queen. My queen once I am king."

She looked up at his sharp features and strange, haunting eyes. Everything except those eyes slipped out of focus. She felt her lips part as though to accept a kiss. A feeling of well being flooded over her. She shivered but it was with excited anticipation rather than fear. *I could,* she thought, *do worse.*

Leirbag squeezed her hand, breaking the spell. "We have lost Arthur," he said. "Disappointing that. We still have twelve seats to fill before our court is complete, but we will fill them, my princess. We will fill them." They were at the door to the throne room, Alice looked along the length of the table. Only two places were set. "Yes," she replied, "we will."

"Yes…my king."

There was just the hint of a taste.

Alice bowed her head. "Yes, my king." The taste disappeared.

Seven

They were all old men, their bodies bent and compacted with age. There were ten of them. They were sitting cross-legged in a circle around a blazing log fire. There were two gaps in their circle; central to these, two candles flickered but added nothing to the illumination of the tent.

The only sounds were the sizzling of the sap that dripped from the freshly hewn logs onto the fire, and the flapping of the thick canvas walls of the tent that kept out most of the freezing wind that lashed down from the surrounding mountains and across the barren plain on which they were camped for the winter.

One of the candle flames spluttered and died. A sigh of despair travelled clockwise around the circle. The flames of the fire shrank back toward the wood that fuelled them as though in sympathy.

"Ranorth is lost." The old man looked down at the extinguished wick. A string of white smoke curled up from it to the roof of the tent, and then like a dying breath it was gone.

"Aye, Ranvile, and Leirbag still lives. We have failed."
The answering voice was full of despair.

Mumbles of agreement rolled over the weakened fire
from the bowed heads that surrounded it.

~ * ~

Wilson looked around at his new surroundings. It
couldn't be real. He closed his eyes, shook his head, and
then looked again. The walls of the gorge rose vertically
to either side. To his front, a narrow track wound steeply
and erratically upward until it was lost in a swirling bank
of dark cloud. From out of those clouds, a bitter wind
roared past his ears, and pricked his exposed face and
hands with needles of ice. He turned away from its attack,
and looked down at his hands. They at least were how he
remembered them, so were his brown brogues and the
chalk smudge on the knee of his trousers.

North lay on his back a few feet down the track. His
body was contorted, and his eyes stared, unblinking into
the onslaught of cold air and ice. Beyond him, Rubek was
on his knees, and struggling to his feet. His lips were
moving but the wind carried his words away down the
gorge and over the bleak moorland plain beyond.

Wilson stopped fighting the wind, and allowed it to
push him along the path. He glanced down at North's
body as he passed. "Another fine mess you've gotten me
into," he said, as he edged alongside the American on the
narrow track.

Rubek shrugged but the shadow of a smile curled the
corners of his mouth. "Let's just get out of this..."
Something bounced off his temple. He dropped to his
knees, and then keeled over sideways.

Wilson's attention flicked from his fallen companion to the object that had caused his fall.

A carved wooden club, dumbbell shaped and weighted at either end with a band of grey metal had become wedged between two jagged rocks. He bent to examine it. Another grazed the top of his skull, and clattered against the gorge wall beyond. He turned.

There were four of them, amongst the boulders behind and above him. They were big men, very big men, tall and broad, with wild unkempt hair and beards. All were clad in loose woollen jerkins patch-worked in greys and browns.

Wilson's eyes darted left, and then right, searching for an escape route. Upward and into the wind would be impossible, but down with the wind behind him... He concentrated on that. There was a large egg-shaped boulder. It was big enough for him to crouch behind, and as far away from him as he was from the giants. He turned to face them, not wanting the direction of his gaze to give him away, and edged sideways half a pace. One of the men grunted. Wilson registered a barely discernable flick of a wrist. Something whirled toward him. He slumped to the ground next to the prone American.

~ * ~

Alice rolled over, and felt the empty sheet next to her. She sat up shaking the hair from her eyes. Leirbag was standing at the foot of the bed, looking down at her. She had not felt him leave her side. He was dressed once again in the flowing, black and silver gown. His expression could have been affection, or, just as easily disdain.

"Come," he said, "there's work to be done." His face brightened, lighting up his haunting eyes.

Alice smiled back. "Yes…yes, my king."

He turned, and strode from the room.

Alice rolled onto her back, and stared up at the rough timbered ceiling. It had been wonderful, then scary, wonderful, and then scary again. She shuddered. There was a tall enamel jug next to a washbasin on the table across the room. None of these, she was sure, had been there before. She needed to make herself clean. Her hand slid beneath the sheets to the moisture between her thighs. Her body quivered at the contact. She pulled her arm free, and turned her fingers in the light from the window. There was blood.

She swung her legs over the side of the bed. The suddenness of the movement made her head swim. She hesitated, and then pushed herself to her feet. There was work to be done

~ * ~

"They say the strangers killed Ranorth." The old man looked around the circle until his eyes came to rest on the extinguished candle. "The only talk is of revenge. Already they are preparing for it."

"They will do nothing without our blessing, Ranvile, scared as they are."

"They captured them next to his body near the entrance to Ardam's Gorge. They can see no other truth. And it was we, remember, who told them to guard it. We warned them that it was from there that our enemies would appear."

"Ranorth did not die on this world. That we know."

"We know, but they don't, and their faith has been severely tested of late."

~ * ~

Wilson tried to raise a hand to his throbbing temple. It was stuck fast behind his back. There was something else too, something hard against his spine. He opened his eyes. He was in the centre of a circular tent, and tied to its single support pole. His mouth was dry. He licked his upper lip, and caught the taste of blood. The wind tugged at the loose entrance-flap, and he caught a glimpse of a pair of woollen-clad legs beyond it. He looked around as best he could. There was no sign of Rubek. He flexed his fingers, and was relieved when a tingling at their tips confirmed that he had managed to get some blood circulating to them once again. He kept up the movement until the sensation stopped, and then concentrated on freeing himself. It took only a few seconds for him to realise that his efforts were futile.

The tent flap moved again, not the wind this time but a hand pulling it aside. A man crouched at the entrance, and studied Wilson before he advanced, and straightened.

Wilson looked up at him. His hair was long, blond and matted, so was his beard. He could have been one of the men who captured them in the gorge. Wilson was not sure. He concentrated his policeman's mind on the man's features: wide, honest, eyes, one grey the other blue, a flattened nose with gaping nostrils. A bushy moustache covered the man's mouth. Wilson had the feeling that it would be large with full lips. His arms were long and although covered by loose woollen sleeves the square shoulders above them suggested that they were well muscled. Wilson's scrutiny continued its downward path to two large weather-beaten hands; one held a large wooden club, the other a long, barbed and lethal looking dagger.

There was a noise from behind the man, and he stepped aside. Two others entered the tent. They could have been brothers of the first, only their hair colour, redder, and somehow more intimidating, was different. "He is to be taken before the Council first," one of them said.

The first man grunted. He was not, Wilson surmised, at all happy with this.

The dagger twirled around the man's fingers, and his eyes locked onto Wilson's.

Wilson shuddered, knowing that the man would be happier cutting his throat than his bonds, but when he stepped around him, it was rope rather than skin that the big man severed. The two others stepped forward, grabbed an arm apiece, and hauled him to his feet. Only when standing did he get a perspective of the size of the men. His eyes were below the shoulders of those to either side of him. The man behind him had been taller still.

The two giants at his side grabbed his arms above the elbows, and thrust him through the tent-flap, into a bitingly cold wind.

From a tent opposite, Rubek, flanked by his own two guards, was pushed to face him. There was an ugly swelling to the side of his head. From this, a trickle of blood traced the line of his cheekbone. His captors dwarfed even the tall American.

"You okay?" Wilson asked.

"Never been better." Rubek smiled. "Nasty bruise."

"You too."

The men at his side pushed Wilson through ninety degrees, and then forward. He looked from side to side, more tents, hundreds of them, stretched away to both sides for as far as he could see across the open, grassy plain. More people: men, women and children moved between them. Those closest stopped and looked as they passed. The adults paused only for a moment before their gazes dropped to the ground, the children stared less self-consciously, and for longer.

They rounded a corner, and entered a clear area of tussock grass centred by a much larger tent than any they had seen previously. In front of it, a group of men were erecting a wooden scaffold. Children ran in and out between their legs and the supports of the structure.

"For us, you think?" Wilson asked.

"Seems likely," Rubek, replied.

The giants guided them around the work party, and then pulled them to a halt in front of the entrance to the tent. One stepped from behind them, and slid through the tent flap but allowed them no view of whatever awaited them inside. A few seconds of uncomfortable shuffling followed, and then the giant's matted red hair reappeared. He nodded twice, and then withdrew.

Wilson and Rubek were pushed toward the hanging leather flap, and then through it.

~ * ~

Alice crossed, and then uncrossed her legs. They were, she thought, keeping her waiting for too long. Anger welled up within her. They should show more respect. She was on Leirbag's business. But they didn't know that. She smiled, counted slowly down from ten, and smoothed down her skirt. It was new, tailored and businesslike. The hot summer sun had persuaded her to leave the matching jacket in the car. She regretted this decision now in the tiled and windowless room. The canvas-slung, metal-framed chair was uncomfortable. She stood. As she did so, the dark blue, steel door of the room swung inward.

"Sorry to keep you waiting, ma'am."

The warder stood ramrod straight in the doorway. Everything about him shouted perfectionist, the shine of his buttons and shoes, the symmetry of the knot at his throat, the angle or rather the lack of it of his peaked cap.

"This way, ma'am, if you please."

Alice picked up her tan leather briefcase from the floor, and followed the square shoulders of her escort from the room, and along a harshly illuminated, tiled corridor. The smell of disinfectant overlay but could not completely hide an undertone of stale urine. They passed door after identical blue door. At regular intervals, barred doors were unlocked, and swung open at their approach, by men as immaculately uniformed as the one she followed. None of these spoke. The only sound was that of their footfalls on the white tiles of the floor. At the end of the corridor, another blue door faced them. Below its swivel-shuttered peephole, a rectangular plastic sign announced that this was interview room No. 4.

Her escort unclipped a heavily laden key ring from his belt, unlocked the door, and then stepped aside to allow her access.

Alice stepped into a brightly lit room.

"Just knock when you're through, ma'am."

Alice did not turn. The door slammed closed behind her. The sound echoed around the white tiled walls, and then she heard a key turn in the lock.

In front of her, and sitting behind a plain metal table was the reason for her visit. Sydney Weaver, convicted drug trafficker, gunrunner, racketeer; thirty-seven year convicted.

"You the new brief?" His accent was East London trying not to be. His eyes played up and down Alice's body. He smiled, narrowing his eyes to slits. The tip of his tongue appeared, and smoothed across his upper lip.

Alice shuddered, then composed herself. "I'm here to get you out, Mr. Weaver. It will take more than a brief to do that." She pulled the room's only other chair from beneath the table, and sat, crossing her legs.

Weaver's eyes followed the action, and stayed there.

Alice swung her briefcase onto the table, and clicked it open. Her hand dipped inside, and pulled out a roll of parchment.

"So what do you want?" Weaver's eyes were on the parchment now. Alice could read both curiosity and hope in his face. She smiled, in control now. Leirbag had said it would be easy. Alice was starting to believe him. "Your son, Mr. Weaver, your son for your freedom." Before he could reply, Alice unrolled the parchment, and pushed it across the table.

Weaver took it.

Alice watched his eyes scan the tight lines of gothic script. Then he laughed.

"This is bollocks," he said. Who'd believe this crap?"

"You'd better believe it, Mr. Weaver, and in the next ten seconds or you'll have thirty-seven years to wonder." Alice reached out her hand to retrieve the parchment, holding it steady as she counted to ten.

Weaver's eyes flicked from the lines of print to Alice's hard-set face and back again. "I just sign this, and I'm free?"

"As simple as that."

"And if nothing happens?" He studied Alice's face.

She shrugged. "What's to lose?" Her hand dipped back into the brief case, and withdrew a chunky fountain pen. She unscrewed the top revealing a hidden scalpel blade. "Except a couple of drops of blood of course."

"This is just crazy. I mean it's Hammer Horror stuff." Weaver leaned back in his chair, and sneered.

Alice reached across the table. This time her fingers gripped the corner of the parchment, and started to pull it back.

Weaver's hand stopped its progress. "Hang on. Okay, okay." He held out one hand to take the blade, and looked down at the thumb of his other. "Crazy, crazy," he said, as he drew the blade along the length of its ball. Drops of blood trickled onto the tabletop forming a small pool. He dipped the gold nib into it, straightened the parchment, and signed.

Standing, Alice retrieved the pen, and reassembled it before she tossed it back into her case. Then she rolled the parchment, and slotted that away too.

Before she clicked the briefcase closed, she dipped her hand inside, and withdrew a die cast model car. It was a bright red, rally-liveried, Mini Cooper. She held it out toward the bemused prisoner. "Your wife was kind enough to provide this."

Weaver took it from her.

She was pleased to see a shadow of indecision darken his face. She smiled. "But it must be given by you."

He stared down at the toy, turning it over in his fingers.

"Or the deal's off," Alice added.

Weaver handed it back across the table. Alice dropped it into her case, and snapped the twin locks closed. "Thank you, Mr. Weaver." She stood to leave.

"Aren't you supposed to say, you won't regret it?" Weaver smiled.

Alice's gaze locked onto his. "Oh, but you will, Mr. Weaver. Believe me, you will." She turned toward the door, and raised her hand to knock. A key turned before her knuckles made contact. She stepped back as the blue metal swung toward her. The warder had been watching through the spy hole. She turned, and looked back at Weaver. Her body, she decided, would have hidden most of the transaction from the prison guard's prying eyes.

"All through, ma'am?"

Alice spun on her heels, and faced him. Her face was set hard, and her eyes blazed red.

He stepped back, uncertainty conquering the arrogance in his expression.

"Yes, thank you." Alice smiled, and lowered her eyes. Killing him would only complicate things, and anyway, she had accomplished her mission.

Eight

Their trek so far had not been a pleasant one. Wilson and Rubek, their heads bent into the icy wind followed the broad backs of their guides over gently sloping moorland toward a distant escarpment. Three more armed giants followed. None of their escort had spoken since they left the tent of the Council. The thought that they were heading for the wind blown, icy hell of the gorge in which they had been captured did nothing to lighten Wilson's mood.

They had escaped the scaffold but only because the men escorting them thought that they were leading them to their deaths anyway. Ranvile, the only member of the Council who had spoken during their meeting had explained this in a quiet voice that Wilson had interpreted as sympathetic. He had explained other things also. Wilson thought back on them, and his concentration diminished the discomfort inflicted by the bitter wind.

The gorge in which they had found themselves was called Ardam's Gorge. Generations earlier a wind had started to blow from it, an icy wind that changed the climate of the plains beyond it, and destroyed the herds and crops of those that inhabited them. Ardam had been leader of the Council then. He had led an expedition into the gorge to trace the source of the wind that was starving his people. Not one of them had returned. A rescue party was despatched, as tradition dictated this consisted of Ardam's wife and those of his twelve companions. They too had entered the gorge, and they too had never returned, but the wind had stopped, and slowly the land had begun to prosper once more.

A whole folklore had developed around the place. It had become in turn, the entrance to Hell, the mouth of the earth itself, and finally the gateway to the home of the gods. These gods had been angered. Two expeditions had been sacrificed. The gods had been placated, and all was well with the world. Until Leirbag that is. He had been elected to the Council, its youngest ever member. His fellow members had not welcomed him unanimously. His ideas were radical to the point of being sacrilegious, and he wasted no opportunity to broadcast them. He was as well versed, however, in the magical rites that kept his people safe and prosperous as some with four times his years, and so he was tolerated. Then, two harvests ago, Leirbag had disappeared. Many would have been relieved had he not taken with him Worldroot, the ancient gnarled timber that had lain amongst the flames of the Council fire since before even their folklore could recall, and from which most of the power of the Council emanated.

~ * ~

The wind was strengthening, and growing colder. The first pricks of ice stabbed at Wilson's cheeks. He pulled the folds of his woollen jerkin more tightly around his body, and clung onto the comfort that the provision of the garment suggested that the Council at least wanted them to survive. The only blessing in the wind was that it carried the smell of the oily wool back the way they had come.

At the entrance to the gorge, their leading two guides stood aside, allowing Wilson and Rubek to continue alone. The two giants watched them pass in silence, and then settled down to wait. They would, Wilson had been told, guard the entrance for three days, by which time they could be certain that the two strangers had, one way or another, passed from their world.

~ * ~

For hours they clambered over and around the loose boulders of the barely discernable track. Their eyes were closed to slits, and their bodies bent against both the steepness of the ascent and the onslaught of the weather.

Wilson no longer felt cold, just tired. A feeling of peaceful well-being began to engulf him. He thought that if he was just to curl up where he was, and sleep a peaceful, peaceful sleep. He forced the temptation away. The respite that sleep would bring, he knew, would be permanent. He looked around at Rubek, and knew that the American was fighting the same battle. He forced a smile of encouragement, and the corners of Rubek's lips twitched in response. Then Wilson turned back to his task, and forced his aching legs onward.

They trudged on through the night, and into the following morning, slowing their pace but not daring to rest lest sleep overcame them, and progressed inexorably to death. Then the wind stopped. Wilson's whole body had been fighting against it. He pitched forward onto his knees. Rubek stumbled into him but managed to maintain his footing.

With the wind went the cold. Wilson stood, and forced himself upright for the first time in hours. His legs and back ached. The stench from his jerkin found his nostrils. His face wrinkled in displeasure. In front of him, a wall of solid rock rose vertically into the clouds. To either side of its base identical, rounded cave mouths disappeared into blackness. He looked around at Rubek. "Some climb."

"And how."

"Which way?" Wilson's eyes flicked between the two equally forbidding alternatives.

Rubek leaned back against the wall of the gorge, and considered the problem.

Wilson stepped toward the cave to his left. He was able to peer into its entrance without bending. Its damp, grey walls were visible for only a few feet. He took a single step forward. He could hear running water. It was cold. *Normal in caves*, he thought, and then retreated to see if the alternative looked any more promising. It didn't, not immediately, but as his eyes became accustomed to the gloom, something small and white caught his eye. He took another step. It was a shoe, a trainer; there was red also. *A Nike Swoosh*, he thought, as he strained his eyes into the darkness, and then, less discernable, but becoming clearer an ankle and the bottom of a blue denim trouser leg appeared.

"Bill," he called back toward the entrance. The light disappeared as the tall American ducked into the cave behind him. "Give me a hand here."

They located a second foot, and pulled the body into the light.

"Molloy," Rubek said, as the features of the young man became discernable and then unmistakable.

Wilson bent over the boy's face, and felt warm breath on his cheek. "He's alive anyway." He slapped the side of the young man's face gently, and then again with more conviction.

Molloy's eyelids fluttered, and then opened.

"Arthur," Wilson said, his excitement at the discovery overcoming any concerns regarding the boy's welfare. "Arthur."

The boy sat up, and shuffled back toward the darkness.

"Hey, there," Rubek said, "stay easy. We're not going to hurt you."

They helped Arthur Molloy to his feet, and guided him out into the daylight.

"Were you going in or coming out?" Wilson asked.

Arthur looked confused.

"The cave," Rubek added.

"Going in," the boy replied.

"Why that one?" Wilson took over again.

"There was a light, a warm light. I was so cold."

"And then?"

"I fell asleep."

"That's the way then," Rubek nodded toward the cave. "Some more answers first though, I think" He returned his attention to Arthur. "How did you get here?"

"I don't know."

"What do you remember, think, anything?"

"There was a pub…and a woman…a beautiful woman, long legs, long hair."

"Blonde?"

"Yeah, blonde, and then a man, tall, grey, weird eyes." Arthur's face contorted as though he was in pain.

Wilson moved toward him but Rubek held him back.

"And then?"

"I was in an airport, it was Heathrow I think." His brow furrowed. "There were queues everywhere, hundreds of people. I walked into the middle of them. I had to. I knew that I had to. There was something in my pocket, a button thing. I pressed it." He blinked. "Then I was here." He glanced from Wilson to Rubek. "No… Not straight here. There was the man again. He hit me…yes, he hit me, and then I was here."

Rubek looked at Wilson. "Well, we have Arthur. The woman… Alice Craven, it's got to be. The man , Leirbag maybe." He returned his attention to Arthur. "The man, was he tall, long grey hair, sharp featured, distinguished?"

The boy nodded.

"The barman in London," Rubek said. "Ranvile in the tent, now Arthur. We know who our man is."

"So all we've got to do is find him." Wilson took a step toward the mouth of the cave, and then turned. "Are you two coming?"

~ * ~

Alice drifted from sleep. Someone was calling her but her ears were not receiving the message. Her mind was. She swung her feet over the side of the bed, and stood. The hem of her gown dropped around her ankles. She looked down at it. The same silver symbols she had seen on Leirbag's decorated it. His had hung in loose folds. Hers was tightly tailored to the waist, and then dropped, straight to skim the boards of the floor.

"Alice." The call was in her head. She turned, and walked toward the door.

~ * ~

Leirbag was at the head of the table. His arms hung loosely over the sides of his throne, and his legs stretched out, ankles crossed, beneath the table. A young man was sitting to his left. His back was straight, his head bowed. His arms hung stiffly at his side.

"Alice, my dear." Leirbag stood as she entered the room. So did the newcomer.

"Alice, this is Rodney." Leirbag nodded toward the youth. "You met Rodney's father I believe... Rodney, meet Alice."

Rodney Weaver looked to be in his mid-teens. His complexion was pale and freckled, his hair mousey-blond. He turned toward her, and looked to be about to speak. Then he doubled forward, and clutched at his stomach.

"Your queen, Rodney, your queen."

The boy straightened, rounded the table, and dropped onto one knee in front of Alice.

She held out a hand.

Rodney Weaver's fingers contacted the tips hers. He bent his head, and his lips brushed her knuckle. "My queen," he said.

Alice looked along the table to Leirbag.

He laughed. "I told you, Alice. I will be king. You will be my queen and the whole of creation will worship your beauty. But now I think that Rodney is hungry." His tone suggested that Alice should know how to act.

"Thank you, Rodney," she said. "I know you will serve me well, but now you may eat."

The youth stood but made no move toward the table until Alice had taken her own seat to Leirbag's right. Then he regained his seat but did not eat until Alice nodded a smile in his direction.

Leirbag was still smiling. "Good, good, it has started. Eleven more, my queen, and the whole world will be kneeling at your feet."

Alice looked across the table at Rodney as he tore into rolls of bread as though he had not eaten for months. He looked youthful and healthy but something was not quite right. It was his eyes, she realised. There was nothing behind them, nothing in them, no vitality, no life, and no soul. *The lights are on,* she thought, *but there's nobody home.*

"Alice." Leirbag's voice drew her attention back to him. He was holding the lip of a jewel-encrusted jug over the goblet in front of her.

She was sure that neither had been there before.

Leirbag poured. "Drink, my queen." It was an instruction.

Alice lifted the goblet to her lips. The red liquid was thick and sweet, with a saltiness that curled the tip of her tongue. *Not wine,* she thought. It trickled down her throat, *but good.* She looked at Leirbag. His wide grin was infectious. She returned it.

Leirbag took her free hand and squeezed it. "I have chosen well," he said. "Very well. Together, Alice, we will rule the world—maybe even all of the worlds."

One of the imp carvings, the one that appeared to be sitting on his left shoulder, bent its head toward Leirbag's ear. He inclined his own to listen. His smile disappeared. "Meddlers." He spat out the word, and then looked at Alice. The affection in his eyes had disappeared with his smile.

Alice looked away.

"Arthur gone was really nothing more than a minor inconvenience, but now they have him. That I can't allow." Leirbag stood, and placed a hand onto the back of his throne. It shimmered for a few seconds, and then it was gone, replaced in his hand by a wooden cane with an engraved silver handle.

The imps, shining metal now, laughed at Alice through pointed, silver teeth.

"I'll see to Arthur," Leirbag said, "but now you must hurry also. Our table must be filled, and quickly. Come."

As he passed behind Rodney Weaver, Leirbag tapped the young man's shoulder with the tip of his cane.

Rodney fell forward. His head crashed onto the table, sending bread and cheese tumbling to the floor.

"You're off to Jerusalem, Rodney," Leirbag said. "I'll see you there."

~ * ~

Alice followed Leirbag from the room, along the corridor, and through the door behind which she had seen Arthur disappear. He held out a hand, and Alice took it. Then, as though he were leading her into a dance, Leirbag propelled her into the centre of the floor's ornately tiled design. The thought that the mosaic had not been there before had barely registered when there were colours above her head, and monotone red beneath her feet.

~ * ~

Dazzled by a sudden light, Alice almost tripped down a short flight of wide, red-carpeted stairs. She regained her composure, and looked out across the large room below. It was crowded and noisy. There were huddles of people around all of the gaming tables. Dozens more wandered between them. Above her, the ceiling was ornately, plastered and painted with cherubs and gods, goddesses and mythical animals. Beneath these, crystal chandeliers reflected all of the colours of the spectrum onto the players and spectators below.

Alice reached the bottom step.

"Madame." A black-tied waiter held a silver salver toward her.

Alice picked up a flute of champagne, took a sip, and strode into the crowd. The emotions emanating from those around her swirled in her head. There was so much self-centred greed there that it confused her. She concentrated hard, trying to isolate the flavour of her victim from the rest.

Nine

The air inside the cave was still, and remarkably warm. The smell from the steam that rose toward the roof from Wilson's jerkin had passed the point of being unpleasant, and was fast approaching nauseating. The darkness in front of them seemed impenetrable. Once they lost the fading light from the entrance Wilson knew they would be unable to continue.

He looked back, because forward would become impossible within only a few more paces, and caught a whiff of the air he was leaving behind. The jerkin, he decided, had to go. He shrugged it from his shoulders. It dipped to the left. He felt down. There was something inside it. He smoothed his hand along the outside and then the inside. There was a small pocket. His fingers explored it, and pulled free a piece of wood.

Yellow light flooded the cave. Wilson looked down at his find. It appeared to be a piece of old tree root. He turned it over in his fingers. His brow creased. There was no sign that the light emanated from it, and there was no heat. Still, it was light that they wanted, whatever its source. "Thank you, Ranvile," he muttered, and turned to Rubek. "You got one? A pocket? A light?"

The American took off his own jerkin, and examined it. "No…yes." He pulled his hand free, and held out a smooth amber sphere about the size of a small hen's egg. The intensity of the light around them did not increase.

"Keep it any way," Wilson said, "I'm sure it's not there by accident."

Rubek slipped it into his trouser pocket, and then tossed the jerkin aside. "Done."

They walked along side by side. Arthur Molloy followed in silence.

The cave was high and wide, and its floor smooth enough to have been man-made.

"So what've we got?" Rubek asked as they walked.

They had advanced several more paces before Wilson replied. "Well, we've got the place we just came from, where this Leirbag chap, who matches the description given by the barman in London, disappeared from with some sort of magic thing."

"We've got North," Rubek added. "Who was actually Ranorth chasing after him, and getting himself killed. We've got Alice Craven, who died in Somalia, and then killed hundreds."

"Alice." He had almost forgotten Arthur. "Alice, that was her name, the blonde. She was a doctor. Doctor Craven, the man called her."

"What else?" Wilson asked, ignoring the interruption.

"Magic, you've got to believe in it. If you take away the magic nothing makes sense." Rubek replied. "People don't come back from the dead to blow up other people. People don't come back from the dead period."

Wilson chuckled. "If you leave in the magic, nothing makes sense. Motive, what's our man's motive? What's he gained so far, apart from so many dismembered bodies that I lost count of them six weeks ago?"

Rubek remained silent for the next half-a-dozen paces, as though he was remembering the dead, before he answered. "Well, from what Ranvile told us, if they don't get that Worldroot thing back then his people are done for. He could wait until they're almost finished, walk back onto the scene, save the day, and take over."

"So what about what he's doing to our world? I can't believe he's just having some fun while he waits."

"That's a possible though."

The cave was becoming lower and narrower. They could still walk upright, but the encroaching walls forced them into single file. Wilson led, holding the root at arms length in front of him as though it were a real flashlight. He could hear Rubek behind him and Arthur shuffling along at the rear.

"He's making a pretty fine job of destabilising a few governments," Wilson said, without turning.

"Still don't see the gain."

"What if he destabilises enough of the right ones, returns to his own world with the timing of the US cavalry. Saves the day there. Takes over completely, and then returns with a few thousand faithful giants, and has a go at taking over ours."

"No." Rubek said. "Not possible." His denial lacked conviction.

"Think about it. These bombers of his seem to materialise from nowhere. They're already dead. They can appear on different sides of the world within minutes. How many are there? We only know of two, and one of them's here. What if he's got six or a dozen or a hundred?"

The cave continued to diminish in size as they progressed. Wilson's shoulders brushed the walls on either side, and within a few more paces, he had to turn his upper body sideways. The roof was closing in as well, Rubek did not have to stoop, but he was becoming more and more aware of the hard rock only inches above his head. He could hear the scuffing of Arthur's feet behind him. He tried to turn. It wasn't easy. His body was too hemmed in, his head though…just about. The back of his skull brushed against rock. The tip of his nose scraped that in front, but his head turned. Arthur was only inches behind him. Behind Arthur, was another man, tall with long black hair. His eyes were wide and wild. He drew his lips back revealing white, pointed teeth. His tongue flicked out, black and forked. He was holding a cane, javelin-like, and looked to be about to propel it through the back of Arthur Molloy's skull.

"Stuart," Rubek shouted.

Wilson tried to turn his head but his last few steps had made the space too narrow. Then, without warning, they were plunged into darkness.

~ * ~

"You gave them what?" The old man spun round on Ranvile. The flames of the Council fire flared.

"I gave them Smallroot and Heartstone."

"You gave away
they fail? The people

"If I'd done noth
Ranvile kept his conce
of their broken circle
strongest of us, the on
defeat Leirbag, and brin

"We should have tal
opposite side of the fire.
of the speaker through the

"And we would still b̲   ̲ ̲..ow, Ranvile replied.
"We'd still be talking tomorrow, next week, next harvest."

"We must vote now."

"Vote on what?" Ranvile sneered. "It's done."

"Vote on whether you, Ranvile, have betrayed the
Council, betrayed your people, and like as not killed us
all."

"Vote then, I'm tired. If I have saved the people then
they can judge me. If I haven't then no one will." He let
out a long breath, his eyes closed and he collapsed
sideways.

~ * ~

Prince Weinjyk looked up from the table. The ever-
smiling croupier raked his chips across the table, and into
the machine that would recycle them for the house. One
hundred thousand Euro, the Prince shrugged, it was
nothing. Then he saw her. She was at the bottom of the
staircase, accepting a flute of champagne. She was tall and
slender, long legs, long blonde hair. She was the most
beautiful woman he had ever seen. "The blonde," he said,
"at the stairs, I want her."

shoulder moved away.

ked at his watch, *eleven o'clock*. He
of gold discs onto number eleven. The
. The ball rattled, and a polite round of
e rippled around the ring of spectators.

he croupier pushed a pile of chips toward him. The Prince smiled, nodded, and tossed two golden discs back across the table. His gaze dropped once again to his Rolex. One minute had passed since he had spotted the woman. Eleven plus one, he pushed all of his winnings onto number twelve. The onlookers fell silent. Others in the room, detecting the change of atmosphere, gravitated toward the table. There was a gasp, then silence, and then more applause. The audience was less reserved this time.

The Prince looked around, and smiled. This was what the hangers on came for. The crowd around the game thickened. This was what he came for; everyone was watching him and his money. He glanced across the table. There was a young couple sitting opposite. The girl, brunette and pretty was watching him. Her face flushed. She turned away. The Prince grinned. He was fifty-eight years old, and he could still have any of them.

"Please...please." The Prince recognised the voice of his aide. He turned to the man at his side. "Excuse me, sir, would you mind?" He looked around at Alice. The man's gaze followed his.

The prince smiled. "My lucky mascot."

The man stood, nodded, and backed away from the table. An aide's hand moved, and he pocketed a wad of notes.

Prince Weinjyk looked up at Alice, and gestured to the vacant seat. "Please."

Alice sat.

"You bring me luck, please a number." There was silence around them as people bent to hear.

"Sixteen," Alice said.

The Prince pushed his accumulated fortune across the table.

The croupier was no longer smiling. "Sixteen." His voice had become hoarse.

The Prince looked toward the ceiling. Every security camera that he could see was arcing to target their table. The wheel spun once again. There was silence, it lasted longer this time, and the applause that followed sounded embarrassed.

"You are my angel." The Prince took Alice's hand as he watched his winnings cross the green baize toward him.

"No." Alice grinned, locking her gaze onto his. "I'm the devil."

"Oh!" the Prince chuckled, "I've never slept with the devil."

"There's a price... A very high price."

"Anything." Prince Weinjyk squeezed her hand

"Anything?"

"Anything at all."

Alice stood, leaning forward slightly. The Prince's gaze rose to her cleavage and rested there. Then she swayed provocatively away from the table, her head half-turned toward him, her eyes and smile inviting him to follow.

The Prince stood, bowed to the croupier and strode after her, his hand already outstretched to take hers. Behind him, the casino staff, watched by his own, collected up his winnings.

~ * ~

In the Royal Suite Alice sat at the bedside table, and unrolled the parchment.

~ * ~

Rubek remained motionless in the darkness. Something smashed into his shoulder. Liquid splattered his face. His instincts screamed at him to get down, to make himself as small a target as he could in the blackness, but the cave walls made it impossible for him to bend, even at the knees.

Something grabbed at his sleeve and pulled him onward. *Wilson,* Rubek thought, *it had to be.* There was a groan from behind him, and then other sounds, like an animal feeding. The image gripped his mind like a claw. The darkness only intensified the horror of it. Beads of sweat burst from his brow. Close to panic, he edged his body sideways, something brushed against his hair, the roof. He took another step, and his skull was pressing against rock. He hunched, and lost two more inches. It was enough for three more steps. He stopped.

Wilson was tugging at his sleeve again. He bent his neck to the side and edged on, rough stone grazed against his temple. *Another yard,* he thought, *and my neck will break.* Then he was free. With nothing to fight against, his head shot upright. He reached out a hand and felt nothing.

~ * ~

Wilson maintained his grip on Rubek's sleeve but did not attempt to move. Sandwiched between the walls of the cave it had been easy, there was only one direction in which to go. Now he had a choice. He still held the tree root. He waved it around at arms length, and encountered only air. He reached up, nothing there either.

Behind Rubek the grunting and slurping became less frantic, and then stopped. As the last sound died away there was light once again. For a second it blinded him as effectively as the darkness had. He closed his eyes, counted to three, and then opened them. They were still in the cave. It was just bigger.

"Ranvile," Wilson gasped.

Rubek turned.

Ahead of them, the old man was sitting cross-legged on the stone floor. He was instantly recognisable, and yet strangely indistinct. He smiled at them. "You made poor time."

"It wasn't easy in the dark." Wilson made a point of looking at his tree root. "This didn't work for long." He looked as though he was about to toss it aside.

"Oh, it worked all right," the old man said. "It was working all the time. Leirbag appeared you see, came to reclaim his prize, and he has Worldroot, more powerful than that." He gestured toward Wilson's hand. "Ten thousand times more powerful, perhaps even more." He shrugged. "But now that its influence is gone you should be safe enough."

"Where's this lead?" Rubek asked, looking over the old man's head into the cave.

"Back to your own world, or to another. No one knows. You have Heartstone though, that should help."

"This?" Rubek pulled the amber from his pocket.

"You should keep it in your hand," Ranvile said. "When the time comes it may influence things. Fate is a funny thing you see, always thinks it knows best. Through the Heartstone, it will know where your heart wants to be. It may choose to ignore it of course, as I said, a funny thing."

"So we just carry on walking, and see where we pop out?" Wilson asked.

"Not exactly, you keep on walking until the cave allows you to go no further. Then one of you must take Smallroot and Heartstone, and grip them in one hand, Fate will take over from there. But wherever it guides you, you have only one task, and that is to return Worldroot to my people."

Rubek looked at Wilson, and then at Ranvile. "And how are we supposed to do that when Leirbag is ten thousand times more powerful than us?"

"I don't have all the answers." Ranvile chuckled. "You could steal it I suppose. You could kill Leirbag. You could find magic on your own world, or on another, that is as powerful as his. I really don't know. But if you fail, then my world is doomed, and, I suspect, yours also."

Then the image of the old man began to fade. In seconds, he was gone.

~ * ~

Alice lifted her face into the refreshing jets of warm water, supported herself against the tiled wall of the shower cubicle with one hand, and soaped the stickiness from between her thighs with the other.

At first, the prince had refused to sign. Alice had unzipped her gown, and let it drop to her waist. Beneath it, she had been naked. He had signed. It had been that easy. Her part of the bargain had seemed to take only seconds. Whatever control the prince had over his money and his people he had little over his own body.

She adjusted her position letting the sharp pricks of water cascade over her breasts. Her nipples became erect. Her hand continued its soaping, finishing the job that the Prince had barely managed to start. Then she stepped from the shower, and towelled herself dry.

~ * ~

The prince was still naked when Alice re-entered the bedroom. He turned to face her. In one hand, he held the parchment, in the other a gold cigarette lighter. "You are a foolish young woman," He said, positioning the lighter beneath the parchment, and smiling.

Alice was only feet away from him. She closed the distance before the prince's thumb had time to trigger a flame. She grabbed him around the throat with the long manicured fingers of one hand, and lifted him from the floor. Lighter and parchment dropped to the deep-pile carpet, and the prince's eyes bulged. Alice squeezed harder. Her fingernails punctured skin, and her fingers met her thumb around the dying man's windpipe. She thrust him away, then pulled him back tearing his windpipe from his throat. Blood erupted from the wound splattering Alice's face and the white towel that covered her. She licked her lips, savoured the taste of the precious liquid, and let the body drop to the floor.

"Majesty... Majesty." A rapping on the suite's outer door accompanied the words. Alice turned toward the threat. "Majesty, your son." Alice smiled. Her job was done, another place at Leirbag's table had been filled. The door's handle rattled, and then its frame shook as someone in the corridor launched a shoulder or a kick at it. The wood around the lock splintered. Alice folded her arms, and closed her eyes.

When the door finally gave, and one of the Prince's aides tumbled into the room, Alice was gone.

~ * ~

The security guards hardly gave Rodney Weaver a second glance as he strolled into the hotel foyer. He was light-skinned and blond, obviously a westerner. The young Arab, who followed him from the revolving door, was hauled roughly to one side, and body searched. Rodney strode past the crowded reception desk toward the elevators.

Leirbag watched Rodney's entrance from across the busy street, and then turned away, and disappeared into the crowd.

~ * ~

On the twelfth floor, the function room was buzzing. The meal was finished, and the speeches over. The older guests remained at their tables chatting. The bride and groom and the younger of the guests danced to the accompaniment of a tuxedoed jazz band.

Rodney skirted a circle of laughing girls, and found the centre of the crowded dance floor. The carefully packed bags of nails and explosive around his waist were uncomfortable. He stopped, and turned, slipped his hand into his trouser pocket, and found the detonator. His thumb pushed aside the plastic safety-cover, and pressed downward.

Ten

"It's a dead end." Wilson glanced around, hoping that he'd missed something, then he reached out and touched the damp stone. "The only way is back."

Rubek stepped to his shoulder. "Keep on going, the man said, until the cave allows you to go no further." He held out the amber sphere. "I guess this is it."

Wilson looked down at the yellow jewel sceptically, but took it anyway and squeezed it into the palm of his hand with Smallroot.

"Might as well sit down." Rubek sat.

Wilson lowered himself to the floor beside him. The stones were damp and the moisture soaked through the back of his trousers causing him to squirm.

For what seemed like an age, nothing happened, and then the rock wall in front of them began to lose its substance.

Rubek closed his eyes.

Wilson kept his open. The wall shimmered green and then red, then every colour and then none. He remembered the strange walls of the lab and then he was looking at them. The same colourful squirls, sometimes they were recognisable, more often not. They were back. Somehow, they were back.

"Rubek," he hissed. "Rubek."

The American opened his eyes. "We're back. We're in the lab." He nodded toward Wilson's closed hand. "Those goddam things actually worked."

They were sitting in the centre of the strange chalk design, surrounded by the belongings of the now four times dead Arthur Molloy.

"So it would seem." Wilson pushed himself to his feet. The backs of his trousers were still damp. He pulled the clinging fabric away from his skin and gazed around the room in silence. The memories of his recent experiences were taking on a dreamlike quality now that he was back in almost familiar surroundings.

"What now?" He looked at Rubek, who was scanning the room open mouthed.

"We should file a report."

"That would make interesting reading. They might even be kind enough to let us out of the padded room for a joint retirement party."

"Well we'd better think of something. We came in here...what, two days ago and with North? All the doors are guarded and now we leave without him."

The American laughed. "I wouldn't worry too much about explaining North. He was always, should I say, unconventional? And as for the two days, things are so secret around here that I doubt anyone's even mentioned it for fear of compromising something."

"Would five and a half days be more of a problem?" Wilson twisted his arm so that Rubek could see the crystal display of his wristwatch.

The American checked his. "Could be all that magic power stuff, sent everything haywire."

"One way or another it certainly is. Let's just bluff it out shall we?" He gestured toward the reinforced steel door behind them. "After you."

~ * ~

Two redcaps stamped to attention as the two policemen emerged into a gloomy, mist-laden Yorkshire day.

Wilson glanced at Rubek and chuckled. "Your place or mine?" They had been allocated adjacent rooms in the base's accommodation block.

"Yours I think," Rubek replied. "The scotch is better."

Their escort fell in behind them, around the gravel parade square, passed squat, grey administration buildings to the entrance of the equally uninviting accommodation block.

Their uniformed companions stood aside as the first of the steel double-doors slid open and then closed as Wilson and Rubek stepped through them.

Wilson bent forward and rested his chin onto the rubber pad that ensured that his eyes aligned with the retina recognition device.

"Wilson," he said. "Four, seven, six, nine, eight."

The doors in front of him purred open and he stepped through them into a claustrophobic space no bigger than a two-person elevator. The doors closed behind him. He waited until pressure and heat censors confirmed that only one life force had entered. The door in front of him swung open and he stepped out into much more pleasant surroundings.

Potted palms lined the walls of the foyer and guided incomers toward a wide and curving aluminium staircase. Wilson turned and waited for Rubek to complete his own screening.

"Not much, but it's home," the American said, as he stepped out of the final security obstacle and followed Wilson up the staircase toward their apartments. Wilson glanced up and saluted at the ceiling-mounted camera that arced to follow their progress as they passed beneath it. After all of the checks to get into the place he'd always considered them to be over-kill.

~ * ~

Wilson closed the door of his apartment behind them and gestured Rubek to a small corner settee next to the window that overlooked a bleak stretch of open moorland. Then he bent to extricate a bottle of Glenmorangie from a huddle of other bottles in the cabinet beside the door. He poured two generous measures and passed one to Rubek. Then with his own glass, he gestured across the room toward a sound system. Its LED display shone green. "Five and a half days, give or take," he said.

Rubek took a sip of his drink. "You know, I'm not even surprised anymore. I don't think anything could surprise me anymore." His gaze switched from the CD player to Wilson. "It answers one of our questions though. If two and a half days can become five and a half days, then Bradford, England to New York, USA in thirty-five minutes becomes less of an impossibility."

"If that's how they did it."

"But it's now feasible."

"Double thirty-five minutes is still just over an hour."

Rubek shrugged. "So what now?"

"Well it might not feel like it but we haven't had an update for over five days, a lot could have happened." Wilson put his drink aside, lifted the wall-mounted phone from its bracket and punched three numbers into the keypad on its handset.

"Saville, get the team together in the communications room." He looked at his watch. "Thirty minutes." He hung up before the young policeman had time to launch any questions at him.

Wilson had kept Saville with him because he was a good policeman and because he trusted him. He now thought that perhaps that had not been a good decision. Perhaps he liked the youngster too much, but what he did not want to do was get him involved with all this magic stuff. He drained his glass, refilled it and then topped up Rubek's drink. He would, he decided, use Saville as his eyes and ears at base. If they needed company on their next jaunt, he would find someone else, or better still, he would let Rubek select one of his own. He gazed over the American's shoulder and across the windswept heather to the grey sky beyond. He knew that they were not going to find any answers on their world. They would be making another time-expanding excursion and soon. The thought unnerved him more than any lunatic bomber had ever done.

"I really need to shower," he said, "before we meet the troops." He was still holding the telephone. He looked down at it. He knew that he should call Sarah and the boys. His finger had completed only half of its journey to the keypad when he pulled it back. Five and a half days, he shook his head and slotted the phone back into its cradle. "I don't need the abuse."

"You should, you know."

Wilson turned. Rubek was smiling up at him.

"Hell, I got no one worrying about me 'cept maybe the taxman." He stood and drained his glass. "I'll leave you to it."

Wilson re-took the phone and punched in his home number.

"If it helps," Rubek said, as he pulled the door open. "Blame the Americans. Most of the rest of the world seems to."

Gemma's snapped, "Hello," cut off Wilson's laugh.

"Hi, it's me."

"You Bastard!" He heard the door close, held the handset away from his ear, grimaced and screwed his eyes shut.

~ * ~

The young man writhed across the wooden floor. He had drawn his knees up beneath his chin and his fingernails had punctured skin, drawing blood, where they gripped his tortured stomach.

From his throne, Leirbag smiled down at the youth's convulsions. Next to him, Alice looked on disinterestedly.

"You are a prince no longer," Leirbag said, "and do you know why?"

The boy lay still, his hands still clutching at his stomach.

"I'll tell you why." Leirbag closed his eyes and pointed at him.

The boy's teeth bit through his lower lip.

"Because your father, your own father, sold you to me. Not for money you know, he has more than enough of that. For pleasure, for thirty seconds of pleasure. He thought that he could use my queen, your queen, thought that he could use her like a common street prostitute."

The youth was screaming.

Leirbag raised his voice. "You will pay for his arrogance if you do not obey me in all things. DO YOU UNDERSTAND THAT?"

Tear filled eyes stared back at him.

"DO YOU?"

The boy's spine jerked from the floor.

"DO YOU?"

The boy lay still for a second and then nodded.

"That's good." Leirbag rested his head back against his throne and smiled.

He placed his hand over Alice's on the table and squeezed her fingers.

"I had a dog called Prince once. When I was a little girl," Alice said.

Leirbag looked at her and smiled. For the first time, the warm glint in his eyes seemed to communicate genuine affection.

Alice returned his smile. "A scruffy little mongrel it was. Dad called it Prince because it had no breeding."

"A dog, I like that," Leirbag chuckled. "A dog with no breeding." He threw back his head and laughed. "Prince, you will be then, dog with no breeding, come, join us...Prince."

The youth staggered to his feet.

"Sit there." Leirbag pointed toward a chair along the table to his left. His hand released its grip on Alice's fingers and he lifted it to his temple. His eyes closed as though in concentration. The smile disappeared and then returned. His eyelids flicked open and his gaze settled on Alice. "Rodney has returned. He has done well. You have done well."

Alice felt a flush of pleasure at his praise. She lowered her eyes.

Leirbag crooked his finger beneath her chin and lifted her head. "No modesty Alice, my dear. Modesty never ruled the world now did it?"

~ * ~

Rubek had not feared the worst. He had expected it. Across the globe, international tensions were critical. Five major conflicts at least were on the verge of exploding into full scale wars: India-Pakistan, North Korea-South Korea, with the added bonus of China massing troops at the border, Argentina-Chile, Israel-Syria Jordan and Egypt Nigeria-Cameroon. Wilson shook his head over his hastily scribbled notes.

Those countries that should have been mediating had withdrawn into themselves in desperate attempts to keep their own internal conflicts under control. Wilson scanned the list. The USA topped it: full mobilisation, all internal civilian flights grounded, international flights only allowed to enter US airspace under fighter escort, the Pacific and Mediterranean fleets called home. The situations in France, Russia, Canada and most of South America were little better.

"And our own domestic problem?" Wilson asked.

Saville did not consult his file. "Forty-three," he said, without looking up at his boss.

"Forty-three!" Wilson exclaimed, "forty-three in two…"

"Five days." Rubek said quickly and loudly enough to drown out Wilson's voice.

"The current UK situation." A young agent to Wilson's right flicked open a blue file and extracted a sheaf of papers.

"I don't want to know," Wilson barked and pushed himself up from the table. "Bill, we're out of here." He snatched up his file and was gone, leaving the door swinging open behind him.

Rubek smiled at the wide-eyed, open-mouthed faces around the table. "He's under a lot of pressure," he said, before collecting up his own notes and rising from his seat. "Stay by your phones, gentlemen, and thank you."

~ * ~

Leirbag leaned his head back against the timber of his throne. "They came close," he said. "Those two meddlers from your world." He stretched out his arms and then interlocked his fingers behind his head. "Not that they could do much, but when the buzzing of a fly becomes a nuisance, what do you do?" He smashed his fist down onto the bare tabletop.

Alice jumped.

"You swat it Alice, that's what you do." His fist smashed down once again. It remained there this time, with fingers clenching and then relaxing. "You will take care of this one personally, my dear, and I want you to be seen. When the time comes I want everyone on that world to know that their queen is immortal." He turned over his hand and studied its palm. "You did well before. They will have pieced together the fragments that we tossed to them, but I want them to be certain."

Alice placed a hand over his, ready to pull it back if he objected to the contact. She stroked her tongue across the roof of her mouth but detected nothing.

Leirbag closed his fingers around hers and stroked the length of them. "You are learning quickly, Alice. Soon you will be truly worthy of the role I have planned for you." He stood and looked at Prince. "And you, my young friend are going flying."

~ * ~

Stephanie Kinkladze stabbed her toe at the brake catch on the rear wheel of the trolley and leaned across a row of empty seats to peer out through the small window.

There it was, not long now then. The F-16 held position off and just behind the starboard wing of the Atlanta bound Airbus. She could see the pilot clearly. There would be another, she knew, in mirror formation on the port side. Their presence gave her no comfort. They were there not to protect the Airbus, but to blow it out of the sky should it deviate from its flight plan.

She used the armrest of the nearest seat to push herself upright and slipped backward through the curtain that separated business from economy. There were no business class passengers. She smiled at the stupidity of having to keep up the pretence. There were only twenty in economy and they had all opted for the rearmost seats, believing them to be the safest. She smiled at that too. *Still,* she thought, *if it makes them feel better.*

She turned. There was someone in the window seat of the row next to her.

Her genuine smile stretched into her trained one.

The young man smiled back.

Nice teeth, she thought, *but why has he changed seats?* She moved toward the rear of the aircraft more slowly than she would have liked. Never appear rushed, her job training had taught her, never appear flustered, always remain in control. She head counted as she went. Her smile remained fixed. She reached the rear galley. *Twenty.* Had she counted the youth? She turned and head counted back. *Twenty.* She looked along the cabin at the back of a head of shiny black hair. *Twenty-one.* Now she was flustered. "Excuse me." She was still three rows behind passenger twenty-one.

The young man turned. She took another three steps. He was still smiling. He squirmed in his seat and dug his hand deep into his trouser pocket. The fabric bulged as though he had tightened his fingers into a fist.

The explosion ripped through the fuselage of the Airbus microseconds before destroying its fighter escort.

~ * ~

Bill Rubek was becoming bored of the whole process. He thought that by that time, they must have seen them all, every shape, size and persuasion, but Wilson kept dragging more of them in.

Across the table from them now and looking confident and in control was a girl. *Young woman,* he corrected his thoughts.

She shuffled the pack of cards deftly.

She's casino trained, Rubek thought, and that thought progressed through professional to fraudulent.

She laid out five cards, face up, in a horizontal line, then five more from the far side of the table back toward her self, forming a simple cross. She looked down at the formation and then up at Wilson. "You've been there."

Wilson was not sure whether it was a question or a statement. He held her steady gaze. It was a *statement,* he decided.

She looked down at the display again. "You've been there and returned."

She flashed a look at Rubek, suggesting that she thought this unlikely, that perhaps they were the fakers and had somehow corrupted her powers.

"Yes," Wilson said, reading her mistrust. "We've been there, and obviously we got back. What we don't know is where *there* is."

She collected up the cards and looked about to stand.

Rubek watched her closely because he had caught a sparkle in Wilson's eyes that had not been there during any of the innumerable previous sessions. She was young, mid-twenties perhaps, and attractive with long, raven black hair. A little too much make up perhaps. *Cleopatra,* he thought, *but an Elizabeth Taylor, Hollywood movie, Cleopatra, designed to present a powerful mystical image.*

"What else?" Wilson asked.

She squared the pack of cards in the centre of the table and then snatched her hand away from them. She looked up at Wilson. "You will go back," she said, "not only to that world but to others."

"And?" Wilson looked from the neatly stacked pile of cards to her face.

She held eye contact only for a second and then looked down at the table, for the first time appearing to lack confidence. "If you fail, then the world we know will cease to exist."

"Thank you Karrina." Wilson stood. "Would you be kind enough to wait outside?"

~ * ~

Rubek watched the young woman rise from her seat.

Standing, she looked taller and slimmer than when hunched over the cards. She did not look at him or at Wilson as, head held high, she strode around the table.

Rubek did not like that. In his non-magical world, it said arrogant.

Wilson regained his seat, but remained silent until the door behind Rubek closed. "She's the one," he said then. "She's on the team."

"Hang on a minute." Rubek stood to emphasise his disagreement. "There's a lot she isn't telling us."

"There's a lot we didn't tell her." Wilson retorted. "She's on." He spread his hands. "But we're looking for a team of four. The pick of the final one is all yours."

"From this lot?" Rubek gestured at the pile of resumes of interviewees seen and yet to be seen.

"Not at all." Wilson smiled. "From wherever you like, Navy Seals, Rangers, FBI, it's your call." He pressed the intercom button on the desk and leaned down toward it. "Could you ask Karrina to come back in, please...and send the others home, all of them."

"Yes, sir...and sir...There's been another, Atlanta bound Airbus, blown out of the sky."

Wilson stared down at the finger that was holding the connection open and then flicked it closed. He looked across the table at Rubek. "Tomorrow we go."

Eleven

Leirbag watched the warrior giant attack his meal. There was much that he wanted to know, but he knew that questions before the man's appetite had been sated would be a waste of time. He closed his eyes and tried to focus his thoughts on what he had achieved thus far and on what was still to be done. It was not easy against a background of grunts and slurps. He gave up and studied the man again.

He was only half a head taller than Leirbag but twice as broad. His muscled forearms were as thick as Leirbag's thighs. He was stuffing food into his mouth with one hand while using the other to keep his long, unkempt hair away from his rapidly working jaws.

When his plate was empty, he leaned back from it and belched. Remains of his meal hung from his thick blond moustache. *Probably the remains of his last one as well,* Leirbag thought, but smiled away his distaste.

"Well, Lucan, what news?"

"Ranvile is dead." The warrior wiped the back of his hand across his mouth.

Leirbag already knew this, but he leaned forward, feigning interest.

"Two strangers came from Ardam's gorge. They killed Ranorth, but the council let them go."

"Did they now? What else?"

"The Council gave them Heartstone and Smallroot."

"So, they are powerless now, the Council." Leirbag kept his gaze locked onto the eyes of the giant.

"They still have their own powers, even though now they are only nine. And the people are still with them despite their suffering." The giant's gaze flicked to the wall at his side. Leirbag smiled, Lucan did not like giving him bad news. His own size and strength were as nothing compared to the power that Leirbag possessed and the giant knew it.

"They are all that the people have," Leirbag said, "until I return."

That brought Lucan's attention back to him.

"No, not yet, Lucan, the time is not yet right. What of the granaries?"

"Two weeks, three at the most and they will be empty."

Leirbag leaned back and interlocked his fingers behind his head. "Not long then. And how many have you confided in?"

"Just three. Minded like myself and of my clan." Lucan's eyes begged approval.

Leirbag smiled. "That is good. No more now. Just make sure that they are ready when I need them."

Lucan appeared to take this as a dismissal and pressed his hands against his thighs as though to rise.

Leirbag held up a hand. "Stay a while, Lucan and drink with me." He waved his hand over the table. Two goblets and a large pewter jug appeared at its centre. He filled one and pushed it across the table.

Lucan's eyes widened.

Leirbag's smile broadened. It did no harm to impress, and magic such as that hardly dented his growing reserves of power. "And there's someone I want you to meet." He poured himself a drink, closed his eyes and thought of Alice.

Two minutes later, she strode into the room.

"Alice, my dear." Leirbag stood.

Lucan lurched to his feet. His thighs caught the edge of the table, jug and goblets toppled.

Leirbag thrust out a hand and they righted themselves. "Alice, this is Lucan."

~ * ~

Alice crossed the room, hand outstretched.

The giant took her hand and shook it. His grip was both firm and gentle.

He could, she thought, *crush my bones to powder, should he wish.*

She looked at Leirbag. He was grinning at them with what appeared to be genuine affection. "When the time comes, Lucan," he said. "Alice will be your queen, and you will be her champion. Your life and your soul will belong to her."

Lucan still held onto Alice's hand. He dropped onto one knee in front of her and kissed it.

The moustache was rough. The lips, hidden behind it, were soft and fleshy. Alice fought back an urge to pull her arm away and smiled down at his wild head of hair. "I'm sure that we shall also become friends, Lucan."

Leirbag stepped toward them; placed one hand on the warrior's head and slipped the other around Alice's waist. "Go now, Lucan, we shall not meet again until I am ready to return to my people. You will know when that time has arrived."

~ * ~

"Karrina." Wilson stood and turned toward the door. "Thanks for not running away."

Rubek remained seated and did not turn to greet the girl.

The young soldier, who had ushered Karrina through the door, hung back after she had entered, leaning forward, one hand on the door handle as though frozen in the act of pulling it toward him and himself out of the room.

Wilson caught his eye. "You okay, son?"

"Sir, yes, sir." Then he did pull the door closed.

"He doesn't like witches very much," Karrina said, walking around the table and retaking her seat. "Thinks I'll turn you both into frogs." She crossed her legs and looked from Wilson to Rubek.

Has her skirt gotten shorter, Wilson thought, *or had he just not noticed it before.* "Karrina, we would very much like you on our team."

Rubek snorted.

Karrina looked at him. "And I would very much like to be a part of it." She smiled.

Wilson looked at her. He had never met anyone so mysteriously attractive, interesting and downright sexy.

Yes, he thought, *sexy.* He shook the image away and cleared his throat. "I'll explain as much as I can."

Rubek coughed and shuffled papers.

"Sorry." Wilson could not take his eyes off her. "There are some...formalities to be taken care of before we can continue."

Rubek turned the document he had been toying with through a hundred and eighty degrees and pushed it across the table.

"The Official Secrets Act," Wilson said, holding out his pen.

She signed.

Wilson laid another document on top of the first. "And to keep our American friend happy."

She signed again.

"Good." Wilson leaned back in his chair. "Well..." Suddenly he was lost for words. He looked at Rubek.

The American was looking away from him toward the window.

"If it entails travelling between worlds," Karrina said. "You don't have to sell it to me."

The movement of her lips fascinated Wilson as they formed the words.

"I've always known that they existed," she continued, "and that there are pathways between them, but I've never known quite enough, or had the artefacts at my disposal to cross between them." She glanced from Wilson to Rubek as though expecting one of them to produce the magic keys.

Wilson laughed. "Karrina, we have visited one other world, once, and then we were guided by another who is now dead." He looked at Rubek. He had the American's attention once again. "But we did manage to pick up a couple of things on our travels that may prove useful. I really don't know. What we need is…" He glanced at Rubek's sceptically raised eyebrows. "What I think we need, is someone who can recognise magic when they see it, who can feel it before it has time to do us any harm." He twiddled his pen around his fingers. "And perhaps to recognise magic in objects that we…" His nod included Rubek. "…see only as normal. If you'll forgive the irreverence, we need a pantomime audience to shout *he's behind you!*"

Karrina laughed.

Her eyes are so bright, Wilson thought, *so blue, uncontaminated, toxin free and her laugh, it was infectious.* He joined in.

Rubek stared across the table.

"Mr. Rubek," Karrina said, "is not convinced."

"Perhaps not." Wilson's laugh had shrunk to a grin. "But his job is to hire the muscle and I probably won't like the clean cut G-man he lands us with. But if his choice can protect us from the physical and mine from the magical, then perhaps, and only perhaps, we might just have a chance."

~ * ~

Leirbag was alone. He massaged his temples and looked around the room. Unlike those of any of the others in his tower, its walls were draped with crimson hangings. A single, intricate mosaic made up the whole of the floor area. At its centre images of Alice and him sat side by side on tall thrones. At their feet, giants and men bowed in supplication. Behind them was Leirbag's tower. The yellow and orange rays of a hidden sun filled the rest of the floor.

Leirbag looked down at the design and sighed. The tower was his problem. He could get himself and his people between the worlds with ease. He could even pinpoint now, like onto the Airbus in mid-flight. He smiled. That had been a gamble. But he needed more around his table before he could transport the tower itself.

Two weeks, three at the most, Lucan had said. Leirbag had to assume two. In two weeks, he had to accumulate enough power to transport his tower and all of its contents back to his own world. With that show of power, the people would flock to him without question. The biggest construction they had ever seen was the Council tent. They would not welcome him as Council Leader. They would welcome him as a god. However, being the god of a starved army would be of no use at all. He needed them strong as well as unquestioning.

He could feed them up of course, but that would take time and things on the other world were moving quickly. He wanted them destabilised, scared, and ready to accept any alternative to the unsure hell into which his carefully choreographed attacks had plunged them. What he did not want was to push too many of their leaders over the edge; to have too many of them unleash their weapons of mass destruction and make the whole world uninhabitable.

He strode around the perimeter of the room. His fingers were interlocked behind his back. For the first time he had the feeling that events, even those of his own making, were running out of control. He would rule two worlds, maybe more, of this he was certain, but he had to ensure that there was enough left of them to be worth ruling.

He looked down at the mosaic once more. He could trust only himself and Alice to fill the remaining seats at his table. The others were merely mindless, soulless tools.

Possibilities spun around his mind. What if Alice and he were both away from the tower and the two meddlers, using Heartstone, found it. How much damage could they do? *Not much,* he suspected, but he was not sure.

Alice, he could trust only her to eliminate the threat. That, for a time at least, left only him.

He summoned Alice. He had to feed her some of his knowledge. She would be the one to fill his table whilst he kept the momentum of his attacks going, but first the meddlers from her world had to be taken of.

Could he trust her with so much power? He rubbed the tiredness from his eyes. He had to.

~ * ~

Wilson liked the young marine on sight. He wished that he hadn't, wished that he had the same reservations about Rubek's choice that the American had about his. It would make their partnership easier.

Ackroyd, even the name sounded English. Wilson felt that he had been outmaneuvered somehow. He switched his attention to Karrina.

She had swapped skirted interview suit for t-shirt and blue jeans. "Yes, I do," the printed front of her t-shirt proclaimed. Wilson had seen the back when she had turned to drape her denim jacket over the chair in the briefing room, *But not with you.*

Was the message for him? He wondered. *It was not for the marine,* he decided, when he recognised their instant bonding on first eye contact. *Was he jealous?* He pushed the thought away. "Right, this is Heartstone." He held up the piece of amber. "And this Smallroot. We've used them before, to get back here. We arrived in North's…we arrived in the lab, so that's where we'll set off from. Any questions?" He did not allow time for any. He knew that he would not have any answers. "Right, let's go."

Rubek was standing just inside the briefing room door. As the others filed passed him he handed out bundles of cold weather gear.

Ackroyd accepted his package without question. Karrina hesitated and looked up into the American's face

"Been there," he said

She took the bundle with a smile.

Rubek returned the smile.

Wilson relaxed.

~ * ~

Once inside the lab with the blast door closed behind them. Karrina and Ackroyd turned and looked at Wilson.

Wilson looked at Rubek.

The American shrugged.

"Okay," Wilson walked to the centre of the chalk design. "We sit down in the centre. I hold these." He held up Heartstone and Smallroot. "You concentrate as hard as you can on the objects you were given." Each had a copy of Alice Craven's photograph and an item from her make up bag. "And we see what happens."

Rubek and the marine stepped into the design. Karrina followed but hesitated as she stepped across its border.

"There's power here," she said, looking around the room. "Real power." Her grin looked uncontrollable.

"Karrina," Wilson said.

She joined them and sat down, cross-legged between Wilson and the marine. "We should close our eyes," she said.

Wilson looked at her.

Her eyebrows lifted.

He closed his eyes.

~ * ~

In the base's central control room, Saville was toying with the Times crossword. He had followed the progress of Wilson and his team from screen to screen until the door of the lab closed behind them. There was no camera beyond that door.

"How long this time d'you reckon?" A voice behind him asked.

"It was five days last time." Another answered. "What the hell do they do in there?"

Saville swung around on his chair.

"Sorry," the two soldiers said, in unison.

Saville turned back to twelve across. A chair scraped behind him.

"Where the fuck did she come from?"

Saville turned again and scanned the bank of screens until he found her. Accommodation Block—Foyer, the label beneath the screen proclaimed.

She was looking around and then directly up at the camera. The policeman recognised her immediately. His arm lashed out and his fist punched down onto the red button next to his console. On screens around the room, lights began to flash. Behind him, the blast proof door whooshed closed.

On the guardhouse screen soldiers appeared, strapping on helmets and checking weapons.

On Saville's central screen, Alice Craven walked to the bottom of the staircase. She disappeared and then there she was again, on the next screen along, taking the stairs two at a time.

"How many in there?" Saville snapped.

"Forty-three."

"Shit." He glanced at the display to his right. No one had passed through the security screen, everything registered normal. He looked back. She had moved on a screen and was outside Wilson's apartment now.

She stopped and flicked back the hem of her jacket. She looked pregnant.

"Jesus... No," Saville gasped.

The screen and three to either side of it went blank. On four others, from four different angles, the first floor of the accommodation block disintegrated outward. The two floors above it hung in the air for a few seconds and then collapsed vertically. Then there was nothing but dust.

~ * ~

Wilson heard a dull thud from somewhere outside of the lab. His concentration was broken. He opened his eyes.

The walls of the room were flickering and then they were gone.

"Wow." Karrina stirred beside him.

They were in the centre of woodland clearing. The grass beneath them was short and lush, like a manicured lawn. Around them, and mirroring the shape of the chalk design they had left behind, small grey pebbles were interspersed with regular pyramids of white quartz. The sky above the treetops was an unbroken hazy blue. It was warm.

Karrina lifted her bundle from her knees, looked at it and then at Rubek. "Been there?" Her eyebrows lifted.

"Been somewhere else." Rubek replied.

Ackroyd got to his feet and looked around. His gaze darted left to the surrounding trees and the shadowy gaps between them. "It might get cold after sundown," he said, "might need 'em."

Thank you, Wilson thought, as he stood to join him.

"Which way?" The marine had turned full circle and appeared to have seen nothing that troubled him.

"We should sit down and try again," Rubek suggested. "Try and find that gorge again."

"Why?" Wilson kept his voice light. "We were trying to find Alice Craven." He looked down at Karrina. "Do you feel anything?"

She tossed her bundle aside, placed her hands on her knees and closed her eyes.

"Come on, soldier let's have a look around." Rubek stepped over the line of pebbles with the marine at his side. They took three paces toward the trees and then they were gone.

Karrina gasped, looked to be falling sideways and stuck out a hand to steady herself. Her eyes were wide, "Jesus."

Wilson stepped past her.

"No." She grabbed at his trouser leg. "Stay in the circle."

He was torn. His instincts screamed at him to follow Rubek. His mind told him to listen. He crouched beside her.

"There was nothing at first," Karrina said. "Nothing from the woman. I was going to tell you that she wasn't here and then boom."

"Boom, what?"

"Boom, power, incredible power, from over there." She pointed at the trees toward which Rubek and Ackroyd had been heading.

~ * ~

"We'll skirt around the clearing just inside the tree line." Rubek said. "As deep as we can without losing sight of it."

"AH, huh." The marine, eyes and body alert, kept a steady pace alongside him.

They passed the first of the trees and turned. Wilson and the girl had gone, so had the pebble circle.

Ackroyd's gun was in his hand.

Rubek had not even seen him reach for the concealed weapon. That at least gave him confidence in his choice. "We stick to the plan," he said, "but closer to the clearing."

~ * ~

Wilson helped Karrina to her feet. "They just disappeared. Three paces and they were gone. Can you feel anything now?"

She shook her head.

"Well we can't go back without them. Follow them...foolish I suspect. Perhaps if we go in the opposite direction."

Karrina said nothing.

Wilson stepped toward the pebbles and then over them. He turned and held out a hand.

Karrina took it and stepped over beside him. She did not break the contact.

Wilson did and was surprised by how much he missed it. He had to stop himself from feeling for her fingers again. "Anything?" he asked.

"Nothing."

"Come on then." Wilson counted their steps. On three, he stopped and looked around. Nothing had changed. Four, five, six, he felt Karrina's hand on his sleeve and turned again. The pebbles had gone. "What did you feel?"

"A twinge, nothing more, not like before, nowhere near as powerful."

"Or perhaps your own power was greater inside the circle rather than out of it."

"Perhaps."

Wilson's hand was around her waist. He had no idea how it had gotten there. It was under her jacket. He could feel her ribs beneath the thin fabric of her t-shirt. He pulled his arm away. She seemed not to have noticed. He shook his head clear. "Come on."

They stopped at the first of the trees.

Wilson scanned the forest ahead. His ears strained to catch any sound.

Karrina closed her eyes and opened her mind.

They took another three paces.

"Far enough." Wilson said. "Now we need to skirt around and follow the line that you felt that power coming from." He dropped his bundle to the ground and stooped to untie it.

The camouflage jacket was reversible. Its lining was a screaming, bright; *I'm over here,* orange. He balled it up and placed it where he was sure that they would be able to see it from the other side of the clearing. "Come on then." The tone of his own voice shocked him. He glanced around at Karrina.

She was smiling up at him, eyes bright.

He felt an urge to take her hand again, to apologise for his abruptness, to feel the skin beneath her t-shirt. He turned and strode off through the trees.

Karrina, still smiling, followed. After a few strides, she regained his side.

Wilson felt her presence but kept his eyes forward, and the edge of the clearing, not more than ten feet away, at the periphery of his vision.

Every ten paces he stopped and listened. There was nothing, no birds, no breeze in the treetops above them, absolutely nothing. He pressed on, fighting complacency. "I'm not trained for this," he muttered, and tried to increase his concentration to compensate for the fact.

They both happened at the same time, the stab to the back of his neck, and the electrical impulse that his brain sent out to his limbs, paralysing them rather than spurring them into action. He froze.

"Sorry."

He turned his head.

Ackroyd's pistol was at his temple now. The marine lowered it, and his eyes, away from Wilson's. Behind him, Rubek was crouched behind a tree and smiling. Both men had donned camouflage jackets despite the heat.

They had worked, Wilson thought, *either that or he was not even half as good as he thought he was.* He looked at the faces of his companions, something had changed. They looked like a team, felt like a team. He smiled. "Come on then…and let's try to keep together this time."

They skirted the clearing, keeping just inside the first of the trees until the beacon of Wilson's jacket told him that it was time to turn into the forest and find whatever power Karrina had detected from the circle.

Twelve

Even as Alice jabbed her thumb down onto the detonator clipped to her waist, she knew that she was wrong. There was no one in the apartment on the other side of the door. She tried to drag time back. It refused to co-operate. Then it was too late. From above, she saw herself disintegrate into unrecognisable fragments of flesh and bone.

She should be gone but she held herself back. Where was he? Then she was above the camp. There was another building. Now she could sense him. She tried to reverse her flight but the camp beneath her got smaller and smaller.

She was on the bed. She hurt.

Leirbag was leaning over her. "Back, Alice, you must go back."

She hurt, not anywhere but everywhere.

He placed an icy hand onto her brow.

She closed her eyes. The bed was hard now. She opened them and recognised the building in front of her. She was on her back on the concrete walkway that surrounded it.

Something ripped into her left shoulder. She turned. Soldiers, dozens of them, were sprinting toward her. Another bullet took her in the thigh. She threw herself at the wall of the building and pressed the fire button.

~ * ~

Lying on her bed in the uppermost room of the Swiss Chateau, Moyasta felt something cold press against her lips. Then there was liquid. She sipped at it and opened her eyes. She was tired. She had begged death away so many times that soon, she knew, it would refuse to listen.

Around and above her concerned faces looked down. Her lips moved without forming words.

Concern turned to smiles. She was still with them.

A hand lifted her shoulders and she felt a pillow slip behind her. She smiled then, through broken teeth, and her eyes, one green, the other brown, took in her surroundings.

All seven were there. All were female.

She held out a hand and someone placed a glass into it. She drank again and felt strong enough to push herself upright. "So, it is done," she said." Karrina has been accepted."

They had done all that they could, weak as they now were. The danger had been foretold generations earlier, when everyone in the world knew the stories and would have had the power to prevent it.

She had tried not to grow bitter. She had failed. Ever since the first power hungry clan had abandoned the truth to fulfil their own selfish ends, since Ardamsfolk had shown mercy to the like-eyes and been rewarded by treachery. Ever since the first, false prophets had turned the people against the truth for their own equally selfish ends. Those with the true power had been persecuted, tortured and burned. There were, however, still thousands of people, spread across the world, who remained true to Ardam. She laughed aloud then. The like-eyes had even corrupted his name.

"We few have done all that we can," she whispered, "Karrina is wise and she is strong."

Heads bent closer to listen.

"We must have faith, and we must be ready to give her whatever help we can from this world. The usurper will be defeated and Ardam's people will once again fill this world as they fill all of the others.

~ * ~

They left the trees behind. In front of them, the land dipped away into a flat-bottomed valley. A thin ribbon of silver meandered along its length.

Wilson stopped and surveyed the scene. There was no sign of habitation and no movement, not even a bird in the sky. The others drew up alongside him. "How far?" he asked.

No one answered.

"Karrina?"

"No idea, but we're going in the right direction."

~ * ~

They had been travelling for over an hour. Still the valley bottom seemed no closer. They had not even reached the crest of the downward slope. They walked four abreast, trying to remain alert in what seemed to be an open and non-threatening world.

Ackroyd watched the front, his eyes straining to catch any movement that might develop into a threat.

Rubek was scanning the horizon line and trying to slot this journey into something that he could rationalise. He was not getting very far.

Wilson was watching his three companions.

Karrina stopped, head inclined as though smelling the air.

"What is it?" Wilson's question halted the other two.

"It's...no nothing." She smiled. "Perhaps I'm just nervous."

"You sure?"

"...Yes."

They continued.

Another half hour and Rubek stopped. "This is crazy, one and a half hours, five, maybe six miles and we've gotten nowhere."

Wilson looked on. In front of them, the valley sloped away. Below them, the silver ribbon of the river was as it had always been, no closer. "We'll rest a few minutes," he said.

~ * ~

The river was no more than twenty feet from the rear garden of Korum's house. The sluices would soon be opened and the life-giving water would be channelled into the orchards and vegetable plots that lined its banks. The town stood further away from the river on higher ground. It had not always been so, but the spring floods had become more regular and more powerful in recent years. The people had moved the town. Korum alone had remained, rebuilding his house on stilts rather than on higher ground. For two months of every year, he was master of his own small island. He had once been master of the Temple and therefore of the people. His own priests had voted him out of office. Casto and his scheming cronies, whose only consideration was lining their own pockets and those of their families, had outmanoeuvred him.

Those priests who controlled the Temple controlled everything. It was easy to know which crops to grow, which ones would increase in price, when, with the magic of the temple, they could bring sun or rain or frost as and when they needed them. Those without connections always seemed to make the wrong guesses. All that was, except Korum, who was still a priest. That, they could not take away from him.

~ * ~

In the centre of the town, people thronged the forecourt of the Temple. They had all heard the rumours. Strangers had appeared from Otherworld. The priests were holding them back for the present, but they were coming.

Casto looked out over the sea of heads. It was not panic yet, but it could turn, he knew, and quickly. Strangers from out of the forest, it was written that this would be the end of the people. He turned back into the room. Eleven other priests knelt in a circle. "What are they doing now?" Casto asked.

"They still come." A single voice from the circle replied.

"Determined then. Who are they?" The High Priest turned away from the window.

"We dare not get any closer. One has power and recognises our presence, and so we pull back."

"And the others?" Casto strode the perimeter of the room.

"From Ardam's world, we think, but not of it."

Below them, the rumblings of the crowd grew louder. Either there were more of them or the ones there were, were growing angrier. Neither would be good.

"We must summon Korum."

Castor rounded on the speaker. "Never."

"He wouldn't come anyway," said another

"Not if he's summoned he won't," added another. "We could try begging perhaps."

Castor felt the tide of support ebbing away from him. He turned back to the window. "Never."

~ * ~

"Well there's no point in carrying on if we're not going anywhere." Rubek pulled at the grass with his fingers.

"And there's no point in going back if this is where we're meant to be." Wilson looked at Karrina. "Where's the power coming from?"

"There." She pointed across the valley. "But faint."

"In the valley or beyond it?"

"In…I think."

Ackroyd stood. "Well we walked this far, no problem. We could stick to the high ground. Skirt the valley and try to drop down into it every now and then." He looked down at the others for agreement. "If we can, great. If we end up back here, we think again."

"Beats sitting here." Rubek joined the marine. "Coming?"

Wilson stood and held out a hand to Karrina.

She took his fingers and the contact tingled up his arm, warm and exciting. The sensation took him by surprise and he pulled back from it.

Karrina smiled and the effect was the same as that of her touch.

Wilson turned away.

~ * ~

They stopped at the stream, which, by the time it reached the valley floor, would have become the river that now stretched away from them rather than across their field of vision.

Four times, they had tried to descend into the valley and failed. The daylight was fading. Wilson's stomach rumbled. "'Scuse me." He patted it.

"Something else we didn't plan for." Rubek said.

Ackroyd unclipped his breast pocket and pulled out a thick bar of mint cake.

"Thank God for the marines," Rubek laughed.

The prospect of food seemed to lighten the mood of them all.

They sat in a circle.

Ackroyd snapped the block into four and passed the pieces round. Dusk was turning rapidly into night.

"The root thing," Rubek said, "you got it?"

"Course." Wilson tapped his pocket.

"Well, it worked in the cave."

Wilson fumbled for it. When he pulled his hand free there was sufficient light to illuminate the faces around him.

"There." Karrina said, pointing out over the valley.

They all turned. Beyond the valley floor and rising up its side to their left there were pinpricks of light, hundreds of them, as though someone had pulled the master switch and lit up a whole town.

"Not just a magic flashlight then." Rubek said.

"Useful," Karrina said, "it reveals what's hidden." She stroked a finger along the root. The light flared. She pulled her hand away and it faded.

"And," Rubek was staring down into the valley, "I'll bet that now we can see it we can walk right down into it."

"Not until morning," Wilson said. "In daylight we should get a perfect view from up here."

"Ackroyd," Rubek looked at the marine, "light or dark?"

"Light. The place will be laid out like a street plan. Karrina might even be able to pinpoint the power source. I say we wait. But we could do with being hidden now."

Wilson slipped Smallroot back into his pocket. The light disappeared, so did the town.

~ * ~

The circle of priests opened their eyes as one. Their defences, so powerful and reliable until then had crumbled without warning.

From his seat at the window, Casto felt a change in the atmosphere around him.

"They see us." One of the circle said, before the high priest had time to form a question.

"The one with the power?" Casto sat forward as though by getting closer to the window he would be able to see what was occurring on the hilltop beyond the town.

"No, she hadn't enough."

"Something new then." Casto returned his attention to the room. "Something hidden, even from us."

"Apparently." The circle was breaking up. With their focus gone, they looked around for leadership. All their gazes settled eventually onto Casto.

"Why did they wait? Why now?"

"Perhaps they were testing our strength."

"Perhaps they were waiting until dark."

"Perhaps they didn't have the power until just now."

The theories assailed the High Priest from all sides. "What are they doing now?" He barked.

"Nothing." Only a single voice had the courage to speak out.

"They weren't waiting for darkness then." Casto looked toward the window. Night had cleared the forecourt. He had until dawn at least. "I will go to Korum," he said, not raising his eyes to meet those of the men who had aided him in the overthrow of the ex-High Priest.

~ * ~

Leirbag looked down at Alice. Her sleep was not a peaceful one. Her arms thrashed around on top of the bed. The rips on her body were healing; soon she would be perfect again.

She had failed, twice. No one had ever failed him twice and there had only ever been one price for failure. He paced the room. He did not want to exact that price. *I must,* he thought, and then, *why? I am Leirbag. I can do anything that I want.* He would, he decided, spare her. He had to. She was to be his queen and beyond that, nothing mattered.

He looked down at her; she was almost beautiful again. He would give her no comfort though. He would do nothing to ease the pain of her wakening. There had to be some price.

Alice groaned and then screamed through her sleep.

Leirbag turned and strode from the room. The meddlers were still an irritant and they still had to be dealt with. But where were they?

~ * ~

Sappers had removed the collapsed roof of the lab. Saville had never seen the inside of the building and was unable to build any sort of a picture of what it had once been from the fractured pieces of tile and plaster that remained.

Around him the careful hands of white-overalled forensic teams sifted through the rubble in search of the remains of Wilson and his companions.

Saville wanted to help but couldn't. His bandaged fingers were torn and bloody from his initial attempts to claw through the smoking pile.

He did not feel anger or loss, that would come later, he knew. Now he was just tired. "Time for a drink, lad." *Why did those words rather than all the thousands of others stick in his mind?* He smiled and the first tear welled in the corner of his eye.

A military policeman placed a gentle hand his shoulder. "Come on, son, nothing you can do here."

Saville allowed the redcap to lead him away, silently thanking him for the 'son'. If it had been 'lad,' he knew that he would have broken down completely.

~ * ~

Dawn emerged from behind the hills and crept down the valley sides. Wilson shook himself awake. Karrina lay on the grass beside him. She looked as though she was dreaming happy dreams. She was beautiful. He did not allow the thought to progress. Rubek was beyond her, sitting but also sleeping. Ackroyd was nowhere in sight.

Wilson coughed. No one moved. He tried again.

Rubek's head jerked.

Karrina stirred and pushed herself onto one elbow.

Wilson stood, stretched the stiffness from his arms and then rubbed some feeling back into his legs.

"We need to cross here."

Wilson jumped back and then stumbled.

Ackroyd smiled. "Farther down it gets too steep and then too wide."

"Jesus, lad, don't do that." Wilson regained his feet.

"Sorry, just thought I'd take a look."

"Well good…thanks, but don't do it again, sneak up on me, I mean, not take a look."

"How far down d'you get." Rubek was fully awake.

"Quarter mile, maybe a little more." Ackroyd said.

"And nothing tried to stop you." Enthusiasm bubbled in Rubek's voice.

"Not a worry." The marine grinned.

"So their defences are down." Rubek took a series of long strides down the hillside, turned and then retraced them. "Piece of cake."

"But the town's still hidden." Wilson stroked his chin. He needed a shave.

"Maybe the town's always hidden. It's pretty vulnerable where it is." Karrina joined them. "And stopping our approach was extra. Once we'd seen them it didn't matter any more."

"I'd have thought that it would have mattered even more. It doesn't make sense." Wilson toyed with the object in his pocket but stopped short of extracting it. "Will we take a look?"

"Let's not make ourselves too obvious though." Ackroyd crouched and then lay down on the ground. "They'll be waking up down there as well, pretty soon."

~ * ~

Korum woke and was immediately alert. His gaze darted around the room and then settled on the uncovered window. Outside it was still dark.

Someone was coming. He closed his eyes, Casto, in the middle of the night. Casto was not good news at any time. Korum swung his legs from the bed and reached for his gown. Another thought tickled the edge of his mind. He tried to grab hold of it. The window, his head turned. There was a light, high up the hill at the head of the valley. No one lived up there. He archived this piece of information and then concentrated on his visitor.

~ * ~

It was not going to be easy; Casto rehearsed his lines as he strode down through the narrow, empty streets of the town and onto the flood plain. "Beg," someone had recommended. "Pah." But he had to ask, not demand. "Sorry to disturb you at such an hour Korum." He mouthed the words. "I have…" He corrected himself. "We have a… No… There's a problem."

Korum's stilt house grew out of the darkness in front of him. It disappeared. "Arrogant old fool." Casto waved a hand and it materialised again. He stopped, composing his thoughts and forcing a smile.

~ * ~

Korum ushered the High Priest into an outer chamber. Not one of the inner ones Casto noted with irritation. Nor had Korum offered him a seat.

Korum sat and smiled benignly up at him.

Casto's fists clenched invisibly beneath the loose sleeves of his gown but he returned the smile. "There are strangers. They come from the forest."

Korum only nodded.

"The people know of them," Casto continued. "They are close to panic."

"So your little band is not as trustworthy as you thought." Korum's voice hovered just on the polite side of mocking.

Anger pulsed behind Casto's temples, but he managed to keep it out of his expression. "That matters little now, friend." His tongue struggled with the word but once said the rest came more easily. "We need your help, Korum. To keep the people calm. To keep us together."

"They are up on the ridge at the head of the river." Korum flicked a wrist in the direction of the window but he kept his eyes on Casto and he was rewarded.

The smile remained fixed but the eyes of the priest told Korum that Casto had no idea how much power he still possessed and was surprised that he could know even that much.

"If they are hostile," Korum kept his voice steady, "and just because they're strangers doesn't mean that they are, then it will be the Power that they seek."

The two men eyed one another.

"And all of the power is in your temple." Korum read scepticism in Casto's expression. "Oh, I've retained a modest amount." He spread his hands as though apologising for the fact. "They will, I expect, approach from the forest. From that direction there are no dwellings until they reach the river."

"We could open the sluices." For the first time Casto's smile looked genuine. "Flood the valley."

Korum did not need his powers to see the picture of his flooded fields and orchards that had so cheered the priest. "That would slow them, true enough. But as they've already come this far I doubt that it would stop them." He stood and crossed the room to where a decanter and glasses stood on a corner table. He filled two glasses and then turned.

"Casto, I do apologise, the lateness of the hour, and gravity of your news have made me remiss. Please take a seat."

"No offence taken." Casto nodded, playing the game. He lowered himself into a chair and accepted the proffered wine.

Korum returned to his own seat, raised his glass in salute and took a drink.

Casto mirrored the gesture, lifted his own glass to his lips but did not take a drink until he was sure that he had seen the other swallow.

Korum watched and smiled. "If it is the Power that they seek and what else could it be." He waited for suggestions. None came. "Then either they can detect it, or they will head for the biggest building. Either way their focus is the Temple. How many are there?"

"Four." Casto spluttered, amazed that Korum had gleaned the information from him with so little effort.

"So," Korum continued, "either very powerful or very foolish. We need to discover which but we must assume the former. Do otherwise and we could be the foolish ones."

Casto nodded, unable to disagree, but searching for a trap and finding none.

"So," Korum took another drink and laid back his head, "to get to the Temple they have to pass my simple house." A wave of his hand took in the room. "If they can detect the Power they may get a glimmer, but not, I suspect, enough to divert them. Not compared with that they must feel from your Temple." He paused, allowing time for the compliment to register.

Casto smiled a smile that was, for the first time, reflected in the eyes above it.

Korum continued. "If they can't detect it, they'll just head straight for the Temple. I'll be at their backs but with insufficient power to aid you."

Casto's eyes darted around the room. He could see the corner into which Korum was arguing him. "We must defend the Temple with all the power that we have. Anything else would surely be foolish."

"We do not know their strength." Korum stood and refilled their glasses. "Sufficient here, with priests of your own choosing to guide it of course, and if their power is real at least you will be warned. We might even be able to inflict some moderate damage ourselves."

"I cannot dilute the power of the Temple." Casto insisted, trying to think of any of the eleven priests who he could trust to be out of his sight and under Korum's influence. *None,* he concluded. "I could send priests here. You could come and help defend the Temple."

Korum laughed. "I don't think so my friend...do you?" He turned toward the window.

A thin line of silver topped the ridge above the valley. "It will be light soon." Korum stood. "Perhaps you should consult your council."

"You are right." Casto hid the displeasure that Korum's casual dismissal of him had generated. "I will hear their views before I decide." At the door he turned. "Thank you Korum." He bowed. "For your knowledge and for your advice."

"Send two," Korum said, "with as much of the Power as you can spare."

~ * ~

As soon as he was alone Korum returned to his inner chamber, lay back on its bed and tried to make contact. It was becoming more and more difficult. Moyasta was old, older than anyone on his world had ever had the good fortune to be. Her knowledge was vast. Sometimes Korum felt that he was drowning in it. She was also powerful, but her ability to maintain contact had waned as the years passed.

After some minutes, he felt her. Just a wisp of consciousness at first, stroking his own. Then he had a name, Karrina, and a picture, hazy, she was pretty. She was one of the last of Ardam's true line and she needed the Power. She needed it to save her own world, Ardam's and perhaps all of the others as well. *Must be quite a girl*, Korum was thinking, when the contact wavered and then broke. A single thought from Moyasta remained in his head. *She is.*

Thirteen

The sun was fully up. The valley below their vantage point looked green, peaceful and empty.

Wilson shuffled around and pulled Smallroot from his trouser pocket.

Barns and animal pens dotted the hillside to their left. Farther away on the far side of the valley a small town of red tiled roofs and white plaster walls clung to the hillside above the floodplain. The pattern of its streets was square and regular. An arched walkway surrounded three-quarters of an open square at its centre. An imposing, four-storey building formed the square's fourth side. There was only one building near the river. It was simple, square and stood above the floodplain on stilts.

A hospice, Wilson thought, *or a prison.* "You still feel the power?" He turned toward Karrina.

"Yes, the big building in the centre. It's so much easier when I can see them. And more, not as strong, not nearly as strong, from that place by the river."

"How strong is strong?" Ackroyd asked.

Karrina looked bemused and then she felt something, from the building by the river. *Her name, she felt her own name.* She smiled.

"How long's a piece of string?" Wilson chuckled.

"Huh?" It was the marine's turn to look confused.

"Never mind, lad, never mind." Wilson patted the soldier's broad shoulder.

"We should backtrack." Ackroyd talked his way back onto familiar ground. "There are no buildings on this side of the river. We should be able to get to the edge of the town unnoticed."

"And then?" Wilson raised his eyebrows.

"Well, the big building if that's where the power is coming from."

"No," Karrina said.

"No? Why?" Rubek rolled onto his side.

"No…I don't know why, just no."

"Well, Karrina, that's what we hired you for," Wilson said. "Intuition."

Rubek's attention switched to Ackroyd. "What do you think, marine?"

Karrina swung around to face the challenge.

Ackroyd looked from one to the other. "Well, if we don't know how powerful, powerful is, then the softer target might be a safer way of finding out."

Wilson relaxed.

"Thank you," Karrina said, looking at the marine.

"For what?" Rubek snapped.

Karrina turned to include him in her smile. "For having faith."

Wilson watched the exchange and was pleased to see the hardness of Rubek's expression metamorphose into what he could almost consider affection.

~ * ~

The three giants looked around the room and then at each other.

"I don't know," Lucan said, "I told you what I was told."

His companions were stroking the stone of the walls, in awe of the building's solidity and size.

"Lucan, good to see you again." Leirbag strode into the room. "You too, friends. Please sit."

The four looked around. The only chairs were those that surrounded the long table in the centre of the room and none of them, except the throne at its head looked substantial enough to bear their weight.

"Sorry, sorry," Leirbag said. "All a bit of a rush." He waved an arm and four bulky timber stools appeared along the wall. "Now, please."

The giants sat, looking toward Leirbag but avoiding eye contact.

Leirbag eased himself onto his throne at the head of the table, wrapped his fingers around its serpent arms and studied his guests. "There are four who would slow our progress." His attention was on Lucan. "You have met two of them, I believe. They killed Ranorth."

The giants looked at one another and growled.

"Lucan, you're sure they never appeared again at the gorge?" Leirbag kept his voice light, for once not wanting it to instil fear.

The giant shook his head.

Leirbag believed him. He was too stupid and too scared to lie. "Well, they're not on this world. They left their own. There must be another. You will go there. You will find them and you will kill them." He stood. "Come, I'll set you on your way.

~ * ~

Alice was not sure whether she was awake or asleep. She knew that she hurt. She opened her eyes. She was in a cell. She could see the bars and feel the earth of the floor beneath her back. She was back in Somalia. Then Tony was there. He was in the cell opposite hers. He was laughing. He had a glass in his hand and a blonde on his knee. It was not her.

She turned over. Her arm had fallen off. She felt for it. No, it hadn't. There was a pain in her head. The noise was unbearable and then it stopped. She was in a hole then, there was dirt in her hair and in her mouth. She couldn't breathe. She was back in the tower. She was on the bed; she flung her body sideways and looked over the side of it. There was a head on the floor. It was hers. She screamed.

~ * ~

The giants had gone. Leirbag hoped that they would not let him down. He would need them later. He heard Alice scream and smiled. He looked along the table. Two vacant faces stared back at him. "Rodney, London. Prince, Rome." He waved an arm and the boys' heads flopped forward onto the tabletop. Then he leaned back against his throne. He would comfort Alice now. He would be the end of her pain. She would thank him for it and then she would fill the remaining seats at his table.

~ * ~

Saville scrambled over the mound of rubble that surrounded what had once been the floor of the lab. His hands were still tender but the bandages had gone and his fingers appeared to be healing well.

Four people had gone in. None had come out. The blast had collapsed the roof. The forensic teams had found nothing beneath it, not a flake of skin, or spattering of blood, no teeth, no bones, nothing.

He sat cross-legged on the cleared tiles, closed his eyes and thought. He thought of Wilson, his boss and more, his mentor perhaps. "Time for a drink, lad." The words spun around his head. *Would they haunt him forever*, he wondered.

He opened his eyes and pulled Wilson's service-issue revolver from his jacket pocket. He had taken it from the ruins of the accommodation block, something solid to hang his memories on. He should not have, but he had and he didn't care. So many things did not matter now, that had seemed so important before. His head dropped. This time when his eyes closed, he did not try to open them.

Fourteen

They edged down the hillside using its undulating contours for cover as best they could.

A few people were moving about the streets of the town. More had congregated on the square in front of the big building. Half the population it seemed to Wilson. Whether Karrina had foreseen this, he had no idea, but he was glad that it was no longer their target.

The ground beneath them began to flatten and became spongy underfoot. Wilson felt his calves begin to cramp. Beside him, Rubek was breathing hard. Karrina and Ackroyd seemed unaffected.

The marine nodded downstream to where a small clump of trees overhung the bank. From the top of the ridge, they had seen that there was no bridge. What they all hoped for was, shallow. "Should be." Ackroyd had said. "It's wide enough and its catchment's not big enough to give it that much volume." Wilson hoped that he was right. He could swim well enough but not fully clothed. He thought of stripping off in front of Karrina and his face flushed. *That would blow it,* he thought. Then he thought of her stripping in front of him, a much more attractive proposition. He looked at her.

She was grinning at him. Her eyes out-sparkled her smile.

She's reading my mind, he thought, and the red of his cheeks deepened. He concentrated on the trees to his front and on the soft ground that sucked at his feet. He tried to think of his wife and the boys, to remember where his affections and his desires should lie, but his mind continually looped back to Karrina.

~ * ~

Moyasta cackled. Karrina was doing well, working her subtle magic on this man, Wilson, with the skill of a woman twice her age.

Korum had made contact too, sooner than she had expected. He had been her friend for decades. She had never seen him or touched him except in and with her mind but she knew him to be a powerful and honourable man.

~ * ~

The four giants gazed, open mouthed, around the woodland clearing. Lucan, more accustomed to Leirbag's magic than the others, stood first and sniffed the air. "This way, I can smell them." He strode across the pebble boundary.

The other three, their fear of losing sight of Lucan overcoming their amazement, scrambled after him.

One looked back. The pebbles had gone. He rushed to regain the company of his fellows and in doing so increased the pace of them all.

~ * ~

Korum felt the strangers. They were much closer now. *Must be almost at the river,* he thought. He would be able to see them from the window. He resisted the impulse to check.

There was power moving too. He concentrated on that. Two priests not close enough yet for him to identify them, but he knew that they would be the least influential and therefore the least powerful. Casto would never have released anyone he considered a threat into Korum's company. They had artefacts too. *One each,* he guessed. The combined power was substantial. *Less than he had hoped*, he smiled, *but more than he had expected.*

~ * ~

Saville shook his mind clear. He was sure that he had seen, just for a second, three men, huge men, scrambling, almost crawling, away from him. The rubble had gone. He looked around. So had the base, or what remained of it following the twin attacks.

He had been thinking about Alice Craven. He had not believed the briefing, despite the photographic evidence, despite the fact that Wilson himself had given it.

Then he had seen her himself, twice, once on the screen when she had destroyed the accommodation block, and then again in the flesh, when they had been called away from their rescue attempts to confront the second attack. She had taken three bullets, maybe four and then there could not have been a single piece left of her that was large enough to take even one. Still his mind had shut out the evidence of his eyes.

Now, he continued his study of his new surroundings, so different from the devastation he had left. *Now,* he thought, *he would believe just about anything.*

His fingers tightened around the butt of the pistol. The force had trained him to use one. But he had never even drawn one, never mind fired one in anger. *Could he,* he wondered. Five words invaded his mind once again, "Time for a drink, lad." Yes, he could. He checked the magazine, full, and flicked off the safety. Then he set off, cautiously, in pursuit of the giants. If they run away, even the wooden tops fresh out of Hendon knew, they are probably worth chasing.

~ * ~

Rodney Weaver squirmed on the hard wooden bench and pretended to read the newspaper he had found there. He had already let two trains go through. They had been half-empty.

A transport policeman patrolled the platform. He slowed and glanced down at Rodney as he passed him for the third time.

Rodney avoided eye contact. It would have to be the next one. A breeze brushed his cheek and beyond the lip of the platform, the rails buzzed. Here it came.

He folded the newspaper and slipped it under his arm.

The policeman ambled away toward the escalators.

The passing windows slowed as the middle carriages of the train approached. It was jammed. Rodney smiled; Leirbag would be pleased.

The doors whooshed open.

A wall of backs confronted him. He squeezed between them and turned into the carriage until the jam of passengers blocked his progress. The doors closed. The passengers around him stepped back as one as the train accelerated toward the tunnel.

In front of him, and pressed against him, a young office girl kept her eyes resolutely forward. He could feel her buttocks pressing against his hip. He turned his body, thrust his groin toward her and felt his hardness grow. He pushed a hand into his pocket and felt for the switch, his other he slipped around her waist. Her body tightened. He could almost read her mind. Was that accidental? Was she being groped? He moved his hand, cupped a breast and squeezed. Her head spun round. Her mouth opened. He flicked the switch.

~ * ~

A solid mass of people filled St Peter's square. The eyes of every one of them focussed on the balcony of the basilica. Prince materialised in the middle of the throng. Those who saw it happen moved away. Some crossed themselves. As soon as he was sure that he was there, he flicked the switch. *Do not hesitate*, was in his mind and he knew, because some of Leirbag's other thoughts had crept in behind the instruction, that the big man himself was for the endgame.

~ * ~

Marcella Thorpe flicked aside the curtain every time that she heard a car pass along the lane at the end of the short driveway of her cottage.

Seven o'clock, the woman had said. It was gone ten after. *One more disappointment*, Marcella thought, *one more dead end, and her resolve would collapse*. There had been so many donors, all willing, all caring, and then, when it came to the final tests, all incompatible.

Darren, only nine years old, was still in the infirmary, more plastic tube and machine than child.

"Before your husband gets home." She had said. He would be in at eight. Marcella glanced at the clock. It was 7.15. The nails of her left hand dug into the loose skin on the back of her right. She looked down and watched the pinched skin smooth back into shape. She did it again, just to feel the pain.

The ring of the doorbell set her heart racing. There had been no car and no footfalls on the flagstone pathway.

In her rush to get to the door, Marcella caught her shin on the brass corner of the coffee table. "Shit." She bent to rub away the pain but kept moving.

Her visitor was not what she expected. She was tall, business suited and, even to a woman's eyes, stunningly attractive. "Marcella Thorpe." She held out a hand. "Alice Craven, sorry I'm a bit late."

Marcella lost Alice's excuse in her rush to get the woman inside the house and comfortably seated at the far side of the coffee table. "Tea? Coffee?" She asked because that was what she always asked.

The woman made a point of looking at the clock.

"Nothing for me," Alice said. "But thanks anyway." She hoisted an expensive looking briefcase onto the table and flicked it open. "Now there are just a couple of formalities."

Marcella did not hear because she was not listening. "Anything," she had said to the woman on the phone, anything to make Darren well again. "Anything."

~ * ~

Leirbag relaxed into his throne and caressed its serpent arms. He could hardly remember when he had last been able to afford himself such a luxury. Everything was running along nicely.

The meddlers were being taken care of. Four giants should be able to handle that. If they couldn't, what use would his army be? He did not let the thought spoil his mood.

Alice had another place filled at their table, and with the help of Worldroot, he had detected enough manageable despair to fill four more.

Rodney and Prince were recovering. They had done well, Rodney especially. Leirbag had felt the boy's excitement, homed in on it. He had shared the feel of the girl before Rodney had blown her away with all the hundreds of others. "Nice touch that, Rodney," he said. He looked along the empty table and then around the empty room. "I'm bored." He thought about the words and then repeated them for their strangeness. How could he possibly be bored? He was almost ready to take control of two worlds and had discovered the existence of a third to be next in line. He needed a little pleasure himself. He could wait until Alice returned and enjoy her closeness. No, he needed her away again. Time was still short. So how could he have fun? His mind toyed with the unfamiliar concept, but at every turn, it collided with Alice. Nothing could be fun, he realised unless she was sharing it with him. She was his queen. Also his subject, his slave, he reminded himself.

What if he freed her? Would she stay? She had to. Would she? Yes, he hoped. *No,* he thought. *How to make her?* He leaned back his head and his long fingers stroked at his brow as he pondered on the problem.

Fifteen

They watched the stilt building from the cover of the trees, more relaxed now that branches and leaves concealed them from the town.

"Shallow enough," Ackroyd said. "We should go." He looked to be about to move off.

"No," Karrina grabbed his sleeve and held him back. "The power has changed."

"Changed how?" Ackroyd turned to look at her.

"It's moved. The big building is weaker, the house stronger."

"Are they mind readers, or what?" Rubek asked.

"Probably," Wilson replied. "Something to think about, or not to think about."

"Well if whoever's in there is getting stronger we definitely go now." Rubek stepped over the lowest of the branches and into the river.

Ackroyd drew his pistol and followed.

Karrina hung back.

"Go on," Wilson said, "rule one, we stick together." He immediately regretted the harshness of his words.

Karrina seemed not to have noticed. She smiled at him and stepped through the foliage into the water.

~ * ~

Wilson felt naked without the cover of the trees. Rushing was not an option with the weight of the water pushing back against his knees. He kept his eyes on the house. There was no sign of life.

~ * ~

The bank on the far side of the river sloped gently upward. Karrina was halfway up it when Wilson reached the water's edge.

Ackroyd and Rubek were already crouched against the base of one of the house's thick timber supports. Ackroyd, gun in hand had all his attention on the single stairway that led to the only door that they had seen. *Easy to defend one door*, Wilson thought, *too easy*.

Karrina was squatting on the damp soil next to Ackroyd and Rubek. Wilson joined her. They were all breathing hard.

"Over to you, marine," Rubek said.

"I'll take the stairs first," Ackroyd's attention was focussed on the bottom of them. He turned and laid a hand on Wilson's shoulder. "You next, then you, Karrina." He nodded at Rubek. "You bring up the rear." He edged further under the house. "Keep close, but keep behind." He swung around the base of the stairway onto the bottom tread and started to climb.

Wilson followed. He could hear Karrina's breathing behind him.

There was a small landing at the top, room for two people but not for four. Wilson joined the marine and

Ackroyd swung his boot at the door in front of them. The wood crashed inward without even a groan of protest. Ackroyd, gun first, was through it before Wilson had time to register the movement. His eyes and his weapon traversed a small hallway. He took three measured paces, allowing room for the others to enter behind him.

There were three doors, one left, one right and one forward. All were closed.

The handle of the one to their front creaked as someone depressed it from the inside and the door began to swing away from them.

"Down." Ackroyd was already on one knee. His gun, held two handed, covered a spot two feet above the door handle. It continued to swing away from him. He adjusted his aim to follow the centre of the growing gap between door and wall.

"A simple knock would have sufficed." The door swung fully open and a tall, white haired man stood framed in the space it had vacated. His arms hung at his sides, palms open toward them and empty.

The marine's posture did not relax.

Wilson raised his head and studied the man. *Old,* he thought, but that was only suggested by the whiteness of his hair and his deeply lined face. Not by his upright stance and square shoulders, or by the brightness of his eyes, one blue, the other brown.

"We could stand like this all day." The man smiled. "I am Korum and this is my home." He looked at Karrina and his smile broadened.

You are welcome, Karrina. She had not seen his lips move and realised that the words were in her head. *Moyasta told me to expect you.*

She was about to reply and then she just thought. *Thank you Korum.* She felt the thought float from her and then she felt its acceptance.

"You are welcome." This time his lips did move. He half turned and beckoned them into the room behind him. Then he smiled down at the crouching marine. "You are cautious, young man, that is good, but there really is no need here."

The barrel of Ackroyd's gun lowered an inch.

"And that wouldn't work in here anyway."

For a moment, Wilson thought that they were going to find out. Then Ackroyd lowered the weapon to his side but did not holster it.

"Good." Korum turned away from them and into the room.

The four looked at one another and then stood and followed. Wilson waited until Karrina was at his shoulder. "Anything?"

"Power, lots of it, but not threatening."

They filed through the doorway. Ackroyd's gun was still in his hand, but that hung loosely at his side.

Korum was in the corner filling glasses from a decanter.

Below the window to the right of the door two figures, dressed in robes more ornate than Korum's, were slumped on a large settee. They looked to be sleeping.

Korum turned back to them. He held a glass in each hand. "Wine?" He caught the direction of Wilson's gaze.

"You see them?" His eyes dropped to the policeman's hand and Smallroot. "Ah. I see, not strong but effective enough. May I?" He handed one glass to Karrina and the other to Rubek. Turned and picked up two others.

Ackroyd accepted one and Korum held the other out to Wilson.

He took it.

Korum's hand remained outstretched.

Something curled around Wilson's mind and he knew there would be no harm. He held out Smallroot.

Korum turned it over in his hand. "Of Ardam's world," he said, "but only a fragment of the whole."

"So we were told."

"Whoever possesses the whole could control the world."

"That's what we're afraid of."

Korum handed it back. "I have two more things for you." He dug into the folds of his robe. "They may not be enough, but it was all I could get." He seemed to be having difficulty locating whatever he was looking for. "You have friends on other worlds you know. People who yearn to see the usurper destroyed and peace return." He addressed Wilson, but Karrina knew, in her mind and in her heart, that the words were meant only for her.

"Leirbag?" Wilson asked. "The usurper. I mean." Korum's silence, he took to be in the affirmative.

After more fumbling, Korum's hands pulled free of his robe. He held one out to Wilson and unclenched it. Nestling in its palm was a small gold amulet. "Wear this," he said, "and you will know truth from lies."

Wilson took it. "Should be standard police issue."

Korum's brow furrowed.

"Never mind, thank you."

Don't worry, Korum's mind, said to Karrina's, *I've done a little work on it myself.* Then he turned to her and opened his other hand. A fine silver chain nestled in his palm. "Wear it around your waist," Korum said. "It will protect you from any power thrown at you and project it back to its source." He looked at the others and laughed. "I give it to the girl," he said, "because tradition dictates that she is the most vulnerable. Not always true I suspect." He looked at Ackroyd. "Feel free, you'll never know if you don't try."

The marine lifted his gun toward the ceiling and squeezed the trigger.

Nothing happened.

"Not always true at all." Korum chuckled

Ackroyd lowered the weapon and stared down at it.

"Sometimes," Korum said, "that which we rely on the most is the first thing to let us down." He spread his hands. "Now drink. It tastes good. It will give you strength and perhaps a little understanding."

Wilson smelled the rim of his glass, not like a connoisseur but like a food taster wary of poison.

Don't worry, something in his head, told him. *It's okay.* He took a drink. It was more than okay. The liquid brought a tingle to his fingers and toes as though he had injected it directly into his bloodstream. The sensation forced his lips into a smile.

The others watched and then raised their own glasses.

"Good, good." Korum looked at the two prone figures. "Now we must go. I will accompany you as far as the forest. We will talk as we go. I can't keep these two hidden for much longer.

~ * ~

Casto swung his body around at the circle of kneeling priests. "What do you mean nothing?" He paced around them. "They can't have turned, not so quickly. They don't have the wits. That's why I chose them."

Only one of the circle had the courage to speak out. "Perhaps Korum had more power than you suspected."

"Than I suspected." Casto's foot lashed out at the kneeling figure and sent him sprawling. "When things are going well you want to be a council." He kicked out again catching the next in line. "When things go wrong, it's me... I suspected." He took two more steps. The next in line fell over before Casto had time to take a swing. "By Ardam's grave, Korum's down there. The strangers are with him. He has the amulet and the belt. Darrus and Rogan are..." He turned back and launched a kick into the ribs of the one who thought that he had escaped. "We've no idea where they are."

He strode to the window, stuck out his head, and then pulled it back again as a well-aimed cabbage bounced from its frame and into the temple. He persevered.

"People...PEOPLE!"

The hubbub below him quietened and then died. He took a deep breath and then continued.

"People, your priests have been working through the night on your behalf." He paused. Bewildered looks crisscrossed the crowd below. He had their attention for a while at least. "We held the strangers back, but..." Murmurings rose up to him. "...But against enemies from

156

amongst us we can do little." There was silence once again. "Korum has welcomed the strangers into his home." The volume started to rise. He held out an arm and it subsided. Casto knew that he had them. "We sent two. Darrus and Rogan, you all know them." He paused for effect. "Korum has killed them and stolen the artefacts that we gave them for their protection." This time when the noise swelled, Casto did nothing to subdue it.

The mob milled around for a few seconds and then it turned and spewed out of the courtyard and into the streets that led down to the river. They were out of control, out of anyone's control. Casto smiled. At least they were heading in the other direction.

~ * ~

Leirbag greeted the newcomer to his table with a blast of pain and a sight of the truck that had been the only possible winner in the head on contest with his BMW.

"Sit." He said. "Marcella wants you to understand. 'Til death us do part.' You said and she said. Well, it has." He thought pain and the man's head smashed backward to an impossible angle and then swung back to sit more naturally above his neck.

"What's your name?"

"Stanley."

There was more pain.

"No, you were Stanley. Now you're Beemer." Leirbag had found some fun. Alice had started it with Prince. She would appreciate it. That minute sparkle of Alice uncontrolled would appreciate it, the part that he wanted to grow without fear of losing the rest.

He laughed. "Well, Beemer, welcome, now eat."

~ * ~

Lucan stumbled from tree to tree. He had never seen a maze like the one into which he had stumbled. It seemed to go on forever.

Behind him, his companions had dropped into single file. Happy to let him realise that he could not squeeze his bulk between the tightly packed trees before they made the same mistakes beside him.

He lashed out at branches in his frustration. Some snapped under the ferocity of his blows. Some stood their ground tearing and bruising the skin of his hands and forearms. Others, younger and suppler, bent away and then catapulted into the faces of those behind. These stretched their line and slowed their progress even further.

Then there were no more trees in front of him. He stopped. He was exhausted. Trickles of blood from dozens of cuts dripped from his fingers onto the grass of the hillside onto which the forest had ejected him. Laboured breathing and curses told him that the others were close behind.

His own breath was coming more easily. He looked out across the gentle green valley and smiled. He could walk country like that forever, without faltering or straining, without even noticing the distance over which his legs were carrying him. First, he had to get that forest and its twists and turns out of his mind, and the tiredness and pain that it had inflicted out of his body

~ * ~

Alice stretched and yawned. She was back. Her bed was soft beneath her and the room warm and airy. She opened her eyes.

This is good, she thought, *this is how to wake up.*

She allowed herself to enjoy the feeling for a while and then she swung her legs over the side of the bed and sprinkled cold water from the enamel bowl onto her face. Then she looked around the room and waited.

Nothing appeared in her mind, no instructions, and no requests. She paced the room, not knowing what to do and then decided to risk it. One taste, one hint of a taste, and she would run back, reclaim the sanctuary of her bed and wait for as long as she had to for instructions.

In the corridor, she kept her pace slow. Her tongue scoured the roof of her mouth for a warning.

At the last door she turned.

~ * ~

Leirbag saw her in the doorway and stood. "Alice, Alice, good to see you back." He left his throne and rounded the table, arms outstretched.

Alice moved to greet him, but slowly.

His arms slipped around her waist and pulled her close.

"Alice, I want you to meet..." He spun away from her.

She noticed the newcomer for the first time and knew that he must be Marcella's husband.

"Beemer," Leirbag said.

"Hello Beemer," she said.

The man looked back at her through empty eyes.

"Beemer," Leirbag, said again.

I heard the first time, Alice thought, and was shocked by that hint of rebellion.

"Beemer."

Alice knew that Leirbag was waiting for a response. She could not think of one. "Strange name." She said, at last, looking into Leirbag's eyes and hoping that she had said the right thing.

"Beemer, Beemer." Leirbag's eyes flashed anger.

Alice stepped back, ready for the pain. None came. The fingers around her waist pulled her firmly but gently around.

She looked up into Leirbag's face and saw only sadness. "Beemer," he said.

Her brow creased. She did not know what to say. But she, for a change, felt his pain and she was touched by it. She slipped an arm around his waist and pulled him close. For the first time, she took him, not because she had to, not because she was scared not to, but because she wanted to.

He pulled away and led her to her seat at the table.

As soon as they were seated, he leaned toward her. "Beemer, Alice, his car, the crash, Beemer, it's funny. It's a joke.

"Ah..." She smiled, and looked again at the sadness in his eyes. And Alice, the real Alice, the old Alice who was only just starting to find herself again, thought that she could ease that sadness.

His hand was on the table. She felt for it and squeezed his long fingers.

Sixteen

They heard the baying of the mob before they reached the doorway at the head of the stairs.

Korum was the first to descend. "So Casto has released the pack. We must hurry."

A narrow wooden bridge spanned the river.

"It can't have been hidden," Wilson said.

"It wasn't." Korum stepped onto the first of the planks. "I just built it." At the far side, he waited until the others had crossed and then waved an arm over it. It disappeared. "A few more seconds gained." He turned and took off up the slope.

Ackroyd followed with long easy strides.

Wilson and Rubek were gasping for breath after only half a dozen uphill paces.

The ascent got steeper.

There was a roar from behind them.

They were visible now from the lower streets of the town.

Karrina, her paces shorter but faster than Ackroyd's, overtook him and then Korum. She crested the rise. She could see the edge of the tree line. In front of it, four huge men appeared not to have seen her. She dived to the ground, flattened herself on the grass and turned, gesturing that the others should do the same.

They did and crawled up beside her.

Wilson looked back. The townspeople were thrashing through the river. Behind them flames licked around the supports of Korum's home.

"I can build another easily enough," the priest said, and then turned his attention and Wilson's to the giants. "Of Ardam's world," he said, "strong but simple minded."

"We've met before." Wilson said.

"And totally loyal." Korum appeared to ignore him.

"To whom?" Rubek asked.

"Ah, now there's the problem. Their judgment is not always sound. Simple minded as I said."

"Do they mean us harm?" Karrina twisted her head to look beyond Rubek and at Korum.

"If they have been instructed to do so they will kill us without question."

"And if not?" Wilson asked.

"Irrelevant, I suspect," Korum said. "They are here and they haven't the power or the wits to get here unaided. You arrived only just before them and from the same direction." He let the implication dangle.

Below them, the last of the mob had gained dry land.

Ackroyd drew his pistol and looked at Korum.

Korum smiled and then nodded.

"Right." The marine took one look at the approaching mob and then spun his head back toward the giants. "We keep low and we angle away from them but toward the trees." He inched forward on his elbows. "At the first sign that they've seen us, we run like hell."

The sounds behind them grew louder.

Rubek scrambled level with Wilson. "This is going to be a close one."

~ * ~

Lucan heard the sounds in the valley below, could not place then into anything he was expecting and so he ignored them.

Then something caught his nostrils. He had the smell of them and they were close. He could not see anything but the scent was strong. He stood.

The others rose behind him. Now he could see them. There were five of them, low in the grass and crawling toward the trees. Five, he hesitated. Leirbag had said four. He was confused. He dare not get it wrong. Leirbag would be angry.

~ * ~

Ackroyd knew that the giants had spotted them. "RUN." He powered himself to his feet, took one wild shot in the general direction of the giants and took off toward the tree line.

~ * ~

Saville crouched just inside the last line of trees and watched the four huge men resting on the grass only yards away from him.

One of them stood and looked even bigger.

Saville rested the revolver on a low branch to counter the shake of his hand. *If they turn round,* he thought, *if they take just one step back toward the trees.*

Something else caught his attention. Further down the hill and more to his left. Someone was running. He heard a shot. More figures appeared. He recognised Wilson.

He remembered the giants; they were all standing now but not moving.

~ * ~

Lucan still hesitated. There should only be four. If there had been it would be easy. Then he recognised two of them. "Two of them killed Ranorth," Leirbag had said. That one and the taller one behind him, they had killed Ranorth. Lucan remembered them.

He roared and broke into a loping run.

~ * ~

A shot rang out from somewhere in the trees. Redness erupted from the head of the second giant. He dropped sideways lay still for a few seconds and then pushed himself to his feet and took off after his fellows.

Ackroyd stopped and turned. He loosed another three bullets into the bulk of the leader of the charge. He was sure that all had found their target but the giant kept on coming. He heard the others pass behind him and took up the rear. Karrina was almost at the trees with Rubek and Wilson close behind. Korum was slowing.

~ * ~

Saville had been aiming at the leader. It was only luck that had felled the one behind him if only temporarily. He tried again. This time the leader slowed, raised a hand to his head and toppled forward.

~ * ~

Ackroyd caught up with Korum, gripped him by the elbow and pushed onward. The others had stopped at the first of the trees. Ackroyd gestured with his gun hand that they should keep going. He glanced to his left. "Fuck." He was not going to make it, not with Korum.

There was another shot, a third giant went down onto his knees, but struggled back up and kept coming.

Wilson leapt from cover and dashed toward them, taking Korum by his free elbow and adding his weight to their charge.

~ * ~

Saville saw Wilson again. He let off one more shot and then edged through the trees toward the point from which his boss had appeared.

~ * ~

Ackroyd shoved Korum through the first branches. Karrina grabbed the priest's hand and pulled him further into cover. The marine turned.

The giants slowed at the trees. They had to turn sideways to squeeze between the ones that Wilson had dashed between. Branches that had been no obstacle even to Rubek they had to duck beneath.

Ackroyd launched a stream of bullets between the trees. There was a roar to his right.

Saville was beside him and shooting in the same direction.

The impact of the missiles slowed and then stopped the giants. Then they stumbled backward out of the trees and into the open. They turned.

The crowd from the town crested the ridge. The sight of the giants stopped their advance.

Ackroyd and Saville were still firing. One by one, the giants fell; this time they remained where they lay.

The mob hesitated and then came on again.

"Come on. Let's move it." Ackroyd lowered his gun and turned. "Back to the clearing."

They dodged through the trees.

Wilson, slipped Smallroot into his pocket, fearful of tripping and losing it amongst the thick carpet of pine needles and broken branches.

Karrina stumbled.

Saville and Ackroyd moved to help her but she was up and running again before they reached her.

Rubek burst into the clearing first. It was green and empty. He could see the bright orange beacon they had left at its far side.

Wilson crashed through the trees beside him, looked around and thrust his hand into his pocket. The pebble circle reappeared as soon as he released Smallroot from its confinement.

Korum was last out of the trees.

"Come on," Rubek said, "The circle."

"Not me," the priest replied. "This is my world."

There were shouted curses from the forest behind them.

"They'll tear you apart." Wilson looked at Rubek. The American nodded. They grabbed an arm apiece and dragged the old man across the smooth grass to join the others.

Wilson felt for Heartstone and clasped it in his hand with Smallroot.

The first of the townsfolk emerged into the clearing. They slowed but only for a second.

Ackroyd raised his gun.

"No," Wilson snapped. "Close your eyes, all of you. Now." He strained to keep his own tightly shut. The voices and pounding feet of the mob sounded to be almost on top of them. Something struck the side of his head. Then there was silence and heat.

~ * ~

Alice snuggled her head against Leirbag's chest and shared the thoughts that he was feeding her. She felt his thirst for power and some of it became her own. His single-minded determination and his ruthlessness, these too became a part of her.

Leirbag looked down at the top of her head, stroked her hair and smiled.

She felt his gaze, opened her eyes and tilted her head to look at him. She returned his smile.

He looked into her eyes. They were big and bright, they always had been, but they were different too, hungry and cruel. *It was*, he thought, *like looking at the reflection of his own.*

He pushed her from him and onto her back. Then he turned himself, eased her legs apart with his knee and rolled onto her.

Alice moaned and closed her eyes. He was not taking her this time, she knew, he was giving himself, and she accepted him willingly and unconditionally.

~ * ~

The smell of burning flesh hung thick in the air. Thirty years on the squad and Ulrik Larson knew that he would never get used to it.

He bent to pick up an arm. Bagged it and sealed it. He rubbed a gloved finger over the soot-stained plastic disc on the back of the seat beside him. Sixty-one, he noted this on the bag's label and looked around. There were no other parts that he could see belonging to the body that had once owned the arm and might or might not have been sitting in seat number 61 when the bomb went off.

Around him, dozens of others were bagging their own gruesome finds. Maybe they had the rest of his, maybe not.

That it could have been so much worse gave him little comfort. A security guard had spotted the man in the foyer of the opera house. Ulrik had watched his approach on the video playback from the security camera. The guard had intercepted him before he got to the door of the auditorium.

They had found pieces of the guard but not of the bomber.

The wounded, hundreds of them, had been ambulanced away.

Reports hit his desk on a daily, sometimes hourly basis. Up until then Copenhagen had been spared. They had had the information and the paranoia but not the horror, not until that evening.

He continued his sifting for the remains of those that life's lottery had allocated the rearmost seats, and wiped the back of his hand across his brow. After thirty years, he had had enough.

Seventeen

Wilson opened his eyes and then snapped them closed against the glare of the sun. His mind was back in Somalia. The heat was the same and the smell of the dust. He tried again, turning his head, assuming that the glare that had assaulted his first attempt was a result of looking directly into the sun. He was wrong but it was not quite as bad. *Diamonds,* he thought at first, *quartz,* his sense told him. The whole of the desert landscape around him was dotted with huge reflecting crystals. Spectrums flashed across the sky, toward him and away from him. He looked around. Apart from the company of the surreal light show, he was alone.

His hand shot out to his side. Karrina had been there and beyond her Rubek, Ackroyd, Korum and Saville. Where had Saville come from? He was supposed to be Wilson's eyes and ears back at base. He could not ask him now. He was not there. He shrugged.

He could, he thought, simply close his eyes again. "No." He remembered the last world, Korum's world. Rubek had wanted to go back because it was not where he expected to be. "No." Wilson had said then because that, he had assumed, was where fate wanted them to be and he had been right. They had befriended Korum, whose powers he had witnessed, and they had two more artefacts to add to their arsenal.

He dipped into his pocket, pulled out the amulet and slipped it around his neck. "This will tell you who speaks the truth and who lies." Korum had said.

"Great." He looked around the seemingly endless crystal desert. "No one here to do either." He took it off and dropped it back into his pocket. He still held Heartstone and Smallroot. Without these, the others would be stuck in whatever world they had found themselves. Or perhaps they had gone nowhere and were at the mercy of the mob. He could not abandon them.

He closed his eyes, folded his fingers around amber and root and thought with all his mind of his companions. All he could see was Karrina. She was beautiful. He held onto the vision. How could she affect him as she did? He could not remember when it had started happening. It was just little things, an odd touch, electric, the bending of his mind, magic. The word bounced loud into his head, charmed, bewitched. Then in his mind, or maybe not, he heard her scream.

~ * ~

The table had become wider in order to accommodate Alice's throne. It stood next to Leirbag's, as bulky but less ornate.

There were six place settings. Another six and their gathering would be complete. With every newcomer, Leirbag's power increased. The walls of his tower grew also, becoming thicker and stronger.

Alice toyed with a bread roll. Leirbag had left her to welcome back his troops from whichever corner of her world he had assigned them. When he returned she would go hunting again and another place would be filled. The giants should be returning soon, too. Leirbag had told her to bid them wait in the mosaic room.

"It will," he had said, "be good to let them see their place in the scheme of things."

A tingling at the base of her skull told Alice that one of the six had returned. She had to concentrate hard to ascertain which. Soon, with practice, she would know instinctively just as Leirbag did. An image formed in her mind. It was Rodney back from Santiago. He had done okay, not well, but okay. She would let him rest awhile and then summon him with her thoughts and let him eat. She liked Rodney; he had been her first. She would find some extra reward for him. Perhaps she would find a girl this time, young and pretty, not too pretty though, slightly plump would be good. She knew Leirbag's taste and was not sufficiently confident of her own position to want to risk bringing temptation to their table.

Soon she would be as powerful as Leirbag and then... She forced the thought away, buried it as deeply as she could. She was not nearly powerful enough yet and if he got even a hint of these thoughts... She brushed her tongue across the roof of her mouth. The taste was only in her mind, a faint memory, but it was reminder enough.

She woke Rodney and beckoned him to the table. Her lips curled into a smile and she leaned back on her throne and waited for the boy to appear. There were footfalls in the corridor beyond the open door. Her smile broadened and then disappeared. Her eyes widened and her mouth dropped open. It was not Rodney.

The girl stopped at the doorway. She was tall and slim, raven haired and beautiful.

Alice flashed her mind around the tower. Rodney was there, still in his room, but coming. Her thoughts returned to the girl. Had she conjured her up just by thinking of an extra reward for the boy? She could not have. She did not have the power or the knowledge.

"Hello Alice." The girl took a single step into the room.

Alice concentrated her mind and sent a spear of pain across the tabletop toward the door.

The girl staggered and then screamed.

Then there was something else. Alice felt her own thought repulsed and then hurled back toward her. She tried to unthink it, but could not. Its rebound caught her high in the chest, flinging her into the back of her seat. She clutched at the pain. The throne toppled backward sending her sprawling.

She could see the girl's legs through those of the table. They were moving around the room toward her. Alice launched another mental attack.

The girl hardly faltered but the rebound, when it came, was a white-hot dagger of pain in Alice's eye. This time it was Alice's turn to scream.

"Thank you Korum." The girl continued her measured advance.

Alice dare not attack again. She struggled to her knees. *Korum, who was Korum?*

Karrina rounded the table.

Alice waited for her to attack.

"Where's Leirbag?" Karrina snapped.

Alice opened one eye and tried to focus it through a mist of pain and tears.

The assault when it came was physical. Karrina launched a foot at Alice's head, sending her spinning across the boards of the floor.

"Where's Leirbag?" Karrina steadied herself and lifted a foot to pursue her advantage before Alice had time to recover. "Where is he?"

~ * ~

The crowd milled around the pebble circle, not daring to step into the area from which their quarry had disappeared.

Leirbag saw them before he materialized, and changed form.

The creature he became was huge, as much lion as bull but with the furled wings of an eagle. The crowd backed away. The beast let out a roar and they turned and fled.

Leirbag pawed the grass with one heavy cloven hoof and then launched himself across the clearing. Before he hit the line of trees through which the last of the crowd had disappeared, he reverted to his true form and jogged into the forest after them.

He found the giants easily and cursed their failure, kicking at their immobile limbs in frustration. Then he sank to the ground. His transformation from man to beast had drained an incredible amount of his strength. He shook his head. He would not try that again, not for a while. Then he felt Alice and his hand shot to the pain in his eye. She was in the tower, his tower. They could not have… His mind reeled. He did not have time to regain the circle. It would take more power than he wanted to lose, but his tower, he had to get back and quickly. He closed his eyes and clenched his fingers.

~ * ~

"He's here, my dear, he's here."

Karrina spun round.

Leirbag was in the doorway. She could feel his power; compared to him the woman at her feet was nothing. She took one backward step, felt him launch his attack and braced herself for it.

It knocked her sideways but she felt it rebound from her body and back toward its source.

Leirbag held out a hand, caught the rebounding force and smiled. He looked into her face and just for a second Karrina saw puzzlement in his. Then she felt the power in his hand grow. This time, she knew, even Korum's gift would not be enough to save her. She backed toward the solid stone of the wall and into… She glanced down. The woman was still on the floor beside her.

Arms closed around her waist and pulled her backward.

~ * ~

Wilson hardly had time to take in his surroundings. He saw Karrina though. She was in front of him. Then he saw Leirbag over her shoulder. He slipped his arms around Karrina's waist, pulled her toward him, closed his eyes and thought as hard as he could about the desert world he had just left.

~ * ~

Worried hands mopped beads of sweat from Moyasta's brow.

Her breath was coming in short laboured pants. Her body tensed. "She is safe," she gasped. "Safe." She smiled then, laid her head back on the pillow and closed her eyes.

Those around her knew that she would never open them again. Something had happened and Moyasta had used up the little strength that she had left to maintain her own life to save Karrina.

Those around her bed stood in silence, their heads bowed, mourning their loss and in awe of Moyasta's selfless courage.

If Karrina was still alive, then there was still hope but none now remained to assist her. For the first time Karrina would be truly on her own.

Eighteen

Leirbag's attack passed through empty air and exploded against the wall of the tower, sending shards of stone flying into the room.

Alice cowered away from it and Leirbag rounded the table toward her. There was a noise behind him. He turned.

Rodney was in the doorway.

Alice felt Leirbag's power focus. "No," she pleaded, and felt him relent.

He held out a hand and she reached toward it.

His hand ignored hers and twisted into her hair, wrapping it around long fingers and then tugging her from the floor and backward over the edge of the table.

Tears welled in her eyes. The hand in her hair wrapped itself tighter. She thought her spine was going to snap. Still he pushed her back and down.

"Your little favourite is he, young Rodney?" Leirbag pushed harder.

Alice's feet were losing contact with the floor.

"Is he?"

"No." She looked into his eyes. They were burning red. "No."

"Rather have him than me would you Alice?" he rasped, beside her ear.

"No," she moaned.

His fingers tightened.

She thought her neck would break.

"Would you?"

"No." She wanted to look away from his blazing eyes, but they held her mesmerised.

He cocked his head to one side as if detecting a distant sound, and then looked back at her. The fire had gone from his eyes and the snarl from his lips. He smiled. "Good."

Releasing his grip on her hair, he stood back from the table and held out a none-threatening hand.

"Good."

She stared at it for a few seconds and then reached out and allowed him to slide her from the table.

His arm slipped around her waist. "You are my queen, Alice; you should not give me reason to doubt your loyalty."

"You need never doubt it," she replied, looking into his face with a forced expression of supplication. *For a minute there, he'd lost control, and in that loss was the hope that if she was careful, she could be free of him.*

She looked toward the door.

Rodney stared into the room through glazed eyes. *She'd saved him once, but if there was a next time she'd have to be more careful.*

"Rodney," Leirbag said.

Was he picking up her thoughts?
"You must be hungry. Come, join us."
Perhaps, not. Alice relaxed.

~ * ~

Rubek smelled his arrival before he opened his eyes. It was a stable smell, old hay and fresh manure. He heard a shuffling beside him and felt a hand on his shoulder. It pressed down, using him for support. He looked.

Korum was pushing himself to his feet.

There was no light source in the barn. Sufficient illumination, however, filtered through the gaps between the slats of its walls to allow Rubek to take in his surroundings.

The building was long and narrow. He looked up. Three, thick, timber pillars supported its steeply pitched roof. There were gaps in this also, which allowed thin, grey daylight to reveal roughly jointed rafters but little beneath them.

The floor was scattered with straw. Here and there larger clumps with square edges, suggested that bales had collapsed and been abandoned.

Ackroyd was crouched against one of the long, sidewalls, his eyes pressed against the vertical gap of light between two planks. A few yards along, Saville was surveying the same scene through a knothole. He turned. "A few scattered huts but no sign of life."

Ackroyd joined him. "Same on all sides."

Rubek stood to join Korum. "Any idea where we are?"

"None." The priest did not look around. "But Karrina isn't here. Nor is your friend."

"Shit." Rubek scanned the barn. He had not noticed.

"But in my experience," Korum continued, "people never turn up where they're not supposed to be."

"And who decides where we're supposed to be?" Rubek asked.

Korum laughed. "If I knew the answer to that one it would be I, not Leirbag who could rule the world."

Ackroyd made a tour of the barn, peering into its corners and kicking at the more solid lumps of straw. "Might as well take a look around outside," he said, transferring a fresh magazine from his jacket pocket to the butt of his pistol.

The door, when Saville eased it outward, swung away from him on rusting hinges. Their tortured screech would have alerted anyone within a quarter mile.

Ackroyd shrugged and peered through the growing gap before beckoning the others to follow him.

The barn was the central structure of a huddle of thirty or so small wooden cottages. The ground between these was well trodden but there were no discernible pathways.

Like the barn, none of the other buildings would have offered much protection from even the lightest of winds. The ones that they investigated were almost identical, two rooms with a small hearth at the end of only one of them, a scattering of roughly carved and jointed furniture, and empty wooden shelves along two walls of both rooms.

"Looks like they all left in a hurry, "Saville said, "Took what they could carry but couldn't handle the furniture."

Rubek joined them from the second room. "No beds," he said, "in any of them."

"Didn't have beds maybe," said Saville, "blankets, animal skins, they could carry those."

They stooped through the doorway and back into the daylight.

"Something else is strange," Korum said.

They looked at him.

"Who was in charge here? The barn's big but it's only a barn, all the others are the same size, small."

They all looked around.

"No headman," Korum continued, "no temple, no authority."

"Could be that this is just a small part of something bigger," Saville suggested.

"And this could well be the only part that's been abandoned." Ackroyd added.

Rubek watched the marine. The hand around the butt of Ackroyd's pistol looked readier somehow. "So we carry on but carefully." His gaze switched to Korum. "Any idea which direction?"

"None." The priest smiled. "But I've a feeling we'll choose the right one."

~ * ~

Sudden harsh light caused Wilson's eyelids to snap closed. His arms were still around Karrina's waist.

She backed into him.

There was a buzzing in his head. His arms tightened. All he could think about was the pressure of her against him. His groin began to tighten. His thoughts focussed on his growing erection. He tried to drag them away but the harder he tried, the more concentrated they became.

Karrina moved against him and turned in his arms.

He opened his eyes and looked down into the blueness of hers. Her mouth was slightly open. The tip of her tongue played across her upper lip.

She slipped one arm around his neck and pulled his head down toward her. Her breath and then her lips tasted of mint.

Wilson remembered his own unclean teeth. He almost pulled away.

Her hand started to stroke and then to massage the urgent throbbing that immediately became the sole focus of his thoughts once again. His mind screamed that this shouldn't be happening. He struggled to conjure up images of his wife; to give his thoughts a focus that wasn't Karrina. He felt her hand take his and guide it to her breast. His fingers stroked a taut nipple through the fabric of her t-shirt. He surrendered.

Nineteen

Alice was on her knees in the centre of the mosaic floor.

Leirbag stood in front of her. His index fingers massaged slow circles around her temples.

Her head was back, her eyes closed and her mouth stretched in a tight-lipped smile. She had never, ever, felt anything this good.

Leirbag's power and his merciless ambition flowed into her. She could feel it fusing with every nerve ending in her body. She felt like a goddess, the strongest, tallest, most beautiful, lithest goddess in the whole of creation. Still it came.

There were beads of sweat on Leirbag's brow. One flowed around the angle of his cheekbone and hung onto the tip of his chin. Another followed its path, reinforced it and both dropped onto the patterned front of his gown, further discolouring the fabric on which their predecessors had landed.

He was exhausted, not by the transfer of his power but by his battle to keep his doubts locked away in the farthest recess of his consciousness. Sometimes they almost disappeared but then they came nipping back on the edges of his main purpose like terriers snapping at the hooves of a shire horse. Was he giving her too much? Should he be giving her any at all? What if she became as powerful as... That one did it. Its tiny teeth had punctured the skin of his resolve.

He pulled his fingers away from Alice's head and staggered backward as the link between them snapped like an overstretched rubber band.

Alice did not seem to notice. Her smile never wavered as she basked in the essence of the new her.

Leirbag dropped to his knees in front of her and watched. Could she ever become as strong as he? He gave her just the hint of a taste.

Her eyes flashed open and her lips dropped apart.

He whipped the thought back and smiled. No, she could not, not whilst he held her soul, and that was hidden where no one would ever find it.

~ * ~

The feeling disappeared so quickly that Alice doubted that it had actually been there. Then there was another thought. Something was hidden, something that she had to find, and then that too was gone. She looked at Leirbag.

He was smiling at her. His eyes were as gentle as she had ever seen them. He looked tired. The sweat on his brow glistened like jewellery.

Alice let her thoughts fold back into the power that he had given her and she smiled back at him. Her smile broadened of its own volition until her cheeks hurt. She felt like a goddess.

~ * ~

183

They left the cluster of buildings behind. The landscape made Ackroyd nervous. It was a mass of small knolls and hillocks. Nowhere could he see a vantage point that would allow him a view of the bigger picture. He did not dare take the easy route, which would have been to skirt the hills and keep to the lower ground. Rather, he led them stealthily to the summit of every one that stood in their path, took in as much as he could of their surroundings, which was always more hills behind which he could see nothing. Then, down the far side, they would bounce before struggling up the next one.

~ * ~

Down is worse than up, Rubek thought, his knees jarring with every step. Ackroyd, with Saville at his side, was only feet in front of him.

"Can't we go round just one of them for a change?" Rubek pleaded.

"No." The marine did not turn.

"Please." This time Rubek was ignored. He looked around for Korum.

The old priest was falling behind.

Rubek waited for him to catch up. "You okay?"

Korum smiled but said nothing.

Rubek slowed, allowing him to keep pace.

"I've a feeling," Korum said, once they had gained the all too temporary luxury of flat ground. "That we are walking a long way to get nowhere."

"How's that?" Rubek looked up to the top of the next hill. Ackroyd and Saville were crouched on its summit surveying whatever lay beyond.

"Because," Korum continued, "whilst you've been looking out and over, I've been looking down."

The ground had begun to rise again. Rubek stopped. "And?"

"And, I've seen the same clump of flowers, exactly the same clump, at least five times. And I probably missed a few before it became obvious."

Saville and the marine waited for them to catch up.

Rubek dropped onto the grass beside them and they listened in silence as Korum repeated his suspicions.

"So what do we do?" Ackroyd asked when the priest had finished.

Korum waited for one of the others to speak. No one did. "Well," he said, "keeping on walking forever won't get us anywhere. Neither will just staying put, here or anywhere else." He paused and studied the faces of the others. They were all watching him. "I'd guess that, whoever they are, they know exactly where we are and exactly what we're doing."

Ackroyd looked around.

"Oh, you won't see them." Korum said. "But we need them to see something that might worry them a little."

The marine shuffled closer.

Korum continued. "There are loose rocks all around the place. We need to collect as many as we can, build a pile of them just here and then a circle around it that we can sit inside. A few flowers and perhaps a small grass fire on top of the pile might help as well."

"Help do what?" Saville asked.

"Well, assuming that they are watching, they might think that we're just trying to leave. Which, I suspect, won't worry them in the least." He plucked a small purple flower from the clump at his side and studied it for a few seconds. "They might think that we're summoning reinforcements." He twirled the flower between his fingers. "They may think that we're summoning sufficient power to break down their defences." He tossed the flower aside. "And that should worry them enough to make them show themselves."

"Let's get to it then," Rubek said, pushing himself to his feet.

~ * ~

Karrina lay on her back on the hot desert sand.

Wilson was on top of her, limp now but still inside her. His head was next to hers and his lips nuzzled her ear.

Her hand was around his neck, stroking at the hairs at its base. Her attention though was on the sky and the flashing, ever changing spectrums that reflected from the crystals all around them. Her gaze was intent, as though she were searching for something in those patterns.

Then she smiled. The jagged colours above her were becoming more fluid and curling into the identifiable shapes of faces. She recognised Moyasta first. In the sky, next to the old woman, was an old man. The lights spun threads of pink and blue through the grey strands of his hair and beard. Ranvile, Karrina knew the name without having remembered it. The image smiled down at her.

A third face began to form. It was behind the first two and larger, much larger.

Ardam, father of all the people. Karrina tensed, fear was now impinging into her feelings of well-being.

She felt Wilson stir on top of her. She pulled his head closer, not wanting him to turn and share the vision. Then she heard Moyasta's soothing voice inside her head and knew what she must do.

She looked into the eyes of the old woman and tensed then relaxed muscles deep in her body. She smiled as she felt Wilson begin to grow hard once again. She held him closer.

He tried to raise his head but she pushed it back down. "Ssh, ssh," she purred, and stroked her long fingers down his back.

He moaned and snuggled into her.

Karrina kept her eyes and her mind on the old woman and on the magic in the sky around her.

At the periphery of her vision, the body of Stuart Wilson began to fade as though it were being absorbed into her own. She felt the weight of him on top of her decrease to nothing. The faces in the sky became indistinct and then vanished. She closed her eyes. Her head dropped to one side and she slept.

Twenty

Alice wandered the rooms and corridors of the tower with all of her senses focussed. Something was hidden, that thought was constantly tugging at her from the just reachable edge of her consciousness, something she must find.

Leirbag rarely left the throne room concentrating, he had told her, all of his time and energy on making his tower stronger, whilst keeping the new power that she was providing locked away until they needed it.

~ * ~

When Alice returned to the throne room from the latest of her searches, Leirbag did not seem to have moved.

The serpent arms of his throne flicked open their eyes when she entered the room, appeared to recognise her, and closed them again, letting their master continue his work undisturbed.

Alice took her place beside them and with a wave of her hand filled the table for those who would soon be returning.

~ * ~

Wilson recognised the gorge and remembered the icy wind that sliced through his clothing and into his skin. Ahead of him, a group of men bent their bodies against its onslaught and trudged up the steep, winding path. Their voices drifted back to him, indistinct amidst the roar of the wind.

He did not know what else to do and so he followed them. At the cave mouths, they stopped and clustered around one of their number. Wilson stopped also. Some of the men faced him but gave no indication that they had seen him.

There was a great deal of gesticulation most of which was directed at one or other of the caves and then the man in the centre of the group strode through his companions and into the one to Wilson's right. The one in which Rubek and he had found Arthur Molloy and from which they had returned to their own world.

Wilson watched the last of the men enter the cave. Then he bent his body against the wind and followed, not hesitating as he stepped into the cave and onto the lush grass of a gently sloping meadow. He looked around. There was a cave behind him. It was larger than the one he had entered but no less dark and forbidding. Below him, the twelve men sat in a circle on the grass. The one that appeared to be the leader was at their centre. Wilson walked toward and then around them. None seemed to notice his presence.

They were all dressed in the same manner as the giants he had encountered previously but they were no taller than ordinary men.

"We must seek the source of the wind." The speaker had his back to Wilson.

"The wind is no more." The man in the centre of their circle said. He looked to be about fifty but a wild mane of black hair and an unkempt beard that hung over his chest could have affected Wilson's assessment by ten years to either side. The brightness of the man's eyes accentuated the darkness that surrounded them. One was blue the other green. *Like the giants,* Wilson thought, *like Ranvile and Korum.*

"How do you know this?" The questioner continued.

"Because I created it."

A gasp circled the group.

Wilson dropped onto his haunches and continued his study.

"You."

"How else was I to justify our leaving of the people?" The man paused and scrutinised the faces in front of him. "Never to return."

"But Ardam…"

The man raised a hand and the speaker fell silent. "With the wind gone our people will soon prosper again. Soon they will elect a new leader of the Council and we will be relegated to myth. All this I learned from Worldroot."

Wilson stood and walked around the circle. No one looked up at him. He stepped between two of the seated figures. Their dialogue continued.

"But why?"

"Because it is now time for us to build a new world here. When we fail to return the Council will despatch our womenfolk to find us and in time this world will become more populous and richer than our old one." Ardam studied those faces that he could see. "I have chosen you twelve to build this new world with me. I know that I have chosen well."

Wilson moved to within a foot of the speaker.

Ardam continued to talk, seemingly unaware of Wilson's presence. "We will wait here for our women and then we will seek a suitable place to build."

Wilson stepped from the circle. As he did so, the men disappeared and the grass was suddenly longer, almost to his knees and topped with heavy heads of seed. Further down the hill, a group of huts circled an area of trodden earth with one larger one at its centre. A crowd had gathered outside this. Children played, laughing and screaming around its edges.

Wilson walked toward the village, dodging away from the children who, blind to his existence, ran past and around him.

He stopped at the back of the crowd. A general murmuring rose from it and then from its midst a single voice spoke out.

"You, Ardam and only you brought this upon us."

Wilson could not see the speaker. He moved to his left and found a spot where the crowd was thinner and he could see the focus of their attention.

There was no mistaking the man that he had seen outside the cave earlier. The one they had called Ardam, even though he was old, very old.

He stood with his back to the door of the hut. A woman was standing in front of him. She had her back to Wilson.

At her sides were two children, one boy and one girl. The woman had an arm around the shoulder of each and their heads rested against her hips.

"We can wait no longer." The hidden voice continued. "They are almost grown now and still they are like-eyes."

Ardam was looking at the children. His shoulders were slumped and his head bowed.

"They must be killed now or the evil will only grow. Already there are three other like-eyed babies."

A man stepped from the crowd and slipped an arm around the woman's shoulders.

Wilson could feel the tension and anger emanating from those around him.

"That they are your grandchildren, Ardam, means nothing." The spokesman continued. "They are like-eyes and they must die."

The crowd roared its support.

"No." Ardam squared his shoulders and lifted his head. "No...not because they are of my blood, but because I will not see children killed no matter how deformed."

The crowd had quietened in the face of their leader's regained authority. Ardam looked around their faces and then locked his gaze onto their spokesman. "The children will be banished from the village," he said, his voice steady and commanding. "They will take the three like-eyed babies with them."

"No." The voice of the woman barely carried to Wilson's position at the edge of the crowd. "They will die alone as surely as if you killed them yourself."

The man beside her pulled her close. "Then we will go with them." He said, half turning his head toward the crowd.

Ardam stared at a spot above the man's head as though ashamed to make eye contact. "You will cross to beyond the White Mountains and then you will walk for seven days and seven nights. Only then will you seek a place to settle. Go now."

The couple turned and the crowd parted to allow them passage. The man and woman kept their eyes to the ground. The children looked up.

The girl's eyes seemed to lock onto Wilson's. He stepped back, thinking for a second that she could see him, but then they flicked away. They were both a sparkling, sapphire blue.

The crowd closed ranks once the banished family had passed through it and Wilson returned his attention to the old man. The meeting was obviously not over.

"And now Ardam." Wilson could hear the arrogance of victory in the voice of the unseen speaker. "Your only son and both of your grandchildren are banished."

The crowd had fallen silent. Most of the onlookers bowed their heads and shuffled their feet on the hard packed earth as though embarrassed at the course that events were taking.

"You are too old now to increase your stake in the future of the people." The voice continued.

A murmuring rose to Wilson's sides.

"I..." Ardam began.

"No old man. You are finished. It is time for another, one with progeny to build this world to take your place."

"Aye... Aye..." The words punctuated the mutterings of the crowd from all directions.

"And who would that be, Charos...You perhaps?" The old man's smile merely tweaked at the corners of his mouth.

"I wouldn't..."

"Charos... Charos." Isolated voices from the crowd moulded themselves into a chant.

"So be it." Wilson lip-read the words as the old man's shoulders slumped and he turned toward the door of his hut.

~ * ~

"Do we close our eyes?" Rubek asked. They were grouped around a hastily erected pile of stones.

"I think not," Korum laughed. "We don't actually want to go anywhere." He stood and with a little concentration and the tip of his finger ignited the small bundle of dried grass and flowers on top of the cairn. Then he regained his position between Rubek and Ackroyd.

The marine held his gun ready and scanned as much of the countryside as he was able. Mentally he was honing his mind against the expected boredom of their vigil.

Rubek was also trying to remain alert but his mind soon began to wander. What had happened to Wilson and Karrina? If that mob had gotten them, he dashed the thought away. He did not want to go there. He glanced at Saville.

The young policeman smiled at him.

Rubek smiled back but only with his mouth.

Ackroyd played his fingers around the butt of his pistol. His gaze dropped to the weapon and he adjusted its

194

position, watching the sunlight play across its barrel. The grass beside him bubbled, and before even his mind had time to react, a hand, skinny fingered and clawed had gripped his wrist and pulled it down into the earth.

More fingers closed around his neck and dragged him backward. He saw Saville beyond the pile of stones. Two skeletal, scaly skinned, saucer eyed creatures were pulling the young policeman down by the shoulders and into the ground.

The marine tried to gain his feet but another hand wrapped around his face. There was a finger in his mouth. He bit down on it. Vile tasting slime flowed over his tongue. He spat it away and then his head was sinking through the grass and into the damp soil beneath. His shoulders followed. His body pivoted and the hands dragged him, headfirst, into the earth.

~ * ~

Karrina opened her eyes. The sky above her was a clear unbroken blue. She edged herself up onto one elbow. The crystals were still there and the sun was still shining but the brilliant reflections no longer played in the air around her.

Wilson had gone but somehow she knew that that was okay. She looked down at herself. She was still naked. Her clothes were scattered on the ground around her. She gathered them together, shook out the sand and dressed. She had been dreaming or half dreaming. It all seemed too real to have been a dream. Ardam, she remembered seeing his face in the sky. That must have triggered it. But the dream could not have been true. Ardam was the father of all her people, almost a god. What she had seen was a broken and defeated man. That could not have been right, not according to all of the lessons and stories of her childhood, but Karrina knew intuitively that what she had dreamed rather than what she had been taught was the truth of it.

She lowered herself to the ground. Other thoughts began to impinge. There were faces, shouting faces full of fear and hatred. Her head felt heavy. Her arm no longer had the strength to support her. She dropped back against the sand, closed her eyes and drifted back into her dreams.

Twenty-one

Alice traced the tips of her fingers around the edges of the stone blocks that formed the walls of the room. Her mind pried into the cracks between them trying to uncover anything that might have been hidden. She found nothing, made a mental note of how far along the wall she had searched thus far and then headed for the mosaic room.

She must, she knew, continue with their work as though that was her main purpose if Leirbag was to suspect nothing. She walked to the centre of the design and sat cross-legged on the small coloured tiles that made up the image of Leirbag's face. She smiled. Even that small act of rebellion gave her confidence. She closed her eyes and thought of the girl that she would bring to their table. She did not want another demonstration of Leirbag's unhinged jealousy, not before she was strong enough to repulse it. She would find a reward for Rodney and set her temporary master's mind at rest. Her smile broadened. *All in all,* she thought, *things are working out rather nicely.*

~ * ~

In the throne room, Leirbag leaned his head against the back of his seat and let tentacles of his consciousness drift between the worlds. The interfering policeman and his friends had become more than an irritation. They had penetrated the defences of his tower, of the very room in which he now sat. There were other worlds also, to be considered, ones of which he had been unaware. How many were there? If there was one, there could be dozens, even hundreds. Wilson and his friends could be on any one of them. They could all be on different ones. He had to bring them to him and for that, he needed bait.

He held up his hand, visualising it through closed eyes. He had caught the power that the girl had flung back at him. For that short time there had been a link between them. If he could just...the corners of his mouth curled upward. It was weak but he could feel her. She was alone and she was sleeping. His mouth tightened into a sneer. She was dreaming. He poured more of himself across the strengthening bridge and felt his body dissolve and follow his mind. Wilson had rescued her once but Leirbag had not been ready. *Next time*, he thought, *I will be.*

~ * ~

The huts around him and then the ground beneath Wilson's feet began to shimmer like heat haze. He felt his balance wavering. He closed his eyes. That settled him. He opened them. The huts had gone. There were houses now, half-timbered and leaning inward above the narrow street of cobblestones that had replaced the packed earth beneath his feet. There was a smell of decay. The central gutter beside him was overflowing with rotting food and excrement. Bloated flies buzzed in a knee-high swarm above it.

People passed him by; all were heading in the same direction, up the street and then into another that joined it from the right.

Wilson braced himself against the smell and followed. He studied the group that walked in front of him and cursed the disinterest he had shown in school history. *Robin Hoodish,* he thought. *When was that?* After the Norman invasion, he was sure, but not long after. He had seen streets like this one before though. In York, he remembered, The Shambles, but this memory did nothing to slot his new location into historical context.

He allowed the crowd to lead him around the corner into another street much like the last. At its far end the façade of a huge church dwarfed the houses and shops toward which he was heading. Between the end of the street and the church was a cobbled market square.

Here the crowd lost its direction. Small groups congregated, exchanged greetings, talked, laughed and then dissolved again. Wilson wandered amongst them unseen. From garbled conversations around him, he heard one word again and again, "Witch."

The bells of the church began to toll. The crowd found a purpose and gravitated toward the imposing front of the building but stopped short of entering.

Wilson edged between bodies that remained unaware of his presence. He considered pushing someone, just to see if he could, but decided against it.

There were three stacks of brushwood on the cobbles in front of the church. Each had a tall wooden stake protruding from its centre. Three clerics holding burning torches were standing at the bases of the piles.

The bells stopped but the vibrations of their chimes continued to buzz in Wilson's ears. The central doors of the building swung inward. Three young women, each flanked by armed soldiers and with their heads bowed walked toward the pyres. At their bases, the soldiers stopped and the girls continued alone, seeming to rise from the ground. *Must be steps behind the piles,* Wilson thought.

The girls stopped atop the structures with their heads still bowed. A soldier mounted the steps behind each of them, took their wrists and secured them behind their backs and around the stakes.

The three young women looked up then. Wilson looked from one to another. Simply by raising their heads they had transformed from submissive to arrogant. Their eyes skimmed the heads of the crowd. All were the same in their difference, one blue, and one green. He turned his attention to the priests, then to the soldiers and finally to those in the crowd closest to him. He saw blue eyes, brown eyes and green eyes, but in every individual face, the colours were the same.

There were some words from the attendant clerics. Wilson returned his attention to them. *Latin,* he thought. Then the three men applied their torches to the tinder bases of the stacks. Orange flames licked skyward. Wilson turned away. The crowd cheered. The smell that wafted around him, forced the contents of Wilson's stomach up into the base of his throat. He swallowed hard and walked away.

~ * ~

Karrina dreamed on. Her two sisters knelt beside her on the hard stones of the floor. The thought that she had no sisters flirted with her dream and then disappeared.

She was walking toward the sunlight then. It was bright after the damp darkness of her cell and she lowered her eyes. The flagstones of the building's floor gave way to stairs and then to cobbles. She was mounting steps then. They were wooden and rickety. Someone took her hands and pulled them behind her back, gently though, not with the brutality of her recent inquisitors.

She raised her head. The eyes of the crowd were on her. She scanned their faces. Most of their mouths hung open in expectation and excited murmurings carried up to her.

Then she saw Wilson. At the front of the crowd to her left. She locked her gaze onto him. Hope swelled inside her and then faded. There was no recognition in his eyes. She felt a wave of heat rise around her and the air in front of her shimmered. Wilson turned and walked away. She pulled at the bonds that held her wrists. Her head fell sideways. Her body convulsed. She woke.

The crystals were still there but they looked dull now, more plastic than diamond. She tested her bonds again. They were still unyielding. No, that was in the dream, she tried again. Her arms were locked behind her back. She tried to turn over. She could not move her legs. They were tied at the ankles.

"You'll only hurt yourself."

She twisted her head around. Leirbag was smiling down at her. He stood, legs apart above her his feet straddling her knees.

She turned away from his stare as best she could.

He dropped to his knees, one to either side of hers and lowered himself on top of her.

She swung her head from side to side. The crystals danced and then faded. The sand beneath her lost its softness and became smooth and hard. Then she was being pulled to her feet.

~ * ~

Rubek's arms and legs were still pinned by the creatures that had dragged him down through the earth but he could move his head and his eyes. He was in a cavern and it was huge. Between the hard rock, on which he lay, and the roof, clouds of vapour hung motionless like those beneath a real sky.

To Rubek's right, four more of the creatures held Saville to the ground. To his left Ackroyd's arms and legs strained against the muscle less limbs of his own captors.

Rubek could not see Korum. He might be behind his head or beyond his feet. A suspicion in his mind moulded itself into a probability and then into a certainty, Korum was no longer with them. Wilson and Karrina had gone and they had the artefacts. Now, Korum too had disappeared and he had power, real power, Rubek had seen it. He levered his arms against the skeletal fingers that gripped them. It was useless. He gave up and relaxed into a controlled assessment of his situation. He was in a cavern. How he had come to be there was irrelevant. There was light. Where was it coming from? He turned his head. There was no shadow to Saville's left or to Ackroyd's right. There was no shadow on the ground beneath either of them. Therefore, the light had to be from below, but it wasn't. *More magic*, he thought, *the light was just there.*

Twenty-two

Alice concentrated on the anguish that she had homed into from the mosaic room. It was strong. Alternating waves of despair and frustration drew her through crowds of shoppers and into the entrance of a narrow rubbish strewn alleyway. Featureless walls of grey concrete to either side banished both the sunlight and the heat that had drenched the busy shopping street behind her and the ground was damp and slippery with moss.

Halfway along the alley two yellow dumpsters were piled high with black rubbish bags and empty cartons. Between these, sitting hunched on an upturned orange box, with his head almost between his knees was Alice's target. She stopped and turned to face him. "Stephen Clifford?" she asked, despite the fact that she knew the answer.

The man looked up. His brow furrowed in a struggle for recognition.

"Alice Craven." She held out a hand.

He stared at it but did not move.

"Anne sent me." Alice expected that to provoke a response but got none. "She wants you back, Stephen."

"No." His lips hardly moved. "Not after…" His words distorted into a mumble.

"She wants you back, Stephen. That's why I'm here." Alice saw hope blaze in his eyes and fought back a smile. He would, she knew, do anything.

"What about Sonia?"

Alice lowered her briefcase to the ground and crouched to bring their eyes onto a level. "It's Anne wants you back, Stephen. What would you give to turn time back, for everything to be back to normal?"

His lips moved.

Alice leaned closer. "Anything…good." She clicked her briefcase open.

~ * ~

Leirbag pushed Karrina into the room with such force that she rebounded from its far wall and dropped to the floor. He looked at her for a second and then pulled the door closed and locked it from the outside. He smiled. He had baited his trap, all that he had to do was wait. When Rodney returned, he decided, he would let the boy have Karrina and Alice would watch.

~ * ~

Wilson wandered the narrow streets with his head bowed. The stench from the gutters was still there but the memory of that of burning flesh overpowered even that.

He stopped and looked around. The buildings looked the same but the people had changed, or at least their dress had. Reds and yellows had replaced the drab browns and greens of the market place. There were other changes too, he noticed. The open fronts of the shops were windowed now with small panes of thick glass. He continued, dodging people who could not even see him, curious as to what would happen if he collided with anyone but too wary to put it to the test.

~ * ~

Korum watched the passing crowd from the shelter of a doorway. He had never been invisible before. He had heard of it, but only at the expense of a great deal of concentration and power. He stepped out into the path of another group and waved his arms in their faces as he backed away from them. Their conversation continued. At the next doorway, he dodged away into unnecessary cover and considered his situation. The fact that no one could see him did not mean that he was invisible. It could mean that he was not actually there. Alternatively, perhaps he was but they were not. He smiled, enjoying the conundrum. Then something along the street tugged at his mind. He scanned the passing crowd. His grin broadened. Things were beginning to drop into place. A few yards away, hands in pockets and eyes darting from rooftop to rooftop, Wilson ambled toward him.

If Wilson could see him... He waited until the policeman reached his doorway. "Pssst."

Wilson looked around. "Korum." He stepped into the doorway next to the priest and turned at his side. "Can they see you?" He asked as a family group passed their doorway.

"No."

"Me neither. Why?"

Korum backed further from the street and Wilson shuffled to his side.

"It's becoming clearer," Korum said, "but first tell me what's happened to you since you arrived."

Wilson started with the cave and Ardam.

Korum listened, nodding and shaking his head in turn. When the story was finished, he placed a hand on Wilson's shoulder. "They can't see us," he said, "because they aren't real."

"But we are?"

"Do you feel real?"

"Yes."

"Well, believe it. We're inside somebody's mind. Inside their racial memory."

"Whose?"

Korum shrugged. "We'll never find out from here. We need to get out of their subconscious and into the conscious."

"How?"

"Walking might be a start." Korum took a step toward the street and then stopped.

The people were no longer walking. They had stepped back against the shop fronts. Then Wilson heard the sound of horses. They were moving fast, clattering against the cobbles of the street somewhere out of sight to his right. Then they were passing, two of them, side by side, almost filling the width of the street. The people had backed into doorways or flattened themselves against windows and walls.

The riders wore black cloaks and black hats. Their mounts were as black as their riders' garb. Behind them, tied by their wrists to the saddles of the horses, two women bounced along the cobbles. Their clothes were in shreds and their bodies bruised, bloody and smeared with the filth of the gutter.

The stares of the crowd followed the riders along the street and then they spilled back from the walls to fill the void that the horses had left in their wake. At first, there was silence but soon conversations restarted and the world continued on its way.

Korum tugged at Wilson's sleeve and pulled him into the street. "Come on, we need to get out of town and away from the memories."

~ * ~

Karrina pushed herself to her feet. Her body hurt from its collision with the wall and then the hard stone floor. Her head hurt even more from the vividness of the thoughts that invaded it. All of the tales that she had heard at Moyasta's knee were more real in her head than even the old woman's skilful storytelling had ever made them.

She knew that they must have value or, she would not be seeing them. But what was it? And why, why was she feeling the pain?"

She dropped to her knees. Her wrists were tied but above her head this time. She saw sky, then people, then walls, then stone. She was being bounced and jolted along the ground. Then she was spinning and then she bounced again. There was filth in her mouth and then air. There was sky and then people, then Wilson and Korum. She tried to hold onto them. Her head spun. There was dirt and then more sky. Then there was only blackness and pain.

~ * ~

Rubek heard footsteps approaching but could not twist his head sufficiently to see. Then he heard voices. The fingers that pinned his ankles released their grip. He looked down. The creatures had gone. His wrists were free also. He flexed his fingers and tingling warmth flowed back into them. He sat up and looked around.

A group of men, white skinned and white haired was observing him from a distance. He tried to stand but could not. It was as though the very air around him was holding him still. Beside him, Ackroyd and Saville had also managed to sit but had gotten no further.

The strangers took two tentative steps toward them and then stopped. There were six of them and they were identical. The likeness went beyond family resemblance; *they could*, Rubek thought, *have been clones.*

"You are welcome." Six mouths moved but the words came from the group rather than from six individuals. "We sense no aggression, but why are you here?"

"We didn't mean to be," Rubek said, "we just arrived."

"On the surface anyway," Saville added. "You brought us here."

"You left us no choice," the group said. "Your intentions were unclear."

"That's because we didn't have any. We just wanted to make something happen." Rubek tried to stand once again and then gave up.

"Forgive our caution. We have had no visitors for centuries and the last ones destroyed our world and forced those who survived to seek refuge here." Six pairs of arms spread to indicate the vastness of the cavern. "Only now and only slowly is life returning to the surface."

"But the huts and the barn."

"You created those, not very imaginative, all almost identical. That's when we knew that you weren't powerful enough to pose a serious threat."

Rubek experimented with his limited freedom. He could move his limbs easily enough once he did not try to rise. "How many survived?" He asked.

"Initially a few thousand but with the planet dead and no food or energy source in the caves none would have lasted long."

"You said centuries."

"Our priests were strong. They sacrificed the people, and themselves, to keep the Power alive."

"And now?"

"Now." The group laughed. "Now, we are as many…"

A sea of identical faces stretched as far back into the cavern as Rubek was able to see.

"…Or as few as we want."

A single figure stood before them smiling. "Now there is only the Power and its memories of those who used to control it."

"Couldn't you return to the surface now, start again?"

"For what?" They were six once again. "We don't exist."

"Then," Saville stroked his chin, "why can I see you?"

"We give the Power a purpose without which it too would cease to exist."

"So you can be as many or as few as you like." Ackroyd measured his words, grappling with concepts strange to his soldier's mind. "Do you always look like you do now or…?"

"We can be anything."

"An army?"

There were thousands of them, silver helmed and armed with swords and spears. Polished breastplates reflected Rubek's image and those of his companions back at him. He turned to look at Ackroyd.

The marine was smiling.

He looked back to the army and saw only six white haired old men.

Twenty-three

Leirbag paced the throne room. "Where are you?" he mumbled, pounding the fist of his right hand into the open palm of his left. "Where are you?" They were, he knew, just like the rest of their stupid world. They thought more with their hearts than with their heads. That was why he would win. That was why they were dying by the thousand under his unremitting attacks. That was why they would die in their hundreds of thousands when the endgame proper started. That would be soon. There were only two places left to fill and then he would be able to launch his full force against Wilson's world and still have sufficient energy left to move his tower and conquer his own.

~ * ~

Alice watched his pacing in silence. She could sense his frustration and did not want to become its target.

Leirbag turned. "Rodney's back."

"Yes." Alice too had sensed the boy's return. Her mind had smelled the burning flesh and seen the shattered flying limbs. The Super Bowl would never be the same again. She smiled. They were bringing the world to its knees. Normality no longer existed, only fear. Countries were tearing each other apart. Some were tearing themselves apart. The terror that they had unleashed had created its own momentum and had become unstoppable. All that their attacks did now was tweak its direction occasionally. Alice stroked at Rodney's mind and tasted the fear and death of its memories.

"Fetch him now." Leirbag's voice broke into her enjoyment. "I'll make the bitch hurt so much she'll drag them here."

Alice smiled. *He's losing it*, she thought. He was letting his emotions rule his mind, just as those did whom he most despised. She would not make that mistake. She would enjoy but she would remain detached. That was why she would win.

"Now."

Alice obeyed.

~ * ~

Wilson followed Korum out of the town and along a deeply rutted track. "How far do we have to go?" he said, to the priest's back.

Korum did not turn.

"Memories," and "fade," were the only words of the priest's reply that Wilson heard. He did not repeat the question but trudged on, half of his attention on the potentially ankle snapping ruts of the track and half on the undulating grassland that spread out all around him. *I must be getting tired,* he thought. The more distant of the low hills had become hazy as though a light mist was falling.

His eyes dropped to the ground and he planned his next few footfalls. He raised them again. The seeming mist had closed in. He walked on then checked down again. The dried mud of the track had become strangely indistinct. There was no mist, he realised. His eyesight was failing. He looked to his side; everything beyond the fringe of the track was a grey-green blur. He jerked his head to the front. Korum stood out as clear as a glossy magazine picture against an indiscernible backdrop.

The priest smiled. "We're just about there I think." He sat down, cross-legged on the track that Wilson could no longer see and patted the spot next to him.

~ * ~

Alice watched Leirbag's lips curl from frown to smile. His eyes were closed. She remained silent, not knowing whether the change of expression was reflected behind their lids.

She leaned her head against the tall back of her throne and allowed herself a smile of her own. Her eyes were still on Leirbag but her mind drifted back over the events of the previous hour.

She had summoned Rodney and the boy had accompanied her and Leirbag back into the corridor to a door halfway along its length to the left. There had, she remembered, been a bounce as well as purpose in Leirbag's step and his grip on her elbow was gentle.

He turned the key and pushed open the door with a flourish.

Alice had searched this room before. It was small and bare, not even having a window to break the monotony of its undecorated walls.

The girl who had attacked Alice earlier was lying on her back in the centre of the floor.

Leirbag bent over his prisoner, lifted the front of her t-shirt, and unclipped a slender chain belt from around her waist. "Now we'll see how brave she is, Alice." He stood back from the girl. "Get up."

As Alice watched the girl undress, she knew that the unquestioning obedience was a sham. The girl was biding her time. It was not Leirbag's power she was witnessing, but the girl's control.

She looked at Leirbag. He was grinning, enjoying his power, apparently blind to that which Alice thought so obvious. With every miscalculation on Leirbag's part her belief that she could escape his influence grew. She smiled.

Leirbag glanced in her direction and returned the smile. The sparkle in his eyes told her that he read their expressions as a mutual celebration of his power. Alice's hopes soared. She just had to be careful.

"Your turn, now Rodney." Leirbag turned to the boy. "Get your clothes off."

When Rodney was naked, Leirbag walked to stand behind him, draped an arm over his shoulder and bent his head to speak into the boy's ear. "She's yours Rodney," he said. "Your reward, a gift from your queen, take her."

Rodney didn't move. His body remained unresponsive.

"I said take her." Leirbag took a step back, raised his arm to strike and then, his fist hanging in the air, he appeared to change his mind.

"He can't do it, Alice." He dropped his arm to his side and beamed at her. "Ha, Ha your little favourite can't do it." He clapped his hands. "He can't do it."

Alice almost expected him to start jumping up and down on the spot. The bulge at the front of his gown drew her attention. It looked so comical. He really had lost control. She laughed.

Leirbag's eyes flickered. He looked down, following the direction of her gaze, and then turned to face her. She felt a twinge of apprehension and then he started to laugh with her.

Once again, he had misinterpreted her. She laughed louder. So did he.

He was still laughing when he lifted his gown. "I'll show you how it's done, Rodney. Watch and learn."

Rodney had no choice. Alice did, and she couldn't watch this. She turned, strode into the corridor, leaned against the wall and rested her head back against the cold stone. Leirbag, intent on his conquest, probably hadn't even noticed her departure. For one reckless second, she didn't care, then she closed her eyes and thought it through. *She'd make him believe that jealousy had driven her from the room. Could she make him believe her? If she couldn't accomplish that one simple thing, she'd be his slave forever. Leirbag out of control might not be the advantage she needed. It made him unpredictable and she needed to out-think him, to stay one step ahead. She needed to make him believe that his control over her was total. That was her only hope.* She opened her eyes, drew a long inward breath and returned to the room.

~ * ~

Wilson had never felt pain like it. His insides were being ripped apart. He fell forward. He was on his knees. His body rocked back and forth. There were tears in his

216

eyes. They ran in unbroken streams down his cheeks and still the pain came. He fell onto his face and scrunched up his eyelids but somehow the tears continued to flow.

The searing pain retreated into a dull throbbing and his breathing eased. He pushed himself back onto hands and knees. His eyes were still closed. He kept them that way until the throbbing had eased further and then he opened them.

He was looking down at a bare wooden floor. Curtains of long black hair blinkered his vision. His head moved from side to side. He was in a stone walled room; of Korum, there was no sign. There was a door, wooden and solid looking. It was closed. His arms pushed him up into a kneeling position and his gaze dropped to his body. He had breasts. Their nipples were brown and erect. Between his legs was a triangle of black hair and nothing else.

He tried to move his hands, to investigate this new body by touch but they refused to obey him.

Then he was standing. His eyes settled on a pile of clothing. He bent picked up a white bra and slipped it on with practiced ease. He slipped on panties and tight jeans; only a t-shirt and denim jacket remained. 'But not with you', he recognised the print as his arms slipped it over his head. His body bent to retrieve the jacket.

I am Karrina, he thought, but knew that he was still Stuart Wilson. *No, I'm just in her mind.*

"Out of the subconscious into the conscious." Korum had said.

He was seeing what she was seeing. This room was where she was. The pain had been hers. Was Korum there also? Was he seeing the same things? How could he find out? He thought that he had shaken his head but the point of focus of the eyes through which he looked had not changed. He wondered what to do next. He could think, he knew. He could see, but he had no control over the body that had become his. No, it had not. His mental dialogue continued. He was only seeing through Karrina's eyes. Could he share her thoughts? He had shared her pain, or had the pain been his? It did not matter; it had hurt like nothing he had ever experienced. Again, he shook a head that did not move. His, her body lowered itself to the floor and sat back against the wall. He could feel the cold of the stone against his back. His attention was on the door. All that he could do was wait. He closed his eyes, but did not; the door was still there.

~ * ~

Alice saw Leirbag's fingers curl and stroke the back of the serpent head arms of his throne. The wooden eyes of the creatures flicked open and their heads writhed with pleasure under their master's caress. Alice almost expected them to purr like satisfied kittens. Her attention switched to his face. His smile had broadened and now there was no doubting its open lipped genuineness.

Leirbag's head turned toward her before he opened his eyes. "They're here, Alice." He pushed himself from the table. "We have them."

Alice scrambled from her seat and had to run in order to be at his side as they entered the corridor.

He stopped outside the room in which they had confined Karrina.

Alice stood away from him, knowing that he was summoning the power for an attack that she did not want to get in the way of.

~ * ~

Karrina watched the door, dreading that it would swing open, but knowing that her situation was not going to change, for better or for worse, until it did. There were only three other things on which she could focus her attention, walls, floor and ceiling. Four, she corrected herself, but she did not want to look at herself, not after what he had done to her. There was dampness between her legs and she knew that she was bleeding. There was something else too, at first she had put it down to the pain and then to shock, but she was calmer now and it was still there. It was as though there was someone inside her mind or there was a conflicting part of her. She rested her head back against the hard stone and stared at one section of the door until it became indistinct under the intensity of her gaze.

She felt Korum first. The priest was inside her mind and he was trying to talk to her. She tried to focus in on him but the harder she tried the fainter the contact became. She shook her mind free and looked around the room. Then she tried again, or rather she didn't. She breathed deeply, exhaling twice for every intake of air. Her lungs filled, her vision blurred and her mind emptied. Then she had his thoughts. Wilson was there too but without Karrina's help, he did not have the knowledge to make contact. Wilson had Smallroot and she needed that. She should wait until the time was right and then she had to get Wilson to release Smallroot.

::How will I know when the time is right?:: She thought.

::You'll know,:: Korum said, inside her head. Then, just before a sound from the far side of the door broke her concentration, he added, *I hope.* Those last two words shattered whatever confidence the contact had initially instilled in her. If Korum with all of his power and knowledge was unsure, what chance did she have?

The sounds beyond the door had stopped. Karrina strained to catch others. For a few seconds there was nothing and then a key turned in the lock. The heavy ring handle turned through ninety degrees and after a moment's inaction, the door crashed inward.

~ * ~

Alice took another step back as Leirbag hurled the door open.

He thrust out an arm to prevent it rebounding and strafed the room with pain, before striding across the threshold to inspect the damage that he had inflicted.

The girl, arms spread to her side, was slumped against the far wall. Her head hung to one side. Leirbag took in the rest of the small room in a glance. There was no one else there. "They were here!" He screamed. "They were! They were!" He took another step and kicked out at Karrina's outstretched legs. They spun away from him. Her body lost the support of the wall and slumped to the floor. "Where are they?" Leirbag's foot lashed out again, catching the unconscious girl in the ribs. "Where are they, bitch?"

~ * ~

Alice remained in the corridor but what she heard told her everything and then Leirbag appeared in the doorway. He looked at her only for a second. "They're here," he said. "They're here somewhere." He turned, stomped to the next door along the corridor and kicked it open. "Come on. Now!"

Alice followed.

~ * ~

Wilson turned the problem over in his mind repeatedly. What could he do? How could he influence anything if all he could do was watch? Then the door burst inward. He tried to jump to his feet. Then there was pain, not from anywhere in his body in particular, not sharp or dull, just pure indefinable pain.

~ * ~

Slowly, Karrina's mind began to function once again. She lay still, not opening her eyes, letting her ears explore the room. She hurt but she pushed the pain away. Somewhere, far off, a door crashed open. She heard shouts and curses, but from her room there was nothing. She listened for a few more seconds and then she opened her eyes and pushed herself back into a sitting position. She looked around. Everything was the same, except...except that the door was open. It swung in a small arc and then corrected itself. She could walk out. "When the time is right." Korum had said. Was it right now? She tried to think but through what was left of the pain, could not.

~ * ~

The door was swinging open. Wilson watched it, knowing that he had no control over the body that could, should, rise to its feet and walk through it. *Korum would know what to do,* he thought. He had to get his head around where he was, what he was. He could not close his eyes to concentrate. He should accept rather than try to control.

He concentrated on trying to sink down into the body he had seen. It didn't work. If only he could control the head, make it look down at the breasts, the long slim legs, and the flat stomach, how he had always longed for that. But without the help of his external senses he found it impossible to give himself the body of a woman, especially when his eyes were open and the door was swinging and then there was the pain, still there, still nagging at the edges of his mind.

~ * ~

Karrina forced her mind beyond and behind the pain. She had to find Wilson. She closed her eyes and thought of his face.

~ * ~

Wilson's eyes closed. He smiled, or thought that he did. Then he heard Karrina's voice. It was faint but growing clearer. "Smallroot, you must find Smallroot." The words repeated until they became a chant inside his head.

Smallroot was in his pocket, his jacket pocket, right hand side. He had no pocket now. He had the t-shirt. He focussed his mind on where the pocket would be if he were still wearing the jacket. Mentally he guided his hand to its flap. He imagined his fingers closing around the small piece of root and pulling it free. He tried again and then again. Then he launched his mind in an answering of

Karrina's chant. *::Jacket pocket, right hand side. Jacket pocket right hand side.::*

~ * ~

Karrina heard his voice. *Jacket,* she thought, and plunged her hand into the pocket of hers. It was empty. "No," she whispered. "His jacket." Wilson's was longer and looser. If he were sitting in the same position the bottom of his would be rucked up on the floor. Would it have creased inward, or outward? She tried to picture the scene and at the same time moved her fingers to the imaginary opening and gripped onto air. On the fifth attempt, her fingers closed around something. She looked down. Her hand was empty but she could feel the gnarled wood resting against its palm. She closed her eyes, squeezed her fingers more tightly and rested her hand in her lap.

~ * ~

Wilson felt his hand close around the familiar shape of Smallroot and he opened his eyes. He looked to his left and his head obeyed. He looked down. His body was back. He unclenched his hand and turned Smallroot over with his fingers, enjoying his regained control of his limbs.

There was a cough to his side. He looked. Karrina was sitting against the wall next to him. She was looking at him and smiling.

~ * ~

Korum relaxed. If he had had a mouth, it would have been smiling. At least, with Wilson back in the real world, he had senses now. He could see and hear through Karrina's eyes and ears and he could communicate with her. He could guide and advise. He knew that they were at the very heart of Leirbag's power. The walls and floor that Karrina could see were solid enough but Korum could feel that they were creations of magic rather than man.

~ * ~

Leirbag stomped from room to room, kicking at each door in turn and then hurling a blast of power and pain through the openings before entering.

In those where his disciples rested after returning from another bloody mission. They were flung from their beds to writhe in agony on the hard wooden floors. Leirbag scanned the rooms without sparing them a thought and then moved on to the next.

~ * ~

Alice followed at his heels, enjoying his increasing lack of control.

~ * ~

Wilson signalled to Karrina that she should remain where she was and then he pushed himself to his feet and took up position behind the open door. He could hear the commotion outside.

Leirbag was on the return leg, smashing into rooms on the far side of the corridor. Soon he would be outside the door behind which Wilson hunched. He could not have been more than two doors away.

Wilson turned in the confining space behind the door and signalled to Karrina that she should slump sideways. He had been counting the seconds that separated the crashing of doors. He would not have long. Leirbag's roars and curses gave him some comfort though. He sounded like a man demented. Then he could see him through the crack between wood and wall.

Leirbag kicked at the door opposite Wilson's hiding place. It flew open. He waved a hand toward it and then strode into the room. There was a scream. *Not Leirbag's*, Wilson thought.

"Bastards! Where are you?" That was Leirbag.

Alice stepped into Wilson's line of vision. He could see the back of her head. She was not going into the rooms. "Shit," he mouthed.

Alice's blonde hair moved back toward him. *She's standing clear*, Wilson thought. Leirbag was coming out. If he saw Karrina and relocked the door, they were lost. Wilson hoped that in his current state of mind Leirbag would not give one more open door a second thought. Alice made things easier. She had backed almost into their doorway, shielding Karrina from Leirbag's view.

Wilson heard footsteps stamping away. Alice's shoulder disappeared from his sight as she followed. He darted around the door, across the corridor and into the room opposite.

~ * ~

Alice remembered the girl. She turned and then stopped. Something… No, she shook her head, just her imagination. She walked back to Karrina's room. The girl was still slumped against the far wall. Her head was on the floor. A long strand of black hair hung over her mouth,

Alice crouched in front of her, wrapped the hair around her fingers and pulled the girl upright.

Karrina gasped and opened her eyes.

Alice glared at her. "I'll have you too, bitch," she hissed.

Karrina felt spots of saliva hit her face.

Alice leaned closer. "For hurting me you'll hurt forever." She traced a line down Karrina's cheek with a long red fingernail and smiled. "An army of giants, one from the front and then one from behind." Her finger retraced its path. "Fucked to death." She bent closer, repeating the words in a whisper and then her lips were on Karrina's. Her kiss was soft. Her tongue played on Karrina's lips, trying to part them.

"Alice! Alice!" Leirbag's scream echoed along the corridor and into the room.

Alice pulled Karrina's head back. Her finger dug into the flesh beneath Karrina's eye and gouged a line downward toward the side of her mouth. Blood flowed. Alice looked at her finger and then sucked it clean.

"Alice!"

She stood and backed toward the door. "Fucked to death." She smiled, turned, and strode from the room, closing the door and turning the key in the lock behind her.

~ * ~

Wilson had watched as best he could through the crack in the door opposite but all that he had seen was Alice's back. He turned and looked back into the room. It was just like the one in which he had left Karrina except that there was a small made up bed in one corner. A low groan came from its far side and then a hand appeared.

Wilson moved around the foot of the bed. Squeezed between its side and the wall was a boy of about seventeen. His face was hideously scarred, as though it had been ripped apart and then stuck together again.

Wilson moved closer.

The boy cowered away. His eyes were wide but there was no life in them, not even fear, nothing.

Wilson crouched and looked into the face. "Who are you?" He smiled what he hoped was a comforting smile. "Who are you?"

The boy pulled his knees up to his chest. His face was mending. One by one, the intricate network of scars was disappearing into smooth, undamaged skin.

~ * ~

Leirbag was standing outside the door of the throne room. "Alice!" he shouted again, even though she was running along the corridor toward him.

She stopped short of him. "The girl, you..." Her eyes dropped to the floor. "...I forgot to lock the door."

Leirbag grunted and then turned away. "Come." He strode the length of the table and gripped the back of his throne. It shimmered, then it was gone and in his hand was the silver handled cane. "They are here Alice and we will find them." He flashed her a look that challenged her to contradict him. She did not.

~ * ~

Alice had left the key in the lock. Wilson sighed. He had not assumed that she would. He had not even thought about it. *What if she had taken it?* He shook the thought away. She hadn't. He concentrated again, on what was happening outside the door. He strained his ears. He had heard nothing for some minutes. He glanced back at the boy. He had pulled himself back onto the bed and was lying on his back staring vacantly up at the ceiling.

Wilson turned back to the door. He would, he decided; give it a few more minutes before he made his move.

~ * ~

Alice followed Leirbag from the throne room. Instead of turning into the corridor, he strode across it to the bare, stone wall between two open doors. Then, gripping his cane by the centre of its shaft, he pressed it flat against the stone. For five feet to either side of him there was no wall. Instead, a wide stone stairway spiralled down into the heart of the tower.

Alice's heart dropped. She had been through every door along the corridor. Her confidence grew with every inch of wall and floor that she searched. Whatever was hidden, she would find it. There was so little ground left for her to cover that she was sure that her search would soon be over. Now there was more but how much more? The staircase might spiral down forever through floor after floor. She had seen the height of the tower from her window. That there had been no windows beneath hers meant nothing.

Leirbag took two downward steps and then turned. "Come on and stay close." He still held the cane around its centre and horizontally in front of him as though it provided protection from what lay ahead.

Alice smiled her assent. *If he needs protection,* she thought, *I'll stay very close.*

~ * ~

Wilson risked a peek around the door. Leirbag and Alice were in the corridor but far along it to his left. They had their backs to him. He continued to watch, ready to pull back his head should either of them start to turn theirs.

He saw the stretch of wall disappear and then Leirbag, followed by Alice, stepped through the opening. As soon as they were out of sight, the wall reappeared.

Wilson tiptoed across the corridor and turned the key in the door of Karrina's room. The click of the lock's release echoed from the walls. He hesitated and then twisted the ring handle and pushed the door inward.

Karrina was sitting against the wall. There was an angry red gash across her cheek. He stepped toward her, checked himself and turned to close the door.

"The key," Karrina said.

He stopped the swing of the door, removed the key and dropped it into his pocket. Then he closed the door and turned.

Karrina was on her feet and then she was in his arms. He held her close saying nothing. He could feel the wetness of her cheek against his. He released her and held her at arms length, looking into her eyes.

She licked a finger and wiped her blood from his face. "It's nothing," she said, seeing his concern. "Won't even scar."

He brushed her cheek with his thumb, careful not to disturb the wound. "Come on." He forced a smile, "Let's explore before they get back."

Her eyes became distant as though she was struggling to hear a far away sound.

Wilson listened himself but could hear nothing.

"Something is hidden," Karrina said. "We must find it."

"Korum," Wilson asked. "Did he tell you that?"

Karrina nodded, stepped past him and opened the door.

~ * ~

Alice thought that the stairway had completed two full turns and then it dropped through the ceiling of a huge circular gallery, spiralled down through its centre and disappeared through the floor. If the size of the room surprised her, its occupants shocked her even more.

There were hundreds of them and they were grotesque. Many had limbs missing. Some had enough but they were the wrong ones. She saw an adult torso with the small arm of an infant. There were loose limbs everywhere, not scattered about the floor but hanging in the air as though they still had bodies attached.

"These are yours, Alice." Leirbag said without turning. "You brought them here."

They continued their descent getting closer and closer to the strange congregation.

Alice saw an armless woman pass a hanging arm. The limb affixed itself to her shoulder as she passed. It was too large and its thick masculine fingers brushed her leg below the knee. The woman stumbled on her way. One of her legs was longer than the other and had attached itself the wrong way round.

"No need to fear these." Leirbag continued, as they neared floor level. "Their loyalty is only to you because you took them." He paused. "And to me of course."

Alice watched his back. He was holding his cane in front of him and was waving it from side to side as though fending off the crowd.

Not as confident as he sounds, she thought, *not by a long way.*

The stairway continued down through the floor of the gallery and within a few feet emerged through the ceiling of another. The room was the same size as the one they had left and its occupants were just as bizarre but there were more of them, hundreds more.

"Rodney's," Leirbag said. "He really has done very well, your little favourite."

They continued down through gallery after gallery of dismembered and mismembered suffering. After the crush of Rodney's room, they became less and less crowded as they descended. The last was empty. There was still one place left to fill.

Leirbag turned. "Quite an army, Alice, don't you think? Can you imagine what they will do on your world?"

Alice smiled. She was imagining. They would be bombed and blasted by artillery and they would reassemble themselves and carry on, becoming less and less human with every attack. That was the power of Worldroot and of whoever possessed it. Soon, her smile broadened, that would be her.

Leirbag placed a gentle hand on her shoulder. "We are a team, Alice, you and I."

His smile looked genuine and his eyes, Alice thought, held as much compassion as she had ever seen there.

He applied downward pressure.

Alice's knees bent until she was kneeling on the stone floor in front of him.

"Now, Alice, go and fill our final place. Then within days we will be ready."

Alice fixed her smile. Her body was starting to lose shape. She held out a hand as though reaching for his.

"Go, Alice, go now and then we will be together forever."

Then just before she was able to curl her outstretched fingers around his, she was gone.

~ * ~

Wilson and Karrina worked their way along the corridor. In eleven of the smaller rooms, they found people at various stages of recovery. All had the same dead, empty eyes, as though their bodies were merely husks, their spirits gone.

One small room had a bed but no occupant. In each, Wilson played Smallroot around trying to conjure out anything hidden by magic. He found nothing.

They moved on to the next door.

"Ah," Wilson said, as he pushed it open. "Now this is different."

Scarlet fabric draped the walls of the room. The whole of the floor was one intricate mosaic; at its centre, likenesses of Leirbag and Alice sat side by side on ornate thrones. A group of people knelt at their feet. Wilson recognised Karrina before he recognised himself. Behind the thrones, an army of misshapen humans and bearded giants stretched away toward a range of black, snow-capped mountains.

Wilson waved Smallroot around the room. Nothing changed.

Karrina stepped away from his side and tiptoed across the design as though wary of displacing the tiles.

"Stuart," she whispered. "Come here."

Wilson moved toward her.

Her eyes were on the centre of the mosaic. His followed. As he traversed the design, it began to change. On the thrones that Leirbag and Alice Craven had occupied, Karrina and he sat side by side, their interlocked fingers forming a bridge between the two seats. Standing behind and between them, Korum had a hand on each of their shoulders. Ackroyd and Saville knelt to either side. Leirbag and Alice Craven lay at their feet their bodies pricked by arrows and swords. Twelve other bent and distorted bodies were scattered across the foreground. Stretching back to the distant mountains were flowers and trees, but no army.

"You think we're looking at an alternative outcome?" Wilson asked.

"Seems likely." Karrina's voice wavered. "Come on let's get out of here." She stepped back toward the door, hoping that Wilson had not seen what she had. Her own image had smiled back toward her from its throne. The delicate flakes of rock that made up her eyes sparkled. One was blue, the other was green.

Twenty-four

Alice had only half materialised. She had practiced this dozens of times but had never dared take it to its conclusion for fear that Leirbag would detect the true extent of her power. Now he had forced her hand. She could not afford to let the final place be filled until she knew where Leirbag had hidden her soul. Until she had that, he would be master.

She concentrated hard, keeping hold of the bridge over which she had crossed and then pouring a small piece of her essence back over it. "Not too much," she whispered. "There, careful." There were beads of sweat on her brow. "Careful."

~ * ~

As soon as Alice had disappeared, Leirbag turned and strode out five measured paces from the bottom of the staircase. Then he tapped the end of his cane on the floor slab immediately in front of him. A square of stone disappeared and a further stairway spiralled down. He took one downward step and then turned. "Alice?" His head cocked to one side. Then he smiled, shook his head, turned back and continued down.

~ * ~

Alice followed Leirbag down through the floor. She was straining to keep control, to keep enough of her essence in the tower to see without being seen. She had also to prevent the fragile bridge between the worlds from snapping. She did not know what would happen if it did, with her senses on one side and her body on the other, but she suspected that it would be the end of all of her ambitions.

The room into which she followed Leirbag was small and square. He did not turn again but sat cross-legged in its centre and laid the cane across his knees.

The walls all around began to shimmer and then some of the stones disappeared revealing small, square compartments. In the one nearest to her, Alice recognised the cigarette lighter and the photograph of Arthur Molloy. She did not wait to see more but let her senses flow back across the bridge and into her body. She had what she wanted but the effort had exhausted her. Her knees buckled and she crumpled to the floor.

~ * ~

Wilson strode around the long table with Karrina at his side. There was a throne at its far end. It was set off centre as though there should have been another next to it. He counted the chairs and remembered the beds.

"There was another one," Karrina said, "bigger and carved."

Wilson turned and looked back along the table. "That would be Leirbag's I reckon. And this..." He patted the back of the one next to him. "...Alice Craven's you think?

King and Queen like in the mosaic." His hand dropped from the back of the throne and hung to his side.

Karrina reached for it and interlocked her fingers with his. "And a court of twelve."

"And we've seen eleven." Wilson said. "He'll make his move once he has them all. We don't have much time."

"Time to do what?"

"To stop him of course"

Somewhere along the corridor a door rattled.

"Come on." Wilson's grip on Karrina's fingers tightened and he pulled her toward the door. He stopped when he reached it and peered around it.

Karrina squeezed his hand. "What is it?"

The eleven they had seen resting, lined the length of the corridor. It took Wilson only a second to realise what was different about them. Their stomachs... "Come on." He pulled Karrina through the doorway and across the corridor to the spot through which he had seen Leirbag and Alice Craven disappear and pressed Smallroot against the wall.

The wood vibrated against his palm. He almost dropped it. Its buzzing increased in intensity, became a rumble and then a scream, like an engine protesting in too low a gear. Then the wall in front of them was gone.

"Quick." Wilson pulled Karrina down the first of the steps.

Behind them the wall re-appeared.

~ * ~

Leirbag concentrated his entire mind on the power that was stored in that room. Here he was at his strongest, more than a king, almost a god. He needed to be if he was

236

to repair the damage that he was about to do in time. But the meddlers would be gone. No, not gone, he smiled. They would be part of his dismembered army and their parts would be spread through eleven of the tower's floors. He buried the vision, pleasurable though it was, and turned his mind back to the task in hand.

~ * ~

After the required time of mourning, they buried Moyasta beneath a giant oak in the grounds of the chateau. There were now over three hundred Ardamsfolk gathered at the retreat beneath the mountain. At other centres throughout the world, there were similar gatherings. They had isolated themselves from the anarchy and turmoil of the times. They took no pleasure from the disintegration of the world around them as the like-eyes destroyed themselves. It was simply destiny. Soon Karrina would return from the old world and Ardamsfolk would retake their rightful place in the scheme of things. She would bring Worldroot back to its people and once again, they would be masters of their own destinies. Whether on the world they had come to know, on Ardam's, or on some other, didn't matter. Worldroot would guide them and protect them. In that, they had absolute faith.

Twenty-five

Wilson and Karrina descended toward the first chamber side by side and hand in hand. They were ten feet above the heads of its occupants before Wilson noticed the deformities. He stopped and squeezed Karrina's fingers.

"Who are they?" she asked.

Wilson was about to say that he didn't know, when suddenly he did. One face he recognised and with that knowledge, another piece of the jigsaw dropped into place. The face belonged to one of the more-intact bodies amongst the crowd. Only one leg was missing. Wilson had last seen that face as it was pulled from the rubble of what had been the Bradford mosque.

"They're the victims," he said. "And if they have them all there'll be thousands of them. For what?"

"An army," Karrina said, "the mosaic."

"Jesus." Wilson's grip on her hand tightened.

Her fingers returned the pressure of his. "There's power," she said. Her free hand rose to massage her temple. "Strong, very strong and below us." Her eyes closed. "A long way below."

"Leirbag came this way," Wilson said. "With Alice Craven." He took another downward step. A blast from behind and above threw him to his knees.

The explosion flung Karrina forward. She tripped over Wilson and then over the edge of the stairway.

He tried to halt her fall but Karrina's momentum pulled him from the stairs behind her. The crowd beneath them scattered before they crashed side by side onto the stones of the floor.

"You okay?" Wilson staggered to his feet.

"I think so." Karrina had pushed herself up onto her knees.

Wilson bent and helped her to stand.

She shook her arms and flexed her legs. "Nothing broken anyway."

The crowd around them shuffled restlessly but did not attempt to close in.

"What was it?" Karrina twisted her neck to look up at the spot from which they had tumbled.

"I think our friends upstairs just blew the roof off."

"Why?"

"I assume, because Leirbag thought we were still up there."

~ * ~

Korum surveyed the scene through Karrina's eyes. He had heard of such things. Worldroot was powerful but it was also amoral, or rather, its morality was gleaned from whoever possessed it. If Leirbag wanted an army of the disfigured dead then Worldroot could certainly provide him with the means to obtain one. The only way they were going to defeat him was to get Worldroot. *::Was Leirbag carrying anything?::* Korum thought.

Karrina verbalised that thought.

"A cane," Wilson replied, "with a silver handle. We heard about it in London too."

::That must be Worldroot,:: Korum thought; *::we must get it from him.::*

"We need the cane," Karrina said. "That's Worldroot."

The crowd began to shuffle toward them but looked unsure of its purpose. Wilson watched them. If Leirbag got a whiff of their presence, he would give the mob a purpose

~ * ~

Leirbag felt the destruction of the top of his tower as though one of his own limbs had been shattered. His eyelids clamped shut. Pain was strange to him and he savoured rather than suffered it. It receded and his mind followed it until it was gone.

He could establish no contact with the eleven that he had unleashed. They would take time to reassemble. There was something though. He probed deeper, unable, at first, to believe what his senses were telling him. The girl, the policeman and the priest were still alive. They were still in his tower. That could only be because they had passed through the wall above him.

He used the cane to push himself to his feet. Around him, the alcoves and their artefacts disappeared behind solid stone. He ran for the stairway. Anger had drained his face of blood and his eyes shone red. "Can I trust no one?" He shrieked at the first misshapen bodies he passed. "Can anybody do anything right?"

~ * ~

"He's coming," Karrina said. "And fast."

"Stay behind me." Wilson took a step toward the bottom of the stairway. The crowd did not part in front of him but they did not look ready for a fight either. He pushed the first two aside. They stumbled into those behind them. The next two followed. He looked around for Karrina.

She was close behind him.

The crowd had closed in at their backs.

Wilson gasped and looked down. A crawling infant had locked its teeth around the back of his ankle. He shook his leg free and then kicked the child away, punching out with a fist at the same time and sending a headless body reeling back into the crowd.

He took hold of Karrina's wrist and pulled her forward whilst his free arm lashed out at those that stood between them and the bottom of the stairway. Then he had a foot on the first step. Behind him, Karrina gasped. He turned and saw her shake her arm free of grasping fingers.

"Come on." He tugged at her wrist and started to climb.

~ * ~

Saville, Rubek and then Ackroyd recounted their stories to the six old men. The strangers listened in silence.

"We will think on this." The six said when the marine had finished. Then they turned and walked away across the floor of the cavern.

Saville tried to stand and toppled backward when the resistance that he had expected failed to materialise. Beside him, Ackroyd did the same.

"What now?" The marine asked.

"We wait." After the efforts of his struggle to stand, it seemed more appropriate to sit. He smiled and sat. "They're thinking on it."

Ackroyd lowered himself next to him, body relaxed but eyes alert.

~ * ~

Smallroot screamed in protest when Wilson slammed it against the wall, but slowly the stones began to fade and they were able to step through the growing gap into what was left of the corridor.

The timber roof had gone, so had most of the internal walls. Beyond piles of debris, holes in the external wall let in a warm breeze and orange tinged light.

"Come on." Wilson pulled Karrina across the rubble-strewn floor toward the nearest breach in the outer wall.

He thrust his head into daylight and looked down. It was a long drop but a massive, conical pile of what had once been wall and roof made it just feasible.

He pulled back his head and looked round at Karrina. "You first," he said. "Feet first. I'll lower you as far as I can. Bend your knees when you hit, like a parachute jump."

"Never done one," Karrina said, peering passed him.

"You've seen it in the movies," Wilson said. "Have a go."

She knelt on the rim of the hole and then turned, her feet dangling over the drop.

Wilson's gaze dropped to the gaping neck of her t-shirt. Her breasts looked...he shook his head clear. "Slowly now. Over you go." He took her hands and lowered her from the hole. His own arms, head and upper body followed for as far as he dared let them.

She was looking up at him. Her eyes were wide and her lips pursed.

Beyond her feet rafters and roof beams protruded at crazy angles from a pyramid of brick and stone. Cruel looking nails stuck out from many. Wilson tried not to think about them. "Ready."

"Ready."

"After three... One... Two... Three." He released his grip and closed his eyes.

~ * ~

Leirbag saw the wall above him reform and knew that they had escaped him once again. They would not be trapped at the top of his tower, not now. He turned on the stairway and held Worldroot in front of him. "Come on then my soldiers." He barked.

The crowd in Alice's chamber moved toward the stairway. It was not a charge or even a rush, but more of an amble. They were indestructible, speed did not matter. Below them, other heads appeared from Rodney's chamber and, Leirbag knew, that from the nine floors below those a misshapen tide was rising.

~ * ~

There was a crash, snapping wood, dislodged stones. Wilson opened his eyes.

Karrina was looking back at him. She had landed astride a timber joist. It seesawed between her weight and

243

that of the rocks that held its farthest end in place. Wilson watched as Karrina edged along it, dislodging a stream of dust and pebbles.

His hand recoiled from the wall. It had moved. He looked. It was rebuilding itself. He could not wait for Karrina to clear the pile. He had to go.

He lowered himself out of the tower until only his fingertips gripped the pulsating stone. Then he let himself drop.

He hit the pile where the end of the beam along which Karrina was edging was buried. It broke free and tobogganed earthward. He heard her scream and then he was bouncing, head over heels, down the rock slope.

He landed next to her on hot, soft sand and lay still. An avalanche of small stones cascaded to the ground around him. He shielded his head with his hands. When he could hear nothing he raised his head and looked around.

Karrina had her back to him. She was on her hands and knees. Her fingers were scrabbled in the sand.

"You okay?" He placed a hand on her shoulder.

She resisted his attempt to turn her head and then she scrambled to her feet, her hands to her eyes. "I'm fine," she said.

Wilson was pleased to see her smile. There was, however, something in the expression that was not totally convincing. "You sure?" He asked, but before Karrina had time to answer, something drew his attention to the tower.

From the numerous holes around its top, already disfigured bodies threw themselves to the ground. He could hear bones snapping as they landed. They lay still for a few seconds and then stumbled upright and moved forward. Others followed, many landing on top of those who had not recovered quickly enough, doing even more damage.

"Come on." Wilson turned away and began to run.

Karrina kept pace at his side. He could hear her breathing but the sound was soon lost beneath that of his own and the pounding of blood in his head.

He stopped and bent forward with both hands on his knees. At his side, Karrina mirrored his pose. Her t-shirt had pulled free of her jeans exposing the skin of her hips. It glistened with sweat.

I'm obsessed, Wilson thought, imagining his hands slipping around that waist. He forced a laugh that turned into a rasping cough.

The crowd came on. Behind it, more were still leaping from the tower. Few of them could manage a run. Wilson and Karrina outpaced them easily. Wilson took three deep, controlled breaths, pushed his hands against his knees and his body upright. He looked around. The horizon was a featureless curve. No direction appeared to be more promising than any other. "Okay," he said. "Let's keep going." His words still came in gasps.

"Where to?" Karrina's breathing was back under control.

"Just going." He took off again, kicking up clouds of soft sand.

Karrina followed.

The air was dry and hot.

~ * ~

Leirbag watched the last of his army leap through the hole in front of him and then let his concentration return to the rebuilding of his tower. When the outer wall had healed, he tossed his cane to the floor and slumped onto the throne that appeared in its place. Then he smiled. Alice had returned and she had brought number twelve. He was ready, or soon would be.

Amongst the piles of rubble that littered the floor eleven more bodies had reassembled. Leirbag closed his eyes. He could afford a few minutes of rest. The meddlers could not run forever. They would tire. His army, already dead, would not.

~ * ~

Alice opened her eyes. She was not on her bed. There was no bed. Only half of her room's walls were intact. The door had gone. She felt a moment of panic. The tower had fallen. Leirbag was defeated, and not by her. Then she felt him, his power, his confidence and his calm. She relaxed. Something had happened but Leirbag was still in control. "For now," she smirked, and stood to join him.

She found him in the space where the throne room had been. His throne was the only piece of furniture that remained. She knelt beside it and rested her hand on his.

He opened his eyes. "Alice."

"What happened?"

"A tiresome interruption, nothing more." He waved an arm, taking in the destruction all around them. "All will be back to normal by the time you return."

"Return?"

Leirbag turned his hand beneath hers and gripped her fingers, whilst stroking them with his thumb. "You have an engagement, my queen," he said, and then chuckled. "Your first official engagement." He lifted her hand from the arm of the throne and released it to drop to her side. Then he stroked the wooden serpent head. Its eyes opened and a forked tongue flicked from between its lips. It detached itself from the rest of the throne and wrapped itself around his wrist.

Alice watched, fascinated. Then the creature was gone, replaced in Leirbag's hand by a gnarled piece of tree root. He held it toward her.

She reached to take it but pulled her hand away as soon as her fingertips touched its mottled surface. It had felt alive.

"Take it Alice, you are my queen."

She looked into his eyes and saw no threat. Her fingers inched toward the root and then, as though coming to a decision of their own, they snatched it from his hand.

Alice staggered. Her eyes had closed. She opened them. She was taller. She felt taller, stronger, fitter, and more beautiful. She took a deep breath but it was power and confidence that filled her rather than air. She laughed and the sound echoed from the walls of the tower. She was more than human. She was... She laughed louder... She was a goddess.

Leirbag stood and took her in his arms. "Yes Alice, this is what we will share." His hands went to her shoulders and he held her at arms length. Then he laughed, too. The sound of his laughter bounced back from the stones alongside hers. Then she was gone.

Leirbag resumed his seat and stared into the space she had occupied. A cloud of uncertainty darkened his features. He shook his head and smiled it away. All of his plans and ambitions were still there and he would achieve them, but now there was more. They would be worth nothing, he realised, if he did not have Alice to share them with.

~ * ~

The table, Alice's throne and twelve chairs had reappeared. Leirbag's own seat propelled itself across the floor and retook its place. He summoned the twelve to their places and smiled when the last arrived. It was a girl, the first. She was pretty in a plain sort of way. Leirbag's smile broadened. Alice had brought her as a gift for Rodney and to allay his own suspicions. She had done it because she wanted him as much as he wanted her. Here was the proof that all of his suspicions were unfounded. He waved a hand and the table filled with food. "Eat my friends, eat." He beamed. "And then let the endgame begin."

Twenty-six

The pain in Wilson's side grew from whisper to scream. He stopped running and doubled over. Then he straightened, hands on hips, and arched his back. That helped, but not much. Hot air scraped his throat like sandpaper and salty sweat stung his eyes and trickled into the corners of his mouth.

Karrina caught up and dropped to her knees in the sand.

Far behind them, the bulk of the crowd continued on. A few, more able than the rest, had broken to the front. One was only yards away.

Wilson wiped the sweat from his eyes and watched the figure approach. Tattered blue jeans flapped around well-muscled legs. The upper body was broad and partially covered by the tattered remains of a running vest. The man's face showed the strain of his pursuit.

Karrina stood and moved to Wilson's shoulder.

The man's pace did not falter. His nearest support was three hundred yards behind. He had no arms. Still he came.

Wilson waited until the last second, sidestepped and stuck out a foot, tripping his would be assailant and sending him sprawling, face first, into the sand. Then he grabbed Karrina's hand. "Come on."

She pulled herself free, picked up a jagged lump of rock and strode toward their attacker.

The man was curled in the sand and struggling to get to his knees.

"No." Wilson thought he said, as Karrina smashed the rock down onto the back of the man's head.

Wilson watched, unable to move, as Karrina brought the rock down again, taking away half of the man's face and turning his left eye to pulp. She smashed it down once more, across the bridge of his nose and then stood back, breathing hard.

Wilson watched the rise and fall of her breasts beneath the sweat stained t-shirt. He wanted her there and then. It was insane, but...

"Come on," she said, and took off at a run.

Wilson watched her back for a second, her legs, her... He shook his head and then set off after her.

The smashed face paid Wilson no heed as he passed. The man was too intent on gaining its feet and carrying on.

~ * ~

The freezing wind blew against the flap of the tent, testing its hide bindings to the limit. Inside it, the old men sat huddled around a weak fire for the little heat it still provided. Their shoulders were hunched and their skeletal fingers gripped woollen cloaks around their frail bodies.

They spoke little now. Despair had overwhelmed the people and then the Council. Children, in their optimistic ignorance, still scraped at the dirt floors of the grain stores for anything that had been missed. Some of the giants still had strength enough to search the surrounding hills for the herds that had abandoned the windswept wastes months before. Then the wind stopped.

Only one or two of the broken circle still had the awareness to notice the change. Only one was motivated to investigate it. He opened his eyes.

The fire was burning with renewed vigour. He relaxed his grip on his cloak and felt the heat finger its way beneath it and into his body. He raised his head and smiled.

A woman was standing in front of the tent flap but there had been no icy blast to signal its opening. She was beautiful, tall and slender. Her blonde hair shone in the light of the re-born flames. Her eyes and smile were bright and full of confidence.

The old man watched her. *He was going to die*, he thought, but his death had been presaged by warmth and beauty. This cheered him.

"No, Arlon," the woman said. "Death is not ready for you yet."

The heat from the fire had roused others of the circle. Weary eyes turned toward the woman. On contact, all regained a sparkle that they thought had been lost forever.

"I am Alice," the woman said, stepping forward. "Leirbag's queen."

Huddled bodies became upright.

"He is about to return and save his people."

Only one found the strength to respond. "Leirbag brought this upon us in the first place." He spat out the words, setting the flames sizzling.

Alice raised an arm in the direction of the speaker. Her eyes blazed red.

The old man clutched at his chest and then fell backward. Blue and green flames licked from beneath the folds of his cloak. The smell of burning flesh tinged the air and then was gone.

"The rest of you may live," Alice said, "but only Leirbag will rule. You have failed the people."

There was a commotion from outside the tent and then the entrance flap flew open. No one noticed the lack of an icy wind. Unseen hands pushed a young boy through the opening. No one else followed but there was a hum of voices from beyond the flap when it fell back into place.

"The strain gore," the boy said, blushed and lowered his head.

Alice placed an arm around his shoulders and pulled him to her side.

He raised his head and tried again. "The grain store," he said, and smiled. "It's full."

~ * ~

Rubek was getting bored. There was not enough in the empty cavern to keep his senses occupied. He had been over the circumstances of their capture so many times that, he knew no fresh answers would be forthcoming.

He only noticed the six old men when they were within feet of him. "They've thought on it," he said.

Ackroyd shook himself awake.

Saville smiled, pleased that the marine too, despite his training, was only human.

"We have considered your story," the six said. "There is much that you didn't tell us."

"But…" Saville said.

Six raised hands silenced him.

"But…we have decided that that is because you don't know very much."

"That's true enough," Rubek chuckled.

"The gaps you left, rather than the story you told, took the time," the six said. "You must be re-united with your friends."

Rubek looked at his companions.

The old men continued. "We will accompany you. There is much to be gained."

Ackroyd stood.

Saville followed. "Let's go."

"Or all to be lost," the six added. "Please sit."

~ * ~

Korum watched the horizon line bounce up and down before his eyes. When his brain was driving his body to run, it compensated for the jarring. It wasn't and so it didn't. It was unnerving. Karrina had been running for what felt like hours and he still had not gotten used to it. Her attack on the armless man still shocked him. He had seen the skull shatter and he had felt the blind exhilaration of the act but he could not condone it. Or could he? She was chosen. This he knew, and by Moyasta who was wiser than even he was. He tried to reconcile the conflict, but the world was bouncing about in front of eyes that he could not close. He gave up.

~ * ~

The tower was complete. Leirbag looked along the length of the table. They were ready. He would never see them again but he needed them now. He went back over his planning. He could not fault it. He wished that Alice were there. Then, if he had missed something, he shook his head. No, he couldn't have.

He would launch the twelve, not as individuals, but all together, at one target after another. He had calculated the time differential between Alice's world, his own and Ardam's, it would be clockwork.

He knew that he could guarantee twelve, full strength, attacks. After these, his force would become depleted. How quickly this would happen he had no idea, but, he smiled, after the first twelve, anything else would be a bonus.

The first, because it happened so rarely, would be the full Congress of the Chinese Communist Party.

The second, he chuckled, had been going to be the United Nations, but the attacks that he had already launched had reduced that organisation to a toothless talking shop. The European Congress had faired little better. That left more scope for what had initially been minor targets, nuclear stockpiles and power plants. The damage that the destruction of these would cause might present problems in the future. He shrugged thoughts of these aside.

Easter Mass at the Vatican, this he had left in. God's representative on earth, his chuckle grew to a laugh. Soon they would be looking their new God in the face.

~ * ~

Karrina could run no further. Her legs ached. The hot air burned into her lungs. She was thirsty. She could no longer hear Wilson's footfalls behind her. She stopped and slumped to the ground. She lay still for a few seconds and then raised her head and looked around.

Wilson was crawling across the sand toward her. He looked to be suffering even more than she was. Behind him and closing the distance between them, their armless, half-blind pursuer came on.

The man reached Wilson, kicked out, catching the policeman below the ribs but also overbalancing himself and falling onto his back.

Karrina launched herself toward him.

Wilson rolled onto his back.

The heel of Karrina's shoe was poised above the man's one good eye. He squirmed away. Karrina laughed and repositioned herself.

"No, Karrina." Wilson gasped and swung his arm at her supporting leg, sending her tumbling also.

The man let out a roar and aimed an easily avoided bite at Wilson's arm.

Wilson grabbed at the tattered remains of the man's vest and pulled it from him.

Karrina had recovered from her fall. "Kill him," she hissed.

"We can't kill him. Don't you see? He's already dead." Wilson sat on the man's flailing legs and tied his ankles together with strips of the vest. Then he looked around.

The main body of the crowd was out of sight behind them but a cloud of red dust showed that they were still on the move.

"Okay," Wilson said, "let's keep going." He stood. Karrina did not.

"I can't," she said. "Not another step."

"You must. I'll carry you if I have to."

"You couldn't."

"Come on then." He set off at a fast walk.

Karrina struggled to her feet and followed.

~ * ~

Leirbag looked along the empty table and then pushed himself from his throne. A flick of his wrist and the cane was back in his hand. He needed to be at the base of his tower where he was strongest and he needed to make his move whilst all of the twelve were still together and under his control.

He ran down the spiralling stairway through the now empty galleries. Then in his secret room beneath the lower floor, he sat cross-legged and concentrated on the first of the moves that all of his accumulation of power had been destined to achieve.

~ * ~

There was singing and there was dancing. The grain stores were full. The wind had stopped. The springs around the tent town bubbled with clear, refreshing water and the sun shone down from an azure sky that the younger of the children had never seen before.

Giants came down from the hills herding sheep and deer for slaughter. The flocks and herds had not drifted back. They had simply reappeared.

Alice moved amongst the tents. The crowds quietened when she passed and moved aside to grant her clear passage. They were in awe of her power and her beauty.

She smiled, so they should be. Even the giants averted their eyes and bowed their heads as though they were embarrassed at being taller than she was.

Only the boy, who the crowd had thrust through the flap of the tent and into her presence, appeared not to be overawed. He followed at her heels, his eyes wide and gazing up at her. Occasionally she would stop and he would almost bump into her. Sometimes, when this happened, she would turn and ruffle his hair and he would blush to the roots of it, his eyes never leaving her face.

Alice stopped at a group of tents that formed a family circle. A whole sheep was roasting on a spit at its centre. Two young girls laughed as they turned it. The smell of the cooking meat wafted over the town.

Alice looked up at the sky and held out a hand to one side.

The boy understood and moved forward.

Her fingers stroked his hair and then tickled an ear. "Tell them to leave their meal and follow me," she said. "Then tell all the others to follow."

The boy scampered off between the tents.

Alice walked through the town. She could hear the people following but holding their distance. She stepped between the last of the tents, stopped and gazed out over the undulating grassland. A breeze sprang up but it was warm and pleasant.

Twenty-seven

Wilson kept his pace steady.

Karrina was glad that he had not attempted to break into a run. Still the going was hard and her calves screamed in protest. Her mouth was dry and her tongue felt to be swelling inside it.

Wilson stopped, peering forward into the heat haze that rose from the featureless landscape.

No one had overtaken them. He would have seen them. They could not have been outflanked; their pursuers had not had the pace or the time. The shimmering air and the distance made it impossible for Wilson to see how many there were or what physical shape they were in. *Perhaps ten*, he thought. Too many anyway, no matter how disfigured, for Karrina and him to take on in their weakened state.

He looked back. Karrina had stopped. Behind her, the dust cloud generated by the advancing army hung in the air.

"They have power," she said, following the line of his gaze. "More than the mob behind. Much more."

"Shit," Wilson said and looked from side to side. He was too tired to contemplate any direction other than directly away from the approaching crowd, which was straight at the new threat. "Shit," he said, again.

"Which way?" Karrina asked.

"We carry on, more slowly though, see if we can get some strength back."

Karrina doubted that she would, but she smiled anyway and kept pace at Wilson's side when he moved off.

~ * ~

The six old men sat in a circle around Rubek, Saville and Ackroyd. The still air of the cavern became disturbed. At first, it was only a gentle breeze brushing Rubek's cheeks but it grew in intensity ruffling his hair and then bringing tears to his eyes and forcing them closed. Its whispering became a roar, hurting his ears. Then there was stillness and quiet. He opened his eyes. The sun was bright. Soft, orange sand had replaced the hard stone of the cavern. Saville and Ackroyd were still in their places at his side. The six old men still formed a circle around them. It was hot.

There were two figures approaching across the barren desert. Rubek strained his eyes into the glare. It was Wilson and Karrina. They did not look to have fared well. Their gait was more stagger than walk. A huge dust cloud billowed skyward behind them. It looked to the American as though Wilson and Karrina were fleeing a stampede.

"We are in time." The voice of the six came from all around him. "That is good."

Rubek looked up at the man next to him.

"You should stand and be seen."

Rubek obeyed. Ackroyd and Saville gained their feet beside him.

~ * ~

Karrina grasped Wilson's hand. "It's Rubek... Yes, and Saville and Ackroyd." Her voice sounded parched.

Wilson blinked to clear the sweat from his eyes and recognised them, too.

The sight of their companions gave Karrina renewed life. Her legs quickened and her fingers pulled Wilson along. As they neared the group, the figures that surrounded their friends fanned out behind them. Wilson saw that they were all old men.

~ * ~

"Where's Korum?" Rubek asked, as Wilson and Karrina approached.

"He's here," Wilson, panted. "He's in Karrina's mind."

Karrina shook her head as though trying to shake the priest free of it.

::Don't do that,:: Korum thought.

She laughed, but stopped.

::Thank you.::

"How many follow?" Six voices said.

Wilson looked at Rubek.

"Friendly," Ackroyd said. "And powerful."

"I don't know exactly." Wilson switched his attention to the old men. "But thousands, certainly."

"Then we must send you on your way. We will take care of them."

"You can't kill them." Karrina said. "They're already dead."

"Then it will be a long fight. Sit now, close together and we will lend you some of our strength."

They lowered themselves onto the sand. Wilson's knee rested against Karrina's. The contact thrilled him. He placed a hand on her thigh and squeezed.

She looked at him and smiled before placing her hand over his.

Korum felt a moment of confusion and then his mind cleared. It was Karrina that Moyasta had sent to him. It was for her that he had become involved with all of this and her agenda, he now knew, was different to that of Wilson and his friends. Korum did not like it but he knew that before it was over it would be he and Karrina against those who up to that point he had considered his allies. *::If it comes to that,::* he thought. *::It will,::* Karrina replied.

The clarification did not comfort him.

~ * ~

The six old men closed in around the seated group. Bony hands stretched out to touch every head except Karrina's.

Wilson noticed the omission and assumed that with Korum inside her head she had power enough already. "Where will we appear?" he asked.

"Wherever you are meant to be." The answer came from all around him. An infusion of well-being followed it, making him feel as though he was growing physically larger. Tiredness dropped from him like a discarded cloak and his mind cleared. He knew that he had to defeat Leirbag. *I've always known that,* he thought. To do that he had to reclaim Worldroot. Korum had already told him that. He must reunite the three pieces of Worldroot and make it complete again. Smallroot was one piece. Somewhere was a third. He felt a hand withdraw from his brow. He looked around.

The dust cloud was closer. Close enough for him to make out a line of figures beneath it. He looked to his left. The six old men had broken from their circle and now stood in a line with him and his friends between them and the advancing cloud. Then they were gone. In their place, a vast army stretched across the desert plain. The sun's reflection from shields and breastplates was blinding.

Powerful is right, Wilson thought, and then they too were gone and so was the sun and the sky and the sand.

~ * ~

There were murmurings from the crowd behind her. Alice kept her head high and then, when she sensed that the time was right, she raised her arms. The air in front of her began to creak and groan. She felt those behind her back away. She stretched her arms higher. "You have saved the people, Leirbag." She called, above the noise. "Now return and lead them."

Slowly, from its base skyward, the tower began to materialise. There was a wide, stone staircase now, leading up to large timber doors.

Alice smiled. Leirbag would not make his return at the level of his people. He would be above them and looking down.

The straining of the air eased and then died. No sound came from behind her, not even a cough or a shuffling of feet. The crowd was mesmerised, just as Leirbag had intended. *They'll follow him like sheep*, Alice thought.

Her arms ached but she held them steady. He would not rush, she knew, he would play the moment.

~ * ~

Leirbag closed his eyes. He had arrived, but he would let them wait a while. He could feel the people outside and Alice's power. She had gathered them to greet him. He pushed himself to his feet, just a few more seconds. His throne became his cane; he strode from the room and rapped it against the wall opposite. Then he descended through nine, empty chambers to the doors into Ardam's world. They swung inward as he approached and he saw Alice below, standing straight and beautiful, arms in the air. Behind her, his people stretched away to the outskirts of the tented town.

As he emerged from the doors those at the front of the crowd knelt. Those behind them followed in a wave.

He stopped and raised his arms.

"My people." His voice carried easily across the attentive crowd. "My people." He scanned their faces. Not one showed any sign of celebration at his return. He saw uncertainty and fear but no rejoicing. He frowned and then forced a wide smile. "My people, you are saved. The grain stores are full and the herds have returned. The ice wind is banished and will not return whilst I lead you." He lowered his arms to his sides. "Return to your homes now, eat, drink and give thanks for your good fortune." He paused. No one moved. "Giants, gather your kin from the hills. I have one more task for you before you can prosper in peace. Alice." He held out a hand and she walked to join him.

Twenty-eight

Alice sat beside Leirbag in the throne room. In the first five galleries beneath them, the giants had settled themselves. In the seven below these, Leirbag would reassemble the army from his own world. By now, he thought, they would have run down his enemies and torn them into pieces that would never reassemble.

In the tent town beyond the tower, the remaining members of the Council had been evicted from their tent and dispersed among the people. Leirbag had left eleven giants in their place. They were too dull witted to rule, but not to carry out their one task. To crush without thought or mercy even the slightest murmurings that questioned Leirbag's right to rule.

Leirbag wished that he could witness what was happening on Alice's world. To see the results when he arrived to conquer would be good, but he wanted to hear the screams, smell the smoke and taste the blood.

I could do it, he thought, *and without losing momentum.* It would be like a holiday. A week on Alice's world would only be hours on Ardam's. He had missed Beijing and the U.S. Senate, but he could still make

Easter. That one moment that would turn the faith and hope of millions into despair.

He thumped the table. "I need a holiday, Alice." He stood and throne became cane. "Keep an eye on the new council. If any falter, kill them." Then he was gone.

Alice's mouth dropped open. She stared at the space that Leirbag had occupied, unable to believe her luck. When she was sure that he had truly gone she bounded from the room and across the corridor. From the folds of her gown she pulled the piece of root that Leirbag had given her. She pressed it against the cold stones and closed her eyes, praying silently that it had enough power to replicate the magic of Leirbag's cane.

The wood purred and vibrated against her palm and then she almost fell forward and down the staircase.

Those giants who were still awake stood as Alice descended toward them.

"Rest," she said, as she scampered past. "Save your strength for the fight to come."

At the base of the tower she stopped, her breath coming in short exhilarated gasps. She measured out the paces and then bent and pressed the root to the floor, more confident now that it had proved its magic on the first obstacle.

The wood vibrated beneath her fingers. The flagstone beneath it held its shape. "Come on. Come on." Her frustration communicated itself to the root; its humming increased to a scream. "Come on." She tried to transfer some power of her own. It would have none of it. "Come on." The edges of the stone started to lose their definition. She could see the edge of the stairway. It was taking too long. Her face creased with concentration. The root was vibrating so violently that she feared it would break free of her fingers. She pressed her other hand on top of it and held it firm. That did it. She plunged forward, head over heels, crashing against the sharp edges of the steps.

At the bottom, she lay stunned for a few seconds and then pushed herself to her feet. Her back hurt, so did her hip. She hobbled to the centre of the room and looked around, wary now that she was so close to her goal. Doubts started to nibble at the edges of her mind. She was powerful, but was she powerful enough? She gripped the root and felt some of its strength seep into her. It mingled with that, that Leirbag had granted her and with that from the twelve that she had, secreted away so carefully. That she had kept this extra power hidden from Leirbag for so long increased her confidence. She smiled and the worry lines dissolved back into her brow.

She moved toward the row of niches in the wall to her right, recognising their contents and broadening her grin as she remembered her conquests. She reached into one, halfway along the line and closed her fingers around a jewelled dagger. It had belonged to Prince, a present from the father who had sold him. Alice remembered her fingers closing around that father's windpipe. How she had lifted him, one handed, from the floor. She remembered the taste of the blood that had spattered her face, and how, in that moment, she had realised that she was the most powerful woman in the world.

She lifted the dagger from its home and slid the blade from its silver sheath. She felt the power of Prince's bartered soul flow into her. What she gained now, she knew, Leirbag would lose. He was bound to notice. How long would it be before he realised where it was going? She re-sheathed the blade, slipped the dagger into the folds of her gown and moved on.

~ * ~

Leirbag hovered unseen above the crowd. There were thousands, perhaps tens of thousands, of people crowded into the square. Television crews focussed their equipment onto the balcony high above the throng. Leirbag had recognised four of his twelve before his attention was also drawn in that direction.

Two aides supported The Pontiff into the sunlight; Leirbag laughed. God's representative on earth looked weak enough to be crushed by the weight of the very air around him.

Eleven of the twelve would wait. Leirbag wanted the TV pictures broadcast around the world before he recruited the cameramen, sound engineers, and reporters into his army.

The old man raised a bony hand and all attention became focussed on him. In the shadows of the room behind him, Leirbag saw Prince materialise. Excitement tingled through his body. His mind counted down, three...two...one...Prince disappeared.

Leirbag's essence tumbled earthward. It took all of his concentration to halt the fall and to prevent himself materialising above the crowd. He hung in the air above their heads. Directly below him, next to a white-toothed CBS anchorman, he saw Beemer's fingers tense around the detonator in his pocket, and then Beemer, too, disappeared.

Leirbag's mind reeled. Two had been taken from him. He had been robbed. His eyes flashed around the crowd. "Now!" he screamed, and the ten that remained detonated their charges.

Leirbag did not stay to enjoy the carnage. The meddlers must have breached his tower again, must have penetrated right to his inner sanctum this time. That they had escaped his army and his world did not concern him. They were in his tower. So was Alice, if any thing happened to Alice. He hurled himself back across the fragile bridge to Ardam's world.

~ * ~

Alice slipped Beemer's bundle of cigarette cards next to Prince's dagger and moved on. Her fingers had just touched against those of a baseball glove when she felt Leirbag's return. "Shit." She pulled back her hand and her eyes darted along the wall. She had to find whatever of hers Tony had given Leirbag and she had to find it quickly. She passed quickly along the remainder of the wall recognising the contents of all the hideaways as her own trophies. In the last were Arthur's Zippo, wristwatch and photograph. There had to be another, one she had missed. She pulled the root from her gown and slammed it against stone after stone; hardly giving its magic time to reveal what might be hidden beneath before moving on to the next.

~ * ~

Leirbag materialised on the run and crashed into the wall of the mosaic room. He shook his head clear and ran for the door. He did not look down at the patterned floor as he sprinted across it. There was only one throne and

Alice Craven smiled down from it. His own twisted body lay at her feet.

~ * ~

"Come on, come on." Alice continued her frantic search. There was sweat on her brow and tears of frustration crept down her cheeks. "Come on... Yes, yes." The stone beneath the root shimmered gold and then disappeared. She plunged her hand into the space beyond and pulled out a pair of black silk panties. For a second, hatred of the husband who had sold her, blinded her to what she had to do before she could revenge herself on him. "Bastard." Her fingernails dug into the delicate fabric. "Bastard." Her legs buckled beneath her. She fell to the floor. Her tongue swelled and her mouth filled with soil. Her hair hung, lank and matted, over her face. "No," she groaned. "Not there. Not back there."

~ * ~

Ackroyd felt his pistol reappear in his hand. Blackness still surrounded him and there was no noticeable support beneath his body. His mind was clear though. He curled his fingers around the weapon's familiar butt. He assumed that it had been returned to him because he was going to need it.

He focussed his mind on being ready to react to whatever he encountered when the lights went back on. In his mind, he redrew the positions of his companions. Karrina was behind him with Wilson next to her. Rubek was in front. He would block the marine's line of fire. Saville was to his right. Ackroyd dropped his shoulder to the left, ready to roll as soon as anything happened. He screwed up his eyes. He had been plunged into bright sunlight before and that second's delay caused by the sudden glare could, he knew, cost them dearly.

~ * ~

Wilson too was in limbo. He could feel Karrina's fingers in his. He squeezed and felt an answering return of the pressure. His sense of time was real. He reflected on this because he could not remember being aware of time during any of his previous journeys. He felt that they had been suspended in black nothingness for hours. *A watched kettle*, he thought, *but what if they had simply been taken out of the fight whilst Leirbag grew in power and wreaked his horrors.*

Karrina's fingers twisted free of his and stroked along the inside of his thigh. Then another hand pushed him backward. He felt her hair, brush his face and then her lips were on his. He thought of pushing her away. They had to be ready. His head pounded. Her tongue forced its way between his teeth. His eyes could see nothing, but in his mind, there was only her. Her fingers released the buckle of his belt.

Whilst Karrina concentrated on getting her mind inside that of Wilson, her fingers worked their own, more primitive, magic.

~ * ~

Leirbag ran down the spiral stairs paying no heed to the giants who lumbered to their feet as he passed. He could feel Alice below him. She was in the trophy room. She was in pain. She must have followed them, tried to protect what was his. They had hurt her. His dash down the stairs became reckless. His rage increased with every jolting step, blinding him from the realisation that Alice was no longer truly his.

~ * ~

The power within Alice filled out her gaunt features and quenched her thirst. Her mouth emptied of soil. Her matted hair straightened and regained its sheen. She pushed herself up onto one elbow. Leirbag was almost upon her. She could feel his rage. She must be ready. Her back still hurt. She could live with that. The power of Leirbag's emotions rolled over her in waves. It terrified her at first and then she smiled. His fury was not directed at her. She had fooled him. She could hear him then. She lowered her head to the stones, closed her eyes and lay still. She felt a disturbance in the air behind her. Leirbag's footsteps rang on the stairs above. She draped an arm over her head, hiding her face, and waited.

~ * ~

Ackroyd rolled onto his shoulder. There was a girl lying on the floor. Was she hurt, dead? He could not tell. Beyond her were stairs, then a man, long white hair, features distorted with rage, wild red eyes, and a cane.

Ackroyd fired. A third red circle appeared above the two at which he had aimed. The impact of the bullet hurled the man backward.

~ * ~

Leirbag saw Alice. There were three men behind her. He raised his cane. Something hit him on the head. His feet lifted from the floor and he crashed backward onto the stairs. There was pain. He had only felt pain once before. This time it shocked him. They had hurt him. They could not have but they had. He struggled to recover. It could not be happening. How much had they weakened him? How many souls had they stolen? He needed to think. He did not have time. There was another flash from the man's weapon. Leirbag threw himself out of the world and spun crazily across the bridge back to his own.

~ * ~

Ackroyd fired again. The man disappeared and the bullet rebounded from the stone on which his head had rested.

Alice's mind was reeling. She had sensed three arriving behind her. Leirbag was there, too. She heard a shot, then another and Leirbag was gone. She kept her head down and her eyes closed.

Rubek saw the man, heard the shot from behind. The man fell. There was another shot and then he was gone.

Rubek looked round.

Ackroyd was lying on his stomach with both his arms outstretched. His hands gripped the butt of the pistol that he was still aiming at the now empty staircase. Next to the marine, Saville looked on wide-eyed. His hands fumbling to retrieve his own weapon.

Wilson and Karrina were not there. Rubek turned to look back into the room. There was a girl lying on the floor. She looked to be hurt. Her arm and a curtain of blonde hair hid her face from him. He crawled across the flagstones of the floor toward her.

Alice felt a hand on her shoulder.

"You okay?" The voice was American.

She faked a groan and fluttered her eyes open. "I...I think so." She turned her head.

Rubek recognised Alice Craven. She was the bomber. She was also a victim. Leirbag had stolen her soul. "Can you get up?" He asked, standing and holding out a hand.

"I think so." She tried and winced. The pain in her back was real. "He took my soul." She opened her fist and a ball of black fabric expanded out of it. "I took it back." She half smiled and then, knowing that the American would catch her, she buckled her knees.

Rubek's arm shot to her waist and held her upright.

Ackroyd, gun still at the ready, was at the bottom of the stairs and looking upward. "He's got to be up there somewhere." He took the first two stairs, stopped and looked around.

Alice knew that Leirbag was nowhere on that world but she allowed Rubek to guide her toward the stairs. Saville, still looking bewildered, followed.

~ * ~

Wilson laid his head back against nothing and bathed in Karrina's closeness. She was everything. He had never been so happy. He was in love. "Love." He mouthed the word and revelled in the feel of it.

Karrina pulled her mind back from his and smiled into the darkness. At last, she had managed to blind him. His senses of duty and patriotism were now a distant second in his order of priorities. She was first and now she would win. 'And love is blind', she remembered the words of the song. Her father used to play it all the time. 'Or so it seems, to make me offer you my dreams'. Horselips, she remembered, that was the name of the band. She sat back from Wilson and combed her fingers through her hair.

"Karrina." Wilson sounded half-asleep. "I love you."

"I know." She bent and kissed his forehead. "I know."

~ * ~

Korum took no pleasure in Karrina's victory and he did not understand why. He was glad of the darkness though. He could live with her thoughts and ambitions but kissing Wilson held no appeal to him. *Perhaps,* he thought, *Moyasta had recruited him as a control mechanism. Maybe the old woman had inkling as to Karrina's personal ambition. That made sense.* He felt Karrina's mouth curl into a smile and then a laugh. *Yes,* he thought, *that's it,* Moyasta wanted to save her people. She did not want to annihilate the like-eyes or to subjugate them.

Karrina's laugh became louder inside his head. Moyasta was dead and Karrina was laughing at him. He had to get out of there. The laughter continued and beneath it, almost hidden, was the thought that she had him exactly where she wanted him, Wilson, too.

Korum tried to withdraw into his own private thoughts. *Could he hide them from her,* he wondered. The laughing stopped. He felt her concern. Yes, he could. Now his mind smiled. Karrina's mouth did not.

~ * ~

Leirbag hung in the air above his army. His head hurt. Below him was carnage. His army was being hacked to pieces by the well-armed and disciplined mass that spread across the desert in front of them. Most reassembled themselves and carried on the fight. Those that had been taken by the souls that had in turn been taken from him did not. They lay, broken and distorted where they fell with the desert flies feeding on their blood.

Leirbag could sense who had taken them. Prince's and Beemer's victims lay still, and Alice's also, he realised. There were not many of hers, New York, Bradford, Dublin, the base where she had failed him twice.

He scanned his army again, just to be sure. They could not have found Alice's soul; Smallroot was not nearly powerful enough only...He did not want to believe it. Alice had reclaimed her own soul. She would only do that if...How much power did she have? She had what he had given her. Had she added Prince's and Beemer's? If she had then she had not been saving herself or protecting him. She had been plotting against him. For how long? Had she been giving him all that she captured? Was she... "No!" he screamed, above the noise of the battle... More powerful than he, never.

Below him, his enemies fell and died but as they did more appeared at the rear of their lines. Two indestructible armies could fight until eternity, he thought, but if he lost more souls, if he lost all of the souls.

Alice had betrayed him. He had loved her. He would have shared all of the worlds with her, and she, from the start, had been plotting against him. He must return, he decided, and this time there would be no consideration for anyone but himself. "Like the old days," he said. She had blinded him with her beauty but now he could see again. All might not be lost.

He concentrated on thinking clearly despite the pain in his head. He would ease himself back across the bridge. Alice was now his enemy and she was powerful. He did not want her to sense his approach. It was almost a relief only having himself to think about. "Like the old days," he said, again, "when victory was assured."

~ * ~

Ackroyd stopped at the entrance to the gallery. All of the lower ones had been empty. This one was full, full of unkempt giants.

The barrel of his pistol traversed the room. There were hundreds of them.

"Jesus." Rubek had stepped up to the marine's shoulder.

"They're prisoners, too," Alice said

"You sure?" Rubek did not sound convinced.

"Leirbag took them to keep the people quiet." Alice held Rubek's gaze. "Any sign of dissent and he has one of them thrown from the top of the tower."

"Nice guy." Ackroyd said.

"Evil bastard," Alice replied. "Go on, they won't harm us."

They had taken the first two stairs. Giant heads turned toward them but none approached. Ackroyd kept his gun at the ready anyway. Rubek was still supporting Alice.

She twisted away from him. "Take them."

Ackroyd had time to let off a dozen shots. Three giants fell but the odds were hopeless.

Alice smiled, turned, and retraced her steps toward the trophy room. "Kill them," she said, without looking back.

~ * ~

The room was empty and gloomy, but after hours in total darkness even the little light that there was caused Wilson to blink.

Karrina was by his side but somehow the image of her inside his head seemed more real. He tried to take in his surroundings but thoughts of her interrupted his concentration. He tried to ignore the images and look at the real thing. She was smiling, she was beautiful and, to him, she was everything.

"Smallroot," she said, "give me Smallroot."

There was a buzzing inside his head. His hand dipped into his pocket, pulled the root free and held it toward her.

Her fingers closed around it. "Thank you."

He looked into her eyes. There was something strange. For a second he maintained his grip on the root.

She smiled.

His suspicions dissolved. His fingers relaxed their grip.

Karrina skirted the room pressing Smallroot against the stone slabs of its walls and then moving on. On her fourth attempt the stone beneath the wood disappeared revealing an empty cavity. "Damn," she said, stepped to the next and then the next. Her second success revealed a small teddy bear. It had only one eye and tattered fabric ears.

~ * ~

Alice felt the change in the tower beneath her. She had not felt Leirbag return. She increased her pace. She needed to reclaim as many of the trophies as she could before he did.

~ * ~

::I'm a priest,:: Korum thought; ::I should be able to think my way out of this.::

::Not a hope,:: Karrina thought in reply

He watched her fingers close around the stuffed toy and then he pounced grabbing three quarters of the power held there.

"Yes," Karrina gasped, feeling what remained flow into her.

Korum almost relaxed, but quickly dragged his concentration back. She had felt the power but had not known how much to expect. If he could just beat her to every one that she found he would remain three times more powerful than her.

~ * ~

Wilson was watching Karrina. Her movements mesmerised him. She was all that mattered to him.

~ * ~

Alice felt another soul disappear and broke into a run.

~ * ~

Half way back across the bridge Leirbag felt it, too. *The bitch has another,* he thought, but despite the temptation to rush, he maintained the stealth of his approach.

~ * ~

Karrina had gained another three trophies but Korum had managed to hijack most of the power of them all. She had just revealed a fourth when Alice ran down the last of the steps.

"Karrina." Wilson shouted a warning. She had her back to the stairs. Her hand gripped a baseball glove. She pulled it free of its hiding place and turned.

Korum was ready to make his move. He watched the glove emerge from its compartment through Karrina's eager eyes. He waited for the moment when it came free and then Wilson shouted. Karrina's eyes spun away from her prize. Korum lost track of its progress and lost his chance of the power it held. Then he saw Alice.

She raised her hand.

Korum sensed her power focus and forgot about everything but defending himself. He saw the bolt of energy launched from Alice's fingertips. He concentrated his entire mind on freeing himself of Karrina's. The extra power that he had tricked away from her made the difference. He leapt free of her at the very moment that Alice's attack took her high in the chest and flung her back against the wall. Her shoulders hit first and then her head was catapulted back against solid stone. She dropped the glove and sank to the floor.

Alice ran to reclaim the prize.

Wilson's mind cleared when Karrina's head hit stone. He launched himself at Alice. She was bending to pick up the glove. He barged into her butt, snatching the glove from the floor, she spun away.

He turned but Alice recovered and sent a spear of pain hurtling into his eyes. He staggered blindly away from the attack.

Alice scrambled across the floor toward Karrina, prised her fingers apart, took Smallroot and pressed it against the root that Leirbag had given her.

The two pieces of wood hummed and fused into one.

Alice let the power flow into her. All she needed now were the rest of the trophies. She bent toward Karrina's prone form and reached into the unconscious girl's jacket pocket.

Wilson crouched in the corner of the room. He rubbed his eyes with the balls of his thumbs but could not clear them of the blinding red pain.

Korum was spinning out of control in a kaleidoscope of colours. He was free of Karrina but he had to regain his own body. He tried to remember where he had last inhabited it.

"Alice, my dear."

Alice forgot about her prizes. She had not sensed Leirbag's return. She whipped her head around.

He was standing on the third from bottom step and smiling down at her. He held his cane two handed across his chest.

She was still crouched on the floor, despite all of her power she felt submissive. She eased herself to her feet, never taking her eyes from his. She raised a hand.

Leirbag laughed. "Do you really think that you're powerful enough?" His eyes shone, not red with anger but bright with confidence. "Do you really think I'm that stupid?"

Alice hesitated but kept her arm outstretched.

"Go on then, if you think you can." Leirbag cocked his head but did not attempt to close the distance between them. "If you fail I'll have you back in that pit, Alice." He took one downward step. "But you won't die, Alice. You'll live that final moment for eternity."

Alice's backward step mirrored his downward one. Her heel banged against Karrina's outstretched leg. The girl groaned.

"She has power, too Alice. And she's behind you." Leirbag advanced another step.

Alice flicked her tongue across the roof of her mouth. It was clear. *Leirbag,* she thought, *would have backed his threat with a taste. Unless,* she smiled, *he was bluffing.*

Wilson's vision was still tinged with red but he could see them now. They were intent on each other. He shuffled to his left without distracting the attention of either of them. He would never be able to reach Karrina or the staircase.

"We could still rule together, Alice." Leirbag narrowed the distance between them by one more step. "We could divide the worlds between us."

"Would that be enough for you?" Alice's smile remained constant. *He's worried,* she thought. "Or for me, I don't think so."

Wilson looked from one to the other. He tensed his body. He could see no way out but something had to happen. When it did, he wanted to be ready.

Karrina groaned and kicked out a leg.

Leirbag's eyes left Alice's and flicked downward.

Alice attacked with all the strength that she had. She had been focussing on his power. His cane flashed white-hot and leapt from his hands. Before it hit the ground, Leirbag countered.

The root was wrenched from Alice's grasp.

Wilson saw all of this in slow motion. The two pieces of wood arced toward each other above him. Leirbag stumbled backward and sat down on the stairs. Alice screamed and tripped over Karrina's legs. Wilson leapt forward and caught cane and root, slamming them together between his palms. They felt alive. He felt more than alive.

Leirbag tried to stand.

"Stay where you are!" Wilson barked. His eyes flashed to Alice. "And you." He did not have a clue what to do with the power but he knew that he had it, and he knew that they knew that he had it. "Now, over there both of you." He nodded to the corner of the room farthest from the stairway and from Karrina. "No, don't stand, crawl, both of you."

They did, not looking at him but at one another. Their expressions were identical and Wilson had never seen such hatred. "Now stay there." He edged across the room; not taking his eyes from them, crouched next to Karrina and laid a gentle hand on her shoulder. "Karrina."

She opened her eyes.

"Give them to me, Karrina, the things you took."

She felt his power washing over her and obeyed without question.

Wilson stuffed his pockets and then tucked the baseball glove into the waistband of his trousers. Then he turned toward the corner. "Now yours, Doctor Craven, if you please."

Alice glared up at him.

"Now."

She tossed dagger and cigarette cards across the floor and Wilson saw power and confidence drain from her. Then she opened her other hand and stared down at the ball of crumpled fabric.

"That you may keep," Wilson said, picked up the others and felt what Alice had lost transfer to him. Then he collected those that remained in the wall and spread them about his pockets. He turned to Karrina. "Now young lady, follow me and keep quiet." At the bottom of the staircase, he stopped and looked back into the room. "Try not to kill each other."

Worldroot looked heavy and ungainly but it hung, well balanced and light in Wilson's hand. He mounted the stairs with Karrina at his heels.

She had not spoken.

Behind them, the floor of the tower sealed itself.

The first giants they encountered backed away from them when they sensed the power Wilson carried. Rubek, Saville and Ackroyd lay on the ground. Their heads lay at impossible angles. Their necks had been broken.

Wilson knelt over Saville and stroked back the young policeman's hair. Tears welled in his eyes. He closed them and wished more than he had ever wished for anything that he had never gotten the boy involved. "I'm sorry," he sobbed.

"For what, Guv?"

Wilson opened his eyes.

Saville was smiling up at him.

He turned to Rubek and laid a hand on his brow.

The American snorted.

Wilson moved on to Ackroyd.

The giants shuffled uneasily around them.

Wilson looked up. "Go home," he said. "All of you." Then he looked back at his companions. "What?" he asked.

They were staring at him, open-mouthed.

He looked down at himself and at Worldroot gripped in his hand. There was a cough from behind him. He turned.

Korum was descending from the gallery above. One of the old men followed at his heels.

"So, you didn't need me after all." The priest laughed.

Wilson looked at Karrina.

Her eyes dropped to the floor.

"I think that perhaps we did." Wilson held out a hand toward the girl. "Karrina."

She lifted a hand to her face, dropped the tinted contact lens into it and held it toward him.

"Keep it," he said, smiling. "If you still need it."

She dropped it to the floor and looked up at him. "I..." she began.

"I..." Wilson interrupted, "don't want to know."

The old man stepped around Korum and stood, head bowed, in front of Wilson. Then he knelt at his feet.

"No," Wilson said, "it's over." He held out Worldroot.

The old man raised his eyes, stared at it and then up into the policeman's face.

"Take it," Wilson said. "It was once yours."

The old man reached out. As soon as his fingers touched the wood, Wilson staggered backward as the power that he had so recently attained drained from him.

He barely regained control before his knees buckled beneath him.

The old man stood. He was taller than Wilson, taller even than Rubek. His hair was still white and his features wrinkled and gaunt but there was strength in them now as well as wisdom. "We must let them rest," he said.

Wilson emptied his pockets and handed the trophies, one at a time, to the old man.

As soon as his bony fingers closed around them, they disappeared. "Keep that," he said, as Wilson emptied the last pocket. "The room with the mosaic floor will get you home." He turned and, with Korum at his side, walked toward the downward stairs. "We have work to do here."

"Alice Craven?" Wilson asked.

"Yes," the old man replied without turning. "She will decide her own fate."

~ * ~

"So what was it all about?" Saville asked as they mounted the first of the stairs.

"There was a God," Wilson said. "The God, capital G God. Now there is again."

~ * ~

They sat around the mosaic. The white haired old man on the throne in its centre smiled up at them.

Epilogue

Tony Craven stroked the head of blonde hair that lay in his naked lap. His other hand lifted a flute of champagne to his lips. He rested his head on the back of the sun lounger, closed his eyes and concentrated on the feel of the girl's breath on his thigh.

"Tony."

He opened his eyes and saw the gun before he saw Alice. She was holding it two handed and steady. He could see down the barrel.

The naked girl looked round, gasped and scrambled from between his legs toward the swimming pool.

"Alice," he croaked.

She looked down at his face as incomprehension turned to fear. She lowered her aim and her eyes to his exposed groin.

"No, Alice." He shrank back into his seat. "Please, Alice, no." His glass slipped from his fingers and shattered against the marble surround of the pool. His hands dropped to protect the focus of her attention.

"Hands behind your head, Tony." Alice's voice was as steady as her aim.

He did not move.

"Now." Alice's finger tensed against the trigger. "Now, Tony."

He whimpered and obeyed.

Alice raised her eyes to his face.

His bottom lip was trembling. "Please, Alice." Tears trickled and then coursed down his cheeks.

"Say, 'I'm sorry, Alice.'"

A series of mumbled sounds emerged from between his quivering lips.

"I can't hear you, Tony. Say 'I'm sorry, Alice for selling your soul.'"

Again, there were no words, only an incomprehensible blubbering.

Alice took a step toward her husband, her aim never wavering from its limp target. "I'm losing patience, Tony. Say..." Her gaze flashed to the blonde by the pool.

The girl crawled backward, away from her.

Tony Craven's eyes were on the barrel of the gun. A trickle of amber liquid flowed onto the seat of the sunlounger.

Alice snorted and then tossed the gun in wide arc over the swimming pool. It landed with a splash and disappeared beneath the dancing reflections of the water's surface. "Forget it," she said, turned and walked away.

~ * ~

Karrina walked up the tree lined drive toward the chateau. At the ancient, gnarled oak, she stopped and looked at the roughly carved block of granite that marked Moyasta's grave. She bowed her head and closed her eyes. "I'm sorry," she whispered. "I wasn't clever enough, wasn't strong enough." A breeze brushed her cheek.

"You did well, Karrina. You were cunning and you were strong. The one power is back and now all can live in peace."

Karrina swung her head around. She was alone. She looked up and, just for a second she saw Moyasta's face in the clouds above her. The old woman was smiling and then she was gone.

~ * ~

Wilson, Rubek, Saville and Ackroyd, walked side by side, across the lawn in front of the Senate Building. Rebuilding was almost complete. Their reports had been filed away. *Very deeply*, Wilson thought.

The world could be put back together. "Won't be easy." The president said.

"Well at least now there's a God." Wilson replied.

"Always was. Some just lost faith is all."

Wilson smiled at Rubek.

The American's eyes laughed his response.

Wilson dropped his hand into his pocket and wrapped his fingers around the small amulet. He had forgotten about Korum's gift until the end. He smiled. He had turned down the opportunity to be God but he could still be the best policeman in the world. He looked at Saville and slipped an arm around the young man's shoulder. "Time for a drink lad."

Meet

David Toft

Born in Bradford, England, David gained a degree in education at Kesteven College before going on to work in London and Warwickshire. He now lives in South County Dublin, Ireland with his wife Mary

VISIT OUR WEBSITE
FOR THE FULL INVENTORY
OF QUALITY BOOKS:

http://www.wings-press.com

Quality trade paperbacks and downloads
in multiple formats,
in genres ranging from light romantic
comedy to general fiction and horror.
Wings has something
for every reader's taste.
Visit the website, then bookmark it.
We add new titles each month!